Itinerary

for the

Hopeless

Cymru Roberts

ITINERARY FOR THE HOPELESS Copyright ©2017
Line By Lion Publications
www.linebylion.com

ISBN: 978-1-940938-85-1

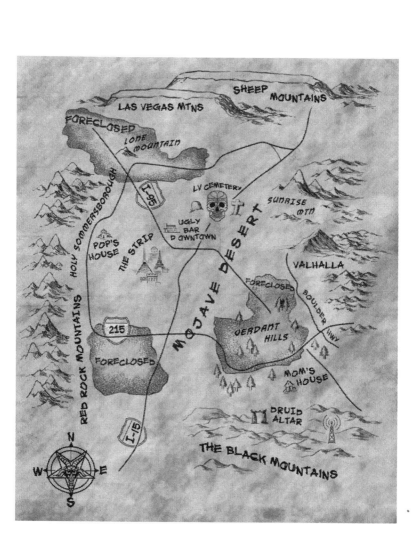

"Well, Sisterworld is not a pronoun. It's not a world we made for everyone to enter on our terms. Sisterworld is an alternate state that any person creates in order to help them deal with life on their own terms."

-       Aaron Hemphill, Liars

"There's no other world."

-       Mount Eerie

ONE

By twilight he was deep in Verdant Hills. To the east the purple sky was gaining ground. To the west the sun had set below the mountains, the vibrant shock of its ultimate rays hanging in the sky a muted wound, like a nuclear bomb had just exploded beyond the horizon. Palm trees scattered along the street leaned on their thin grassblade stalks, caught in the shockwave.

Cameron stood at the foot of the oil-stained driveway and looked at his new house. The front yard had been dead a long time. Only renegade weeds of Mormon tea and a wily creosote bush had managed to survive the brutal summer. The FOR SALE – BANK OWNED sign fluttered on its wooden stake in an evening wind that brought with it the faint smell of rain and dust.

He walked around the side of the house and

calmly looked around. No one was on the street in either direction. From the yellowed paint on the houses both occupied and vacant to the tired branches hanging lifeless from the brown trees it was impossible to tell if any life existed at all. The only signs of occupancy were the rusty metal skeletons of cars and trucks in the neighbors' driveways, some stacked on top of one another in the front yard, looking like they hadn't been driven in years.

He hoisted himself over the stucco wall, avoiding the spikes of the wrought-iron gate, and landed on the gravel in the backyard making more noise than he had wanted to. A dog barked somewhere in the distance. His eyes alert, nerves taut. Through the top layer of filigree brick he could see into the neighbor's backyard. Nobody home. He'd left the sliding glass door cracked and without further hesitation he slid through the opening into the living room.

The house was completely empty and lay in utter darkness. He had explored it in its entirety when he first came there two days ago but found nothing in the bedrooms. In the bathrooms only broken mirrors and bathtubs bathed in dirt. He'd shat in one of the toilets but like the electricity, the water had been turned off so he couldn't flush and now the watery waste just sat and drew flies. Other than frayed cable cords coming out of the walls the only thing the previous owners left was a kitchen table made of thin plywood. It sat in the corner of the living room gathering dust. Cameron wondered if they'd been in a rush to move, or if they were forced out without being able to pack completely. Maybe when they bought the table they never had any intention of keeping it. Maybe they didn't eat dinner anymore.

He sat against the wall next to the kitchen table and looked out into the backyard. Dusk poured into the house an imposing blue light. From the other end of the house, deep purples and reds shone into the hallway from the ornamental stainglass window on the front door. In the fast approaching night the house stood in multicolor shadow like a forgotten domicile used as a satanic church in secret. He breathed in the putrid smell of emptiness.

"Vampires," he said to himself. It was a visceral fear of the outside world that kept him rooted to the floor. A fear of the evil that had taken control of the city, an evil that was most certainly gaining power globally and was destined to plunge the world into an era of darkness. Foreboding filled him so thoroughly that he was afraid to even look into the hallway.

He tried to think about other things, like what his friends were up to. The parties at the bars and clubs and friends' houses. He both wished he was there and realized how much he would hate it.

Untold miles of walking had tired his body to the bones. As dusk succumbed to night so did he to the darkness of the house and his mind. Cockroaches skittered past him unimpeded, their shiny orange thoraxes gleaming like gold coins pouring forth from the black. He did nothing to bat away the ones which tread over his ragged jeans, threatening to crawl into his jacket and across his face. They were tenants here just like he was. Waiting to be stepped on or gassed out, while he sat there flashing in and out of the sleep of the habitually perturbed waiting for the transparent incubi to float through the glass and slash his throat.

In the morning, he thought, as he fell deeper and deeper. In the morning I'll get out of here.

TWO

Morning came as it no doubt had to. The sun shone through the flowers and trees in greens and bright yellows; even indoors all that had seemed so sinister the night before was rendered laughably innocuous in the new day. Cameron rose from his coiled slumber and stretched away the creaking stiffness in his joints. When he exited the house through the front door, he felt relatively refreshed and insouciant.

He clicked his heels as he passed the rickety foreclosure sign, smiling at the old woman next door who was doubled over pruning a patch of begonias. She watched in horror as Cameron came out of the abandoned house and traipsed by her, tipping an imaginary hat like some imposter aping a Pleasantville father. Her eyes kept darting from the house to Cameron, then steadily on Cameron's back as he walked by, her mental computer frozen by how calm and self-assured he'd been. She looked at the sign in front of the house but didn't see SOLD anywhere. By the time she realized he was a squatter he was already at the stoplight at the end of the street, still smiling from ear to ear.

The trail of Highland Avenue took him past the condominium complex that he and his friends used to sneak into for its Olympic-sized hot tub, and into a valley of mansions where friends and acquaintances once lived. The houses looked untouched by the blight of economic downturn, tucked as they were in a cavity of the city's physiology where the virus had passed over. No faded paint, no uprooted trees. It had been years since Cameron had been by these houses and he had no idea where any of his friends and acquaintances had gone off to. College, or wherever. It didn't matter. The neighborhood had remained the same but his life had changed. It was he who was different. Or was it that life that passed him by? He didn't know that either.

At the corner lot of a curved street sat the house

where Emily Plaskin used to live. Many iconic moments of youthful mischief had taken place at this house. The nighttime pool parties, the fights, the girls. The ouji board that made the lamp turn on inexplicably. It had seemed like magic to be in that house, knowing that you were part of a premier high school party. Looking at it now, with the curtains drawn on the bay window that faced the front yard, it was a peculiar feeling to stare at something that no longer had any meaning. Ultimately, however, it was just another house on the street. It would be so throughout the many iterations of tenants and time and before long no one would ever know what had once happened within and no one would care.

He stayed only briefly, wondering if the curtain would part to reveal Emily's little sister at the piano in the living room. She used to sit at the keyboard and tinkle away little Russian melodies while the older kids lounged on the couches. No, she never did that, but Cameron used to imagine she did. Sometimes it was he who was at the piano, punching the ivories like a young Phantom of the Opera while his friends whizzed by to the tune of teenage romance.

He was out of the neighborhood and walking up

the Sunset Avenue hill toward Smith's soon after. The rumble of his stomach was stronger than his powers of reminiscence.

The grocery store was one of the very few shops that still drew business in the depleted shopping center. Once the social beacon of a new and glamorous suburb, Town Center had been liquidated by the city's ever growing circumference. The movie theatre that had been the site of so many group dates sat empty, its doors locked for good. He could only hope that some spirit of the past haunted it, playing the classic films of childhood on the big screen to a crowd of ghosts. A low-end casino, a Starbucks and the Smith's grocery store distinguished the shopping center from those exhibits one would find in cities like Calico and Quartz Mountain, or any of the other ghost towns of Nevada.

Roberto's Taco Shop was the only establishment to have renovated during the recession, adding green booths in place of the rickety tables and chairs. They sat unpatronized when Cameron walked by, no one inside but the two workers behind the counter who watched him with suspicion.

Inside Smith's he walked with purpose. He selected a Gala apple, turkey sandwich and wasabi almonds, tucking the meal into the pocket of his military jacket. In the chip aisle he could only salivate at the new flavors – Spicier Chili Verde, Roast Beef and Red Onion, Ketchup – for he had no room for junk food.

He blended in with the other customers, the gout-ridden buzzing around on their scooters, the elderly anxiously scanning the shelves for pimento cheese. Everyone had a trace of mental illness in their appearance and this made Cameron confident he was securely camouflaged. The young employers with their pimpled faces paid him no mind. The store had lain off all their secret shoppers. It was only the security sensors that always made him nervous. As he left the grocery store the old black woman guarding the slot machines regarded him impassively. Crossing the threshold back into the morning, nothing happened.

Behind the shopping center Olympic Avenue was a perfect example of what the city had become. Before him sat two buildings: Country Sports Club and the signless decrepitude of Fountasia. Country Sports was a staple of Las Vegas' landed gentry, an extremely overpriced health club that spent more money and time on the plushness of their locker rooms than workout equipment. Its parking lot was already filled with Audis and Mercedes. Next door Fountasia negated two acres of land. It had once been a fun fortress, a theme park for kids to go to on special days. The fuchsia panels that lined the outside were gone now, making the base structure look embarrassingly bald. The astroturf lawns on the putt-putt course had died and turned brown, the bumper boat lake all dried up.

Of the two Cameron found the latter more interesting. He walked to the fence where he could see the windows of the main building, just past the go-kart track. Squinting, he peered through the tinted frames, remembering what was once inside. The roller skating rink on the fifth story, we used to do transfers off the half pipe and speedskate backwards during the couple's dance, remember? Oh yeah! What about the waterslide that went from the ceiling and dropped you into a huge can of Energy Rush soda? I can't believe the health inspectors ever allowed that. How much fun was that?! Man, those were the days.

Had he hopped the gate and actually looked through those windows he would have seen a blank space of concrete. All of the machinery had been gutted from the two-story building and sold for scrap metal.

He took Olympic to Verdant Hills Parkway which curved down a hill and became Patrick Lane. At the base of the hill was an empty plot of land where NS House used to be. "NS" stood for "Not Safe." Kids used to sneak into the condemned building and scare each other, chant Bloody Mary in the bathrooms. It was rumored that a crazy bum lived upstairs waiting in ambush for giggling children. Cameron never heard of anyone falling victim to the crazy bum, but he was glad to see such a godforsaken establishment leveled once and for all.

He strolled down Patrick Lane as light as a feather and ate his turkey sandwich. The birds chirping in the trees added a lovely layer of percussion to the version of "Alberto Balsalm" that played in his head. He had things to do that morning. His clothes were in tatters. His appearance had reached a level of slovenliness that was unacceptable. At this rate, soon anywhere he went he'd be kicked out for vagrancy. He wasn't your run of the mill, garden variety hobo. He had standards. He was going shopping.

The trek to Savers took a decent chunk out of the morning. The thrift store stood sandwiched between a

Costco and a Wal-Mart on a ten acre parcel of land that was seventy five percent parking lot. Cars were parked in clusters around the entrances to the chain stores, less so in front of the thrift store and the florist. Thousands of square feet of commercial real estate sat vacant, without so much as a sign of the previous owner.

He knew the area. It wasn't far from his high school. It too had once been thriving. Now, shops like Shepler's Western Wear and Fashion Bug that he'd seen his whole life didn't exist anymore. A tavern called Dive Bar advertised Voodoo Jones Performing Live Tonight.

He entered Savers and immediately went toward the Men's Suits section. Back in the day, when thrift store shopping was chic, it was not uncommon to find an Yves Saint Laurent dress shirt or a pair of Commes des Garcon trousers. It was true that nine times out of ten he left the store with nothing but an itch in the nuts and the smell of socks up his nose, but every now and then he got lucky. He hadn't been there in a long time. He felt his luck had ripened.

Savers didn't disappoint him. After rummaging through itchy tweeds and plastic sportcoats he found his suit of armor. An ash-grey linen number was pinned to the wall next to dangling undergarments and used penny loafers. It emanated a legendary aura, the jacket flap open, arms akimbo, outlining the phantom silhouette of a model's body.

Cameron plucked it from the perforated display board lest someone seize it before him. As if preordained, a silver paisley dress shirt was draped over a rack of clothing right next to the dressing rooms. He grabbed it as well and stormed through the door and into the cubicle.

Inside an old woman lay slumped against the mirror, passed out. A sheer pink belly shirt and cut-off jean shorts were all that covered her leathery skin that looked like an orange peel left out all summer. The woman didn't budge when Cameron burst in. So as not to disturb her slumber, he tip-toed back out and quietly closed the door behind him.

The dressing room next door was unoccupied. Inside, he hung up the new suit and peeled the old pulverized clothes from his body. The military jacket, a gift from his dad, had crusted over from dirt and sweat. The flannel shirt was missing buttons and torn all over. The blue Levi's he'd bought in high school were thin as paper with a hole in the crotch that grew wider each day. When he was only wearing a pair of destroyed tighty-whiteys, he looked at himself in the mirror. Prickles of mustache and light patches of beard covered his sunken cheeks. Where the skin had been exposed it was tanned a dark bronze. Constant walking and a lack of food had shrunken his legs. Lines ran up his quadriceps parting at the knee and halfway up the thigh. Every rib was visible under the skin, his abdomen a flattened stone of jagged sinew. He flexed his stomach, bounced his pecs. Not an ounce of fat on his body. Years of forced diet and strenuous exercise had never made him look this good. He smiled at his reflection.

The suit fit him like a glove as he knew it would. He adjusted the cuffs of the dress shirt and slipped his bare feet back into his green and white Diadora tennis shoes. Picking up his apple and almonds he looked one last time at the pile of clothes in the corner. It was a pinch of almost sadness that struck him, knowing he was leaving them behind forever.

"It's just clothes," he reasoned. "It's stupid to hold any sentimental attachment to such things."

Leaving Savers, past the long lines at the tellers, he crunched into his apple and headed back out into the morning.

Now that he had accomplished his main task for the day he had to figure out something else to do.

Having shed society's schedules and assumed a life of complete independence, he often found himself with nothing to do but fight with his boredom. What had he done before, when he was back at his mother's house sitting in front of the TV? What did he do when he couldn't think of anything else? He ate. Luckily for him Chapala's was in the same shopping center and he knew the bartender.

When he entered the bar Ryan was leaning against the refrigerator chewing his bottom lip. Above him La Liga Mexicana was blaring on the TV. Neither Ryan, nor the regulars at the video poker machines were watching.

Cameron pulled up a seat and waited a while for Ryan to break from his reverie.

"Shit, well hey there, buddy," Ryan said after a while.

"What's up, amigo?"

"What are you doing here?"

"I was in the neighborhood."

"Alright. What're ya drinking?"

Cameron sucked air between his teeth. "I actually had a hankerin' for one of your bloody beers."

"Good man. You take Bohemia right?"

"That's correct."

Ryan set to making the drink. "You're lookin' spiffy. What are you doing these days?"

That question. That fucking question. He knew Ryan was well-meaning, but all the same his answer was a deflection.

"You're lookin' at it."

Ryan gave him a brief once-over. "This is true."

"How've you been?"

"Same shit."

"How's your brother?"

His brother Rory and he had been an epic duo. They were known all over the city as experts at cheating death. The car accidents, the stabbing, the hard-drinking lifestyle, it would have killed lesser men.

"He's good, I suppose. Taking care of his new baby daughter."

"No shit."

Ryan nodded and daggered some olives. He slid the bloody beer over to Cameron.

"See how that tastes."

Cameron took a sip. It was spicy and good. "Oh yeah, baby."

Ryan nodded.

"Can you join me for a brew?" Cameron asked.

He remembered seeing Ryan drink thirteen 32oz. High Lifes in one night. Ryan once drank over a hundred poppers in Mexico.

"Nah. I don't drink anymore," Ryan replied, definitively.

"Oh."

This was something. The answer and the way Ryan said it called attention to something missing from his appearance. He had always had such a jolly attitude, always wore a smile, whether with friends or unknowns. That was why he was such a dear friend to so many. The Ryan that stood behind the bar now looked deflated, like the joy had been sucked out of him.

"What else," Ryan said. "You hungry? You look skinny."

"I could eat. I don't have much cash on me right now, though."

Ryan looked offended at the mention of money. Cameron ordered a carne asada torta with an egg on it and fries. When the meal came he devoured it ravenously. The rich egg yolk and salty meat reignited an animal hunger that forced starvation had stymied. He smeared the fries in the leftover grease and would have licked the plate if no one was around.

They talked little while Cameron ate. He brought up the stabbing, it had happened at some random party in Verdant Hills. Things turned sour and some hood had knifed Ryan in the belly. Ryan lifted his shirt to show Cameron the scar, a zipper of flesh from his belly button to sternum. He let his shirt drop without ever changing his facial expression.

Cameron finished his drink and another Bohemia. He offered to pay with money he didn't have but was thankfully once again rebuffed.

"Hold up a sec," Ryan said as Cameron stood to go. He reached below the bar and retrieved a pair of Von Zipper Elmore sunglasses.

"Take these, man. They would look sick with your outfit."

Cameron tried to refuse but Ryan insisted.

"Go ahead, try 'em on."

Cameron put on the sunglasses and looked at himself in the mirror over the bar. "These are pretty sick."

"They're yours."

"I can't. Really, man."

"I got 'em for free. Take 'em."

After a vociferous thanks for everything they shook hands and Cameron walked out the back door. He turned around to see Ryan once more but the mirrored door had closed and it was only his reflection and that of the outside world.

THREE

By the time he reached the sidewalk his stomach was already gurgling. It was past noon and the air was thick and smoggy from the traffic that congested Tropicana Avenue. He figured he'd walk across the street to Paradise Park, maybe take a nap or watch people play tennis.

When he got to the park, the field lay before him in expansive disrepair. Like most vegetation in the city, the summer had not been kind to the lawns. The grass spread out past the County building that served as a Rec Center and the pool that was closed for the end of summer. Picnic benches were scattered next to the basketball and tennis courts. At one of them a bum was setting out the day's findings in a makeshift picnic.

Cameron trampled the dehydrated blades

underfoot in sluggish steps. Midway through the field he came upon a circle of gypsies. Their backpacks and sleeping bags were strewn about where they had made camp. Their leader sat on a paint bucket strumming a flimsy wooden guitar, singing an old punk ballad.

> *Demon I am*
> *And face I peel,*
> *See skin turned inside out, cuz*
> *I gotta have you on my wall.*
> *Gotta have you on my wall.*

Altogether the group joined in for the chorus, Cameron along with them:

> *I want your skuuuullls,*
> *I need your skuuu-hulls!*

The group cheered and the leader slapped the body of the guitar. They took notice of Cameron and seemed to approve of the interloper's participation.

"You know that song?" asked one of the gypsies. He lay on his back with his head resting on a sleeping bag. From Cameron's vantage he could see a machine gun tattooed on the side of his shaved head just below the rust colored ponytail.

"Of course. It's a classic."

"Well I'll be! Fancy pants knows his shit!"

The group had a laugh and Cameron shrugged.

"Shit, you want a beer, mister?"

Cameron accepted. A pudgy teenager with dreadlocks in a red sundress opened a Tecate and tossed it to him. When he caught it beer splashed onto his new suit, but he played it off like it was cool.

"You guys heading somewhere?" Cameron asked.

"Burning Man. Soon as we get the money."

Cameron thought they might hit him up for cash but they didn't. Despite his new suit they seemed to sense his nomadic spirit.

"Well, thanks for the beer," he said, making to leave.

Another gypsy who'd been sleeping broke open his snot caked eyes and called out after him. "Hey, man. You wanna hit the glass dick?"

The sleepy cigani produced a browned speedpipe from his cargo pants.

"Nah, man. I'm straight."

The gypsies laughed to themselves and the bum who offered the pipe fell back asleep. Cameron walked away. None of the gypsies took much notice.

No one was at the tennis courts. He sat at the benches in between them to rest a while. Before long a man wearing a white Sergio Tacchini tracksuit walked into the court area, carrying what looked like full grocery bags in each hand.

Cameron watched as the man sat the bags down on the next bench over.

"Hey, Chang. You want to play?" the man said in salutation.

"Huh?"

"I said 'you want to play, Chang'."

"What is Chang?"

The man stared at Cameron for a moment. He was older, bald, and had the unforgiving face of a Slav. A streak of white ran across his forehead from the tanline of a headband.

"You look like Michael Chang. Tennis player from nineties, you know?"

Cameron had to laugh at this. He had been confused for many races over the years, from Hawaiian to Mexican, but never Taiwanese-American.

"That's a new one on me."

"So you play, yes or no." The man was growing impatient. The corners of his mouth teetered on the verge of a sarcastic smile and seething rage.

"You want to play me in tennis?" Cameron reiterated.

The smile teetered dangerously.

"Sure I'll play. That is if you don't mind losing." Cameron kept a straight face and looked the man dead in the eyes.

The man's lips quivered until he finally broke into a roaring guffaw.

"Oh! You a sneaky, Chang!"

"Yeah, that's me. You don't happen to have extra clothes and equipment do you? Cuz I am not ruining this new suit."

The man perked up and became serious. "Yes. Yes." He began rummaging through the shopping bags, pulling out shirts and shorts, most of which looked like they were still sweaty.

Cameron studied his options and chose a Nike tanktop and some basketball shorts with pockets. Meanwhile the man laid out an array of racquets dating from prehistoric wooden ones to turn of the century models.

Cameron changed into the athleticwear and selected a Head Classic Mid.

"You like?" said the man.

"Yeah, I'm good. My name is Cameron by the way."

"Yes, Chang. My name Bjorn." He clasped Cameron's hand with his own dirty leather paw, then skittered toward the far baseline.

Cameron went to his side, jogging in place and stretching his legs. "Rally a bit first, huh?"

"Okay, Chang," Bjorn replied mischievously. He took a fluffy yellow tennis ball from the pocket of his track pants and whipped a forehand. The ball skirted the net and painted the left sideline. Cameron didn't even move to retrieve it.

"Here we go," Cameron sighed. His inner monologue covered the rest of the match.

GOOD AFTERNOON Everyone and welcome to the Paradise Open! We have a mouthwatering battle for you today as the veteran Swede Bjorn Boravic takes on the young American Cameron Azerian. I'm Nick Lester alongside Robbie Koenig.

Thank you, Nick. Good to be here.

Now, Robbie, this is already Boravic's third match of the day. Do you think fatigue will play a part in his performance?

No, I don't think it will be much of a factor,

Nick. Boravic is well conditioned to playing upward of six or seven matches a day. By now he should just have the blood pumping and elbows greased, ready to face the American.

And what about Azerian? He has had a stellar year, with wins over Gonzalez in Morocco and Misday in Monte Carlo. Is he just too young and too hungry for the aging Swede?

We shall see. He definitely has what it takes to produce sparkling tennis, but it will all come down to execution and focus.

Any way you slice it, it should be a wonderful day of action.

Grab your chocolate digestives and mineral water folks, this is going to be popcorn tennis at its finest!

DUE TO TIME CONSTRAINTS WE PICK UP PLAY LATER IN THE MATCH

Here again we see the unorthodox style of Boravic.

He tosses the ball extremely high and lets it drop almost to his waist before slapping at it with a sidespin forehand. You won't learn that technique at the gaming tables, folks.

It really bothered Azerian early in the match, Robbie, but once he got a read on it he never looked back.

No, he was waiting for it. As we see here, he runs around his backhand and smacks a forehand winner to take it home.

All in all a good match, and a good win for the young American. This one is done and dusted. Azerian wins 6-1, 6-2. For all of us here at the Paradise Open, goodbye.

Back at the benches Cameron let the breeze blow cool over his sweaty skin. Bjorn was less amiable.

"You did not tell me you were good, Chang."

"Dude, you still use a wooden racquet. It's not really fair."

Bjorn threw the racquet in question to the ground and sulked at the other bench.

At the water fountain they took turns drinking from the mineral encrusted spout. Bjorn washed himself with a bar of soap he had brought with him, running the lather over his arms and face. When he was done he slapped the stick of soap into Cameron's hands before he could refuse. Black hairs twisted off the bar and were embedded into the blue and white swirls. Bjorn watched Cameron until he washed himself too.

"I never took lessons or anything," Cameron began explaining. "Me and my friends just play a lot. It's addictive, you know?"

Bjorn wasn't keen on Cameron's attempt at civilized conversation. "Addictive, yes. You know what is addictive? I tell you." He unzipped his jacket pocket and took out a handful of what looked like broken pieces of chalk.

"What're those? Pills?"

"Painkiller. Make you feel very good." He kept his light eyes trained on Cameron, the tiny black dots in the center sizing him up for some unknowable criteria.

"Sure, man. I'm with ya."

"I got to blow off steam sometime," Bjorn said with a sigh. "Jebe ti..." He held out the handful of pills to Cameron. "You take." It was not just intonation that made the words a statement and not a question.

Cameron reluctantly took them in both hands. "Uh, thanks."

"You *take*," Bjorn insisted. That same look of

ambiguous anger had returned to his face. There was something threatening in Bjorn's demeanor, as if the slightest false move might set him off. He had to blow off steam sometimes. But how?

"I need some water first," Cameron said, moving carefully to the fountain. He choked down the pills, hoping that they weren't some kind of meth. When he went back to the bench to change Bjorn had cheered up.

"Oh, Chang. You did not tell me you were good."

Cameron laughed uncomfortably.

By the time he had changed back into his suit Bjorn had left the court area. He had spotted a young kid at the basketball courts and was heckling him for a pick up match. "I have extra racquet, bro!" Cameron heard him yell.

"Crazy motherfucker." He said as he watched. He put his sunglasses on and exited the courts.

He walked far enough into the outfield that he was out of sight from Bjorn, that park legend of dubious nationality. As he lay down the grass beneath him felt like Egyptian cotton, the sun on his skin an ample comforter. He opened the small bag of almonds, sucking off the wasabi flavoring before eating them. It had been a busy day, but a good one. The painkillers kicked in which only added to the tiredness he felt from the match and from dealing with Bjorn. It wasn't long before the warmth of the afternoon tucked him deep into the cozy folds of the outfield lawn where Cameron lay enveloped in the grip of a glorious nap.

FOUR

After timeless sleep he woke to the setting sun. He removed his sunglasses to greet the lassos of flame that slashed across the periwinkle sky and obscured the remaining sunlight into the shadows that covered the field. He stretched the tiredness from his muscles in a brief paschimotanasana then stood to go. He would head south for the night. Lately it was always south. He reckoned it was because he knew that side of town the best. It was just as decimated as any other area in Las Vegas which meant there would be plenty of abandoned properties to squat in for the night. If all else failed that was where his friends lived; someone would let him crash. The disconcerting thought did go through his head that while he had the whole city, the whole world even, if he were resourceful enough, to traverse, he still stuck to the same old patterns, the same parts of town as always. Now was not the time to tackle that conundrum, however. The breeze in the air was neither warm nor cold. The beautiful colors of dusk filled him with a nameless energy. He left the park and headed south without debate and without anxiety.

On Eastern Road the traffic on both sides was heavy. The headlights of cars made bright an evening that was quickly descending into darkness. On the street people heading home for work jockeyed for optimal position, trying to beat the rush hour. Sealed off in their cars, shut out from the outside world. Cameron pulled his jacket about his neck and proceeded headfirst against the rushing wind of their pursuits.

At length, a digital sign welcomed him to Sunset Park. It was the closest thing Las Vegas had to a Central Park: a sprawling chunk of land in the middle of town that serviced sportsmen and the leisurely of all kind. A ring of old Stone Pines outlined the perimeter and ran through its various inner pathways, around the baseball fields and running track. There were lawns that dwarfed the size of the ones at Paradise Park where people played Frisbee Golf. A marshland of thornbushes was habitat to wildlife rarely seen anymore. By the rugby fields and volleyball courts the tall Date Palms and African Sumac that sprung from the earth could easily confuse one to think they had traveled from a mountain forest into a subtropical climate. Like Las Vegas itself, the park was an amalgamation of the cultures and species that surrounded it.

He passed others of the city's homeless in the mysterious twilight as he made his way toward the lake. Away from the crowded basketball courts and the baseball fields lit up by huge fog lights, he walked in the open fields concealed by nightfall. When he reached the lake he walked up a small hill to a gazebo that overlooked the water. An island made of concrete rose from its center much higher than years past on account of the draught.

He sat under the gazebo and watched the water. Concentric ripples barely lapped upon the shore. Few shadows walked lonesome on the other side. A young couple ushered their child in the direction of the bathroom. Other than that he was by himself.

It was evenings like these that he always felt implied some unspoken significance. Regarding his surroundings, if he were to account for the attributes and ascribe to them a feeling, that feeling would be loneliness. It must be for some reason then, that he was by himself. There was opportunity here, if he could find it. He closed his eyes and asked the night for guidance.

After some time he rose from the bench and walked to the edge of the lake. The low tide just made it to his tennis shoes. He looked into the water. The face staring back at him wobbled like the reflection in a carnival mirror. Black sockets looked back at him instead of eyes. The shadows at the temples and under the cheekbones wiggled in serpentine syncopations, completing an expressionless skeletal face that proclaimed the judgment of his sleeping double.

With a deep breath he withdrew his gaze from the black mirror in the water. A willow tree sat like a giant umbrella at the opposite end of the lake, its whiskers whispering in the wind. He thought he could make out a gothic ballerina twirling behind the willow tree's curtains, but in the next gust the leaves parted and she disappeared.

"Phew," he said, exhaling. "What do you think, weepy willow?" He returned his gaze back to the reflection in the water, that silent demon asking its infinite questions.

"Think I have what it takes to answer my shadow?"

In vain he waited for the shadow's answer. The figure underwater could have stood there forever and never grown impatient.

It was too dark to stay any longer. Answers would have to wait for another day, another night. Walking from the lake, an uneasy feeling followed Cameron. He felt that the ghost of his body still stood back in the water like a subtly moving statue, turning only slightly to keep a vacant eye on its master.

FIVE

He awoke the next morning to the sound of a sprinkler slapping against the metal railing of a jungle gym.

"Where the fuck am I?"

The sun had not yet risen. The orchid sky added a preternatural glow to the orange shingles of neighborhood rooftops. A nighthawk flew overhead in slow motion on its way home to sleep.

In a panic he twisted on the park bench, scanning the area until his surroundings became recognizable. He felt groggy from the pills. The events of the previous night came back to him in a sudden explanation: the long walk from Sunset Park to the old Verdant Hills library, contemplating the moon next to the cobblestone snake that sat just outside its doors, walking down the hill on Sunset Avenue past Money

Hills – a patch of desert where bums made homes in the sagebrush and BMX bikers built their jumps – the glowing crucifix atop the highest cliff bathing the land below in its holy synthetic neon light, the way Whitney Ranch Road looked like a tunnel under the black and orange eaves, the soles of his shoes slapping the concrete as he approached the park at the stop sign, the park he knew no one ever went to, the one that had a bench where he could sleep, the blissful pain as the pressure in his bones uncoiled after a day of so much walking…

His recollections were interrupted when a Scottish Terrier dashed through the wet grass and started licking his sockless ankles. Cameron had a mind to kick the dog away until he saw the owner standing on the spongy floor of the playground, tucked semi-hidden behind the slide.

The dog continued to make little suckle sounds as it tried to lick every inch of exposed skin on Cameron's legs. When it shook itself, filthy water sprayed him in the face. He looked over to the dog's owner, whose face was mostly concealed by the hood of his sweatshirt. The man peered sardonically back at Cameron as he wiped a thick string of snot that was dangling from his nose.

Cameron rose from the bench and shook the dog loose from his ankle. Instead of calling his animal, the man became engaged in a kind of bastardized callisthenic, standing with his legs together and bending slowly at the knees. At each repetition, the man closed his eyes and made a face like the movement gave him orgasmic pleasure, then looked right at Cameron. His dog continued to scurry around the park frantically, pissing and shitting everywhere.

Cameron broke out into a jog and left the unseemly duo to their morning, not stopping until he reached the stoplight.

"Jesus," he said to himself. "Not even morning yet and I'm already being hassled by freaks, skeezes and weirdos." His skin was covered in a slime from the morning dew and still crawled from the encounter.

He walked the magic hour aimlessly away, the few cars that passed by on the road and he all sharing a secret ignominy. In a dress shirt and suit at this hour he must be a vanquished prowler, or a premature ejaculator cast out too soon onto the walk of shame. The cars were driven by the drunk, or the still-awake, trying to fight the coming sun lest its first rays induce the inevitable comedown before they reach the safety of their rooms and windows covered in pitch-black flannel. People off to work ungodly occupations, whether necessary to the running of society or not, the construction workers and physicians or the first shift of retail salespeople, all harboring unrelenting feelings of impropriety at their predawn waking. Fitting then, that the magnificent hour when the night has been relinquished and day is not yet lucid, the moment of nethertime that holds in it such promise for the future, should then yield all too quickly the blinding brown and burnt orange nausea of dawn's first moment. Without a trace of alcoholic hangover the sight of the sun rising over Sunrise Mountain made Cameron want to puke, in protest, undigested torta all over the sidewalk.

He didn't vomit however, despite a few efforts at clenching his diaphragm. By the time the sun was fully up he had walked a mile away from where he had slept, over to a drainage ditch that ran along Stephanie Street.

The long trapezoidal half-pipe of white concrete sat empty for all but five or six days out of the year. In the spring a lawn of grass would cover the floor for a few weeks before dying in the summer heat. The only time it filled with water was during the monsoon season of late August, when the storms would come so fast and strong the whole city had to brace for cover. Every year at least one person would get swept away in those flash floods. As a kid, him and his friend McKiscko would cut through the ditch as a shortcut toward the mall. A cop stopped them once and told them they were lucky to only get a warning, on the count of how dangerous it was to play in ditches. But where were all the cops to dissuade the kids during the heavy rains? The day he and McKiscko had been stopped it was the middle of summer and there wasn't a cloud in the sky.

He stood on the sidewalk and looked through the fencelinks into the empty ditch. It ran to where the road went up over a hill, disappearing into a tunnel below the earth. It made a pretty picture, he thought, if you considered the geometry. The evenly divided quadrilaterals in rows of three, one angled on each side and one serving as the base, over and over and over. Outside the fence to each side was urban planning: a shirt-making factory and a gymnastics studio, apartments, flanked as always by the ubiquitous mountains in the distance.

I'll create a series of photographs, he thought. Of all the city's ditches framed in their natural surroundings. Call it *Ditches of Las Vegas*. Some bar or coffee shop would let him display the pictures as a gallery. He'd make a coffee table book out of the pictures and sell it at Urban Outfitters. It would become a disposable product showcasing the contrasting urban environments of his town. He liked the manmade industriousness of the images juxtaposed with the outgrowths of plantlife. He liked the giant cross-sectioned tubes of concrete that lay exposed in the body of the city. *Ditches of Las Vegas* would go places. He thought about how easy it would be to shoot the ditches and how it would give him something to fill his days. People would respect him because shooting ditches would be his life. He would live for his job and although the subject matter would be unconventional, the time and energy and life that he put into his work would show in the photographs. The pictures themselves would relate perfectly the empty fullness of such a life. People would buy the compendium in droves. They would keep it on their coffee tables for a while without ever looking at it until the hulking hardback would become too much of a bother and they'd tuck it into their bookcase or put in a drawer and forget about it completely. That too, he thought, was fitting. That would be a suitable end to *Ditches of Las Vegas*. He could rest happy knowing the beauty of his toils lay unseen and unnoticed in cupboards all across the country.

The new project idea energized him like a shot of espresso. Cameron was awake and ready to go. He just didn't know where. Now that he had figured out what to do with his life in the macro-sense, he didn't know where to start. He figured he would need a camera and most likely a tripod if he wanted to get the perfectly still geometric shots that were in his head. He would get a film camera, of course, because the graininess of the film would be more suitable for the subject matter. Digital cameras were so vulgar, so unnatural. If he was going to use a film camera he would need to get film, and he'd be able to get film wherever he got a camera most likely. They would be able to tell him where to get the film developed too, recommend him to people he could trust to expose the photographs correctly, not like some Wal-Mart one-hour photo that would fuck up the negatives and all that. Where would he put everything? He'd have to find an appropriate satchel, or backpack. He could find one at Savers most likely.

Already the list of logistics was beginning to depress him. He just wanted to take photographs of Las Vegas' ditches. He just wanted simple clean geometric prints of the city's exposed natural body. The gallery and the book deal and everyone's ironic responses would all be bonuses. The important thing was the pictures themselves. The picture in front of him. He had been looking at the ditch for some time now but not seeing it. Instead he'd been seeing what the picture in front of him would yield, the life created out of the present image. His forward thinking had blinded him. He increased the trajectory exponentially and already fast-forwarded to the part where the whole project burnt him out. I'll keep this idea though, he promised himself, because he really believed in the essence of it. One day I'll have the technical know-how and the equipment and the collaborators and the agents and the publicists. He didn't bother about all of that right now. He looked down the ditch for a moment longer. Its magic was all dried up, like a pleasure gland wrung dry of serotonin. It would come back. His taste would heal. He turned away from the inspiration and headed toward the mall, deciding on the way that he would instead go to the casino across the street and try to parlay some free coffee. He needed a pick-me-up; all the morning's dreaming had left him exhausted.

SIX

The casino was already busy when he stumbled through the main entrance. All at once his senses were assaulted: his skin blasted by the cold air conditioning, the intense pungent aroma of air freshener mixed with the clouds of invisible cigarette smoke stuffing his nostrils, a cacophony of ringing and digital voices pounded in his ears while a kaleidoscope of twinkling lights and cheap CGI animation flashed before his eyes.

He walked through the labyrinthine aisles of slot machines. Past retired men and women fused into the casino's nervous system by their player cards that connected from their breast pockets to the games they played like a leash. Cocktail waitresses buzzed around with trays of drinks, handing out shots of vodka and white russians. Time didn't exist inside the casino. You played, you drank, you ate at the buffet. This was a way of life. Brushing past the crowds of people in the narrow aisles, Cameron thought he was the only one to think this lifestyle absurd.

He decided he'd take a lap around the main floor and devise a plan to score some morning joe. As he ambled he kept noticing strange looks from the people that passed him. A couple would walk by and one of them would do a double take. A group of hungover dudes gave him an approving once over and laughed heartily. He checked his fly, it was buttoned. No toilet paper was stuck to his tennis shoe. It was only when he caught a glimpse of himself in the steel reflective casing of a slot machine that it clicked. He looked a right mess. He hadn't taken off his sunglasses, his suit and hair were disheveled. He was roaming the casino like a man who was enjoying Las Vegas to the fullest. To the onlookers, today's early morning wandering was a victory lap. The people weren't mocking him; they were respecting him for taking advantage of what the city had to offer.

He decided to continue impersonating a tourist fresh from a romping night and let everyone else fill in the backstory. Like, for example, he came from somewhere in the Midwest, say Indianapolis. He and his friends had saved up all year for a four-day getaway. They'd gotten a room at Caesars, started the night with drinks and dinner at Spago, shopped for a bit at the Forum Shops before meeting a club promoter. They looked like money so the promoter offered them a place on the list at Foundation Room. After taking a cab to Mandalay Bay it was still too early for the club so they got drinks at RM Seafood, upstairs where it was elegant and quiet. But it didn't stay quiet for long! Shots of Johnny Walker Green were slammed back, the mixologists on staff made specialty beverages that were marveled over. Everyone was in high spirits, tossing around money with reckless abandon. The mixologist asked what their plans were. Foundation Room huh? Good stuff. You guys need any party favors? Cut to the club, a blackened catacomb of dancefloor pulsing deep techno, the hallucinations of walking past hundreds of secret rooms and the silhouettes of the orgies taking place behind the frosted windows. Out on the balcony that overlooked the entire Strip, believing that this was what Vegas was all about, the cute blonde appeared out of nowhere, out of the fog from the dancefloor. They hit it off immediately. He asked her to marry him, at the chapel downtown. Just as a gag. We're in Vegas aren't we?

She said yes. Meet me at Sunset Station. Where's that? In Verdant Hills. Where is that?! Ask the cabby. Two hours. I'll see you there, I love you. Laughing, heart racing. I love you too. Now here he was the next day. He'd looked all over but never found his wife-to-be. He ended up playing no limit poker all night and winning big, then losing it all, mimicking his luck with the beautiful blonde. Now the morning had come and none of that mattered, he'd lived to tell an amazing story of the night before. If anyone asked.

Confident with his backstory he took a seat in front of a penny slot machine. While he waited for a cocktail waitress to walk by he tapped the buttons, pretending to play. He hoped it would be enough to finagle a cup of coffee. He'd say he forgot his player card or something. It was just one cup.

He waited and waited. Cocktail waitresses passed in the aisles next to him but never came close enough for him to call, never made eye contact. He hadn't realized how tired he still was until he felt a finger jab into his chest, waking him up from where he had fallen asleep against the slot machine.

"You can't sleep here."

A cocktail waitress stood before him. With

bleach blonde hair and long eyelashes, her face was pretty despite its disgruntled expression.

Cameron snapped awake and looked at the woman, taking notice of her skimpy uniform, her cleavage, her thick nude nylons, all from the safety of his sunglasses. She could see his eyes through the frames and was quickly losing patience.

"You either play or you leave."

"Uh, I'm sorry, I must have dozed off," he stammered back. He removed his sunglasses awkwardly and gave her a look like a kid caught with his hand in the cookie jar.

"Rough night, huh?"

"Boy, you wouldn't believe it."

"Tell me about it," she said turning her back to walk away.

"Excuse me," Cameron called after her.

She turned and looked at him, clearly impatient.

"Think I could get a cup of coffee?" he asked.

She frowned. His audacity hadn't gone over as well as he expected.

"You have to play to drink."

"I know, believe me I know. I just got lost from my friends, and I don't have anything on me. I don't need any alcohol. A cup of joe would really hit the spot, though."

She looked him over, eyeing his suit, his tattered shoes. She didn't believe a word he said. She sighed the sigh of someone for whom nothing matters. What difference did it make if she got him a cup of coffee? If she stuck to the rules and refused she wouldn't have anything else to do for the next eight hours. At least he wasn't rude or belligerent.

"Here," she said, handing him a red and white checkered five-dollar chip. "Play that a while. If I hand out a drink to someone who isn't playing they'll have my ass."

"I don't wanna take your tips, ma'am."

"Ma'am? Just take the chip and play a while. I'll bring the coffee. Or you can get the fuck outta here."

Cameron humbly took the chip. "Thanks. I appreciate it."

The woman shook her head. "Don't mention it."

He watched her walk away before cashing in the chip at the cage. Five bucks would last him a while on the penny slots. Maybe he'd have enough time to chat with the waitress, maybe she'd be impressed by his story of the night before. He was thinking of possible scenarios when he hit MAX BET without realizing it. The dealer hit blackjack and the money was gone. Triple goose-egg at the bottom. Please enter more credits.

"What?! No, no, no," he complained at the machine. "How could this happen?!" His heart was racing with feelings of guilt.

To his horror he saw the pretty cocktail waitress making her way back toward him. He could even make out the Styrofoam cup amongst the other drinks and know it was his coffee. If she saw the triple zero she would be pissed.

Before reaching him she stopped at a row of machines and handed out drinks to an elderly couple. While they dug in their pockets for tips he made his getaway, jumping from his seat and fast-walking away from the machine. He felt like a cheat. He knew he shouldn't look back but he couldn't help it. The waitress was giving him a dirty look and mouthing, "What the fuck?" She's going to call security, he thought. Act natural.

When he was on the other side of the casino he slowed down. He came to a café and looked through the glass at the people eating breakfast. Coffee and pie.

Scrambled eggs and toast. These people looked sober and happy, from good families. He wished he could go in there and have a normal breakfast.

A young hostess in a black uniform was standing at the entrance and noticed him staring. "Sir?" she called out to him.

"Huh? Yes?" Cameron replied. He was suspicious of her motives for addressing him.

She stood straight and spoke formally. Her appearance was immaculate, from pressed uniform to her black hair pulled tightly into a ponytail. Despite her formality, her face was gentle and she exuded kindness.

"Sir, we are offering a free slice of pie and unlimited coffee for all Premium Club Members. If you would be interested I can seat you."

"Uh, I'd like to but I can't really. No thank you. I'm not a member."

"That's okay, sir. If you want you can sign up for free." Her smile was wide and full of white teeth. "Offer still applies. We have key lime pie, it's really good."

"Key lime pie," he repeated.

"What do you say, sir?"

"No, no, thank you. I already had some coffee today." He had no idea why he lied, especially when it put him at a greater disadvantage. Now he just wanted to get out of the casino as fast as he could. The whole thing had been a huge failure.

"Alright," the hostess replied, disappointed. "Have a good day, sir."

"You too," Cameron said, forcing a plastic smile.

The double-doors of the exit were open and the sun was blinding as it came into the casino. Cameron walked toward the light feeling very regrettable about the way he had conducted himself. He'd second guessed himself at every turn and didn't know why. Deflated, he walked through the light. His stomach growled. He loved key lime pie. He loved coffee.

SEVEN

Outside it was warm. A system of grey clouds was moving in from the north. He headed south. Down Stephanie Street past the strip malls that shuffled their inventory of shops every few years. It was a street he knew well.

At the corner of Stephanie and Santiago stood the gated community where his mother's house was. His old house. He didn't remember how long it had been since he'd left. How ridiculous life is, how pointless, he thought, that he could walk back to his mother's house and go back to living his old life in less than five minutes. The world of his dreams out in the city, the wilderness, the danger, the independence: it could all be gone so easily. He never hinted at what he was doing or explained his journey to anyone. In a month he could even pretend to himself that it never happened.

He typed in the gate code and walked up the little street to his mother's house. It wasn't going to be that easy.

His truck was still parked on the sloping driveway the same as he'd left it. The garage door was closed, the curtains drawn. At the door he knocked three times and rang the doorbell. No one came. He walked around the back and went through the gate into the backyard. His soccer goal wasn't there anymore, but it hadn't been for years now. The grass needed to be mowed and weeded as usual. He reached through the doggy door and lifted the wooden stick that kept the sliding glass door locked. A trick he'd learned in high school.

Inside, the house had an eerie feeling of irreality. This was the house he had lived in for the better part of a decade and yet it seemed like any of the other houses he'd broken into lately. A squatter in his own house. A feeling that wasn't altogether unique to this moment.

His mother hadn't returned yet, that much was evident. Dishes were still in the sink and there was dust on the furniture. In the hallway there still lay the pieces of his cell phone. He gathered them up and re-inserted the battery. A pulse of excitement went through him as he powered it on. How many missed calls?

There were two messages. The first was from his mom, sounding chipper, saying they must have been disconnected. The other a robocall. No texts, a few spam emails. His iPhone had never seemed so useless, such overkill, so disgusting even to hold. It would come in handy, however, so he slipped it into his pocket after shutting it off.

He watched TV on the couch for a while but nothing was on. The pantry was lined with bright-labeled containers of flax, rows of flour and spices, but nothing edible.

Upstairs his room was still there, the soccer medals hanging from the wall, the unmade bed. This was his chance to call it a day. Go back to bed and it will all be over. Nothing seemed more unpalatable. None of it seemed real. He was a vandal. He'd broken into a home that belonged to someone else, belonged in someone else's life.

He left the way he came in, through the back door, putting the stick back and exiting the side gate. Leaving his old community he felt nothing.

Now the entire sky was grey. Everything above

him covered in a hazy sheet of nimbostratus. The road ended perpendicularly at a street named Horizon Ridge. He was at the edge of the world. All that lay ahead of him was a subdivision of mansions built into the rolling black mountains. Much of the steppe was still only terraced shelves of concrete foundations and nothing more.

He stood at the lone stop sign. Wind from passing cars whipped him in the face. A friend of his named Groll lived nearby. If he was home Cameron could kill a couple of hours hanging out in his garage.

Groll was part of a group of younger kids that had run with Cameron and his friends since high school. In that time Groll had risen from the rank of naïve whipping boy to that of social conduit. By college, everyone called him to find out where the parties were. Groll never answered his phone. Cameron walked toward his house halfheartedly, not expecting him to answer even if he was home.

When he got there Groll's car was parked in the driveway. Cameron heard music coming from the garage. Groll played in a couple of local bands, the garage served as their headquarters. Someone was repeating a bassline over and over to the crashing of drum symbols. Cameron banged on the metal garage door to no avail. The bassline repeated ceaselessly and whoever was drumming was lost in the zone. Cameron toe-kicked the garage in frustration, immediately regretting it, thinking it was too rash, but still no one inside heard. He thought about trying the doorbell, or trying to come in through the backyard but it was futile. He sat on the curb outside the house while the jam session raged on inside.

He scoffed. Even when he was willing to interact with the world the world would not oblige. Here he was, his friend so close, and nothing could be done to bring them together.

Disconsolate, he wandered through the neighborhood. The elaborate ditch that ran through Groll's neighborhood didn't attract his attention. In the middle of a street he came to an empty lot between two houses. It lay there as if all the homes were lego models and someone had plucked one of the pieces off the board.

"If I could live anywhere," Cameron said, standing in front of the empty lot. "I'd live at this house." He looked at the blank square of gravel. Wind blew plastic scraps over the rocks. "I call it Ghost

House. It is my Monticello."

The neighborhood was a series of twisting streets that led him around in circles. After walking around for a while he found himself back on a main road. Across the street from where he stood was another gated community where McKiscko lived with his parents. He didn't even consider paying them a visit. He didn't want to answer their questions about his life and what he was up to. He walked back up the road toward Horizon Ridge, because he didn't know where else to go, completing a big meaningless circle.

The afternoon darkened, the sky became dirty with grey ash. Behind the smog lurked true rainclouds but even they were filled with sand. The road curved a few times before the apex stoplight. Cameron walked on the shoulder, along the skeletal fence that shielded the street from the subdivision of undeveloped pummeled rock.

Like ruins from a destroyed volcano the black pumice sat piled in undulating hills. At the horizon of the wasteland was a thin layer of sunfaded homes, then the mountains he called Valhalla visible and imperceptibly far in the distance. He entered the area of rubble at a divot where the fence had fallen and walked toward the center of the lot until he couldn't see the road anymore. The scarecrow appeared out of the skymetal surroundings in perfect crystalline fashion. A face silently screaming hung crucified to a cross of iron. As he approached, it never stopped laughing. The pattern of a demented sharp smile was sewn onto the dummy head that lay to one side, starkly shadowed by a straw hat tejana. Each wrist was wrapped tight in barbed wire, an ear of corn dangling from either cuff to feed the frightened. Black jeans hung limply where legs should be, shoeless and empty. The red plaid shirt pixelized in the weather. He pulled the collar from about the neck. Marc Jacobs in gold cursive letters. He stood behind the scarecrow like its puppet master and surveyed the alien land. Sometimes the makings of a car flashed between the hills of mortar. No one would ever notice this statue out here. There was no reason for such elegance, such trouble.

It made him think of Rik Pollen. Only he had the twisted mentality to do something so pointless. Only he had the resources and will to make it happen. Rik had been a year older and gone to the same high school where he was a kind of outcast celebrity. One hardly remembered seeing him in class yet his grades were impeccable, he played no school sports but Presidential fitness tests showed physical abilities that were off the charts. Cameron knew of at least two separate residences of his, a gothic mansion next to the high school and an elegant highrise condo in the center of town, the latter which he financially maintained himself by selling narcotics. Weed and pills for sure. Certainly other business ventures Cameron didn't know about. And then of course there was the limousine. Rik had a driver that drove him around town in a Lincoln Towncar Limousine and it was just this vehicle that had come to Heff's house on that fateful day. It was Rik who had given Heff and him the opportunity for some quick cash and a chance to prove themselves in a hustler's world. It was he who Cameron still connected with the death of his good friend, Nick Niño.

He sat on the ground next to the scarecrow and recalled his old friend. They'd gone to elementary school together. Nick was the kind of kid that was always there for you; through the twists and turns of puberty and popularity he had remained a stalwart comrade, someone Cameron could talk to about anything. Despite the ruthless struggle to gain power, a quest that now seemed so ridiculous and petty but meant everything back then, Nick had asked nothing of him except to hang out. To meet up at the gazebo where they would smoke and joke around light-heartedly. "Are you still coming?" Nick had asked Cameron that night. As he left the house of none other than Rik Pollen, after his friends and the girl he had fallen for had all forsaken him, he went to go meet up with his last true confidante only to find the destroyed remains of Nick's corpse mercilessly splayed across their favorite hangout. The killer, some teenage Satanist, never seemed to exist in Cameron's mind. To him it was all because of Rik. Rik had made them his devil's offer and it was the dull glint in Rik's eye that he saw as the place where the knife went in.

The rain began to fall in acupuncture needles. He slicked back his hair and bundled up his collar, getting back to the road and taking it to where it ended. At the stoplight he stood in front of the closer mountains, the cousins of Valhalla. Psentaylion radio towers stood erect at their summits beaming their waves down onto the city, as if the sole purpose of their construction was some psychological message. He looked back to the ruined section of subdivision. He couldn't see the scarecrow and wondered if it had ever been there to begin with.

Down the road he walked, past McKiscko's neighborhood and all known haunts and refuge. Strip malls and strip malls, always more developments. In the housing boom even mountains weren't safe from the ravenous expansion. A Roberto's, a Fausto's, a Subway. Pick Up Stix and Wendy's. He noticed all the different restaurants now that the cramps in his gut were becoming more frequent. He hadn't eaten a thing that day.

The phone in his pocket was his savior. In a shopping center he found shop with a sign that read COMPUTER REPAIR.

Inside, an old Asian-looking man sat behind the counter. His expression denoted an ambiguous state of consciousness. Archaic flip phones and motherboards were hung from the walls, cords in boxes stacked on shelves all around him.

"You buy old iPhones?" Cameron asked the man.

The man barely stirred. "What model?"

"3."

"We take 3."

"How much?"

"I give you one hundred for iPhone 3."

Cameron almost squirmed with delight. He put the phone on the counter.

"ID," said the man.

"No ID."

The man studied him. His Asiatic face had a stoicism that gave away nothing. "I get receipt."

He came back and handed Cameron a form to fill out.

"What's this?" Cameron asked.

"You fill out the form we send you the check. One hundred dollars."

"How 'bout I give you the phone and you give me the hundred bucks." Cameron tried not to show his frustration.

"In mail, one hundred dollars."

"Check's in the mail, huh?" He enunciated very slowly, "I don't have a mailing address."

The man sized Cameron up, determining his level of desperation.

They bargained a deal that saw Cameron hand over the phone for fifty dollars cash in hand. He took the money and went straight to Fausto's. He ordered a shrimp burrito with rice and beans and a large drink. He doused the meal with salsa and filled up on carrots and cucumbers, drinking three refills worth of Jamaica.

After eating he found a spot next to an empty dumpster in a shopping center that was finished being built but had never had any tenants. Essentially a movie set sitting idle. The rain had stopped and he found a dry spot under a canopy. He could see the city, pink and gold neon in the distance, coming to light under the overcast. In his comfort he thought about Nick and the rest of his friends, of old times. Like the time they went to the dayclub on the Strip. It had happened the previous summer, only a few months ago, but already it seemed like a distant memory:

It was a Sunday morning and they'd all finally rolled out of bed after a night of gallivanting. Outside, he grabbed the swim trunks, a pair of very short faded neon pink shorts that said Aruba across the butt, from the trunk and hopped in McKiscko's Volvo. The rest of the group – Deni, Junichi and Sean -- crammed in and together they headed toward Uranus, the newest swank topless beach club on the Strip.

On the road he zoned out while trying to listen to Test Icicles' "Sharks" that was barely coming out of the speakers. In the middle of a conversation he picked up McKiscko telling everyone how exclusive the pool was and what a ridiculously good hook up they were all getting.

"I'm not kidding. Last week the Sultan of Malaysia was there and spent 700 grand. Shit's stupid. Justin said they ordered multiple three-liter torpedoes of Dom and shot them point blank at strippers in their cabana."

The whole car had a giggle at this.

"Who arranged this for us again?" Cameron asked.

"Justin," answered McKiscko. "He called it in."

"But it's Zoltán that we have to meet at the door," added Sean.

"Wait, I thought that Zoltán and Justin hated each other?"

"Yeah, remember when they came to blows outside of Cannons?" said Junichi.

"What about?"

McKiscko shrieked a laugh and explained. "It was your standard pissing contest. They were seeing who would throw the fattest stack of ones on the catwalk. They got into a big deal about whose was fatter, I think at one point Justin even brandished a ruler if you can believe it."

"You're kidding me."

"No, I swear."

"Yeah, it was stupid as heck," said Junichi.

"How would you know, Juney?!" McKiscko howled. "You passed out head first in a strippers crotch! You were the reason we got kicked out in the first place and now Zoltán is eighty-sixed for life!"

Roars of laughter accompanied this digression. Junichi turned beet red and tried to look away but he was thoroughly scrunched between Sean and Cameron with his armpits in both of their faces.

"The plot thickens!" cried Cameron.

"Finish the story!" Sean said between a fit of laughter.

McKiscko obliged.

"So why these two chuckleheads are literally measuring the stack of bills they've each taken out of their expensive pink and blue pinstriped D&G suits, not even realizing that the strippers on the catwalk had finished their songs and left the stage and no new strippers had come out, over at our table Juno has been just tanking shots of Jack. We're all sittin' around, mainly laughing at Justin and Zoltán, not really paying attention and then I look over and see Juno straight up faceplant right into this Asian bitch's crotch!"

A booming chorus of cheering disbelief spurned the story on.

"She was trying to get him to buy a dance and next thing you know he's on his knees comatose with his face buried in her pussy like he's giving her head or something and then two huge bouncers just swarm on top of him and it took the rest of us to fend them off! We all almost got our asses kicked."

Sean was nodding, coiled up in uncontrollable laughter. Junichi was squeezed even tighter and jabbed in the sides with pokes. Sean started tickling him which was a particular weakness of his. When he stopped screaming, or rather scream-laughing, all eyes fell to him to tell his side of the story.

"No, let me tell you what happened. I *had* been tanking shots of Jack Daniel's the whole time we were there because strippers kept coming up to me and pestering me about dances and the only way I could avoid them was to make myself a drink. Soon the coke was gone and I was forced to just drink it straight."

"Dude, you were on a mission to kill that bottle, don't lie. More than once you were scolded for fondling strippers!"

"Au contraire mon frère," Junichi protested.

"See, something weird happens every time I go to a strip club. I swear I always get lap dances, completely unprovoked and unasked for, and then there is always a hullabaloo about paying or not paying. I'm not paying for something I didn't ask for! I ain't falling for that shit!"

"Remember that one time that Lithuanian milf spit in your face?" Sean chimed in.

Junichi frowned in his direction and continued with his previous tale.

"Anyway, so this stripper, an Asian yes, she must have seen a brother or a countryman or something," (this joke caused several awkward glances to be exchanged throughout the car) "and she sits right on my thigh and starts gyrating. I swear, as soon as she sits down I tell her 'I am not going to pay you a dime.' Just like that I looked into her eyes and I said 'I will not pay you a god-damned dime.' I hadn't asked for a dance! I was faded and she pounced. Simple as that. So she jumps off me like I'm the surface of the sun itself and starts screaming at me in her language, which was not Japanese I can tell you that even with the little Japanese I know myself. I keep repeating that I'm not paying and I start kind of slurring and the lights and the mirrors and the music just got to be so much and next thing I know I'm in the backseat of Ragan's car while Zoltán and Justin are circling each other like they're going to fight. I swear I don't know what happened."

"So you don't remember being dragged out of Cannons by your arm pits with your fly undone and a huge boner poking out?" screamed McKiscko.

"Nooo, it wasn't like that!"

"It was, it was..." moaned Sean, in pain with tears of laughter.

Junichi looked around dumbfounded, because he really didn't remember and he wasn't sure if they were fucking with him or not.

"So why did Zoltán and Justin end up fighting after all that?" Cameron butted in, bringing the story back around full circle.

"We all get kicked out, luckily without getting our faces kicked in, and the bouncer, someone Zoltán had cultivated a mutually beneficial relationship with, warned him never to show his face in Cannons again. Apparently the people there are a really rough and scary crowd. Looking at it now it is lucky we didn't get in some serious trouble. Anyway, Zoltán was obviously pissed, and he and Justin never got on anyway, and they were already fighting about the size of their wads, and Justin just kept pushing his buttons once we got in the car and were about to leave. He kept taunting him and calling him a faggot and saying that his suits were two-cent Chinese fakes or that only a nigger would wear a stupid suit like that. Justin was in the passenger seat and Zoltán was sitting behind Regan who was driving. Justin kept going on and on and then Zoltán leaned back into his seat and just front kicked Justin in the face hella hard! Justin was turning back to taunt Zoltán and got a dress shoe straight to the mouth. It was crazy! We were all yelling TKO! TKO! And Justin *demanded* that Regan pull over, which he did in a parking lot behind a 7-11 and they got out and basically bumped chests and talked shit and eventually Zoltán called his girlfriend to come pick him up and Justin got back in the car and we left, Juney in the backseat moaning and spitting, Justin in the front crying."

There was a collective sigh as the last laughs slipped out the open windows. They were all frowning into the burning hot wind that blew into the car.

"Jesus," Cameron muttered.

"Well, at least we got the hook up," he added a moment later.

They valeted the car at Caesar's Palace and walked through the casino to the pool. Cameron had to change in a frantic rush, bunching up his clothes and throwing them in the backseat while McKiscko got the ticket. He had to walk the whole way to the pool without a shirt in the ridiculous pink trunks, but he was skinny and ripped from a summer of partying instead of eating, his skin so tan and his hair so dark and long that he actually looked quite stylish. Everyone seemed to be looking at him as he passed and he felt that they all were admiring his physique or complimenting his style. By the time they parted the doors and walked back out into the blazing heat heading toward the pool, Cameron was strutting with his shoulders back and chest out, abs flexed the whole time.

They got to Uranus and McKiscko and Sean high fived and joked with the doorman, a friend of Zoltán's they all knew. He checked everyone's IDs, Cameron was last, and when it was his turn he could only smile dumbly and say he didn't have one. The rest of the group was halfway to the cabana by then and only Sean turned and came back when he noticed something was wrong.

"What's going on?" he asked when he had gotten back to the entrance.

"I don't have an ID," Cameron mumbled.

Sean frowned and talked to the doorman. It didn't look good.

"Fuck," Cameron thought. This was a total buzzkill and he didn't want to keep his friends from the glorious party that awaited them just beyond the doorman.

When it seemed totally hopeless Sean reached into his pocket and slipped the doorman a twenty dollar bill.

"Right this way, sir," the doorman said, smiling behind his spray tan and white sunglasses.

He unhooked the rope and cleared the way for Cameron's entrance. Inside, he could see a heavenly beam of sunlight connecting the sky to the pool. The clouds had parted just for him.

Cameron thanked the doorman and thanked Sean profusely as they walked arm to arm toward the cabana.

"I'll pay you back, I promise."

"No worries, man."

The energy in the pool was high and yet relaxed. Bumping four-on-the-floor house beats skittered over the glistening water and the shining skin of topless women; the muscly men standing waist high in the pool, which was fairly small; and the patrons sunbathing in chaise lounges. Groups of European models walked to the bar and back drinking champagne or Cuba Libres with huge triangles of pineapple clipped to their cups.

"This is paradise, mate," Cameron whispered. "Right?"

The cabana was a cave with an arched roof, the walls completely covered in grass that looked and felt real. A flat-screen HDTV was perched in the corner of the ceiling, playing La Liga. Across the green plasma Cristiano ice skated through defenders. Soon a beautiful cocktail waitress in what could be called a bathing suit arrived and took their drink orders. McKiscko told them they were with Zoltán and after some speaking into her wrist intercom and listening through invisible ear buds like some Secret Service agent posing as a cocktail waitress, she smiled seductively and said that everything was compliments of Mr. Lexus and please, enjoy.

"A bottle of Grey Goose is on the way, and if you would like anything else please let me know," she added. She had a soft, hypnotizing voice. "If you want to order from the bar just tell them Cabana 2 and say that you're LGX and it will be taken care of."

She left and returned and the bottle was poured and drank, two more were ordered, and cup after clear plastic cup of Rosé was ordered from the bar and consumed. They ordered steak quesadillas and Cobb salads and grilled squid. They collapsed on the daybed and watched as Madrid hammered the ball into the upper 90.

"Pillow party in the grass canyon," Cameron said without thinking. It just came out as he stared at the grass ceiling and fingered the soft plastic blades, drunk and burned totally by the relentless, beautiful sun.

They got into the pool, and drunk as they were, began play-fighting, splashing and wailing with no regard for anyone around them, but no one seemed to mind; those they shared the pool with were like extras picked from a fashion show paid not to care. In a fit of inspiration Junichi punched Cameron square in the cheek, hard enough to cut the inside of his mouth as it squished against his teeth. It would turn into a wicked canker sore but for now it was hilarious and they kneed each other in the stomachs and fought like animals.

An hour later it was still sweltering, the kind of hot that burned away any care you could ever have. Cameron lay in the chaise longue and watched the people around him. He couldn't believe how many beautiful women were topless and careless. In the middle of a group of particularly sexy specimens a man stood facing elsewhere, completely frozen like a statue. It looked like his entire body was covered in Vaseline, even his hair and glasses. He was impeccably cut, not a single muscle failed to protrude and take shape within the form of his body. Low-rise Armani trunks fit his sculpted thighs perfectly. His hair was spiked and bleached pure platinum.

"Who could ever make themselves up like that?" Deni asked, noticing where Cameron was looking. "The dude literally looks like a Ken doll. I bet his package is just a smooth ridge of nude colored plastic."

"I think he's trying to embody a symbol," Cameron responded.

"Symbol for what? The ultimate faggot?"

"For the perfect man."

Deni scoffed and put a straw hat over his head, his fingers never leaving the cup of champagne at his side.

Cameron watched the man a little longer. He never moved and never looked at anyone. You work toward some idea of perfection, Cameron thought, and when you get there you lose all your humanity. He didn't know if this was a good thing or bad.

"Paradise Circus" by Massive Attack came on, some remix of the song Cameron had never heard but immediately took a desperate liking to. He bolted off the chaise and made his way over to the DJ, a hefty black man wearing a purple shirt and extremely expensive headphones tilted over his head.

"Excuse me," Cameron said to the DJ.

The DJ looked at him like he was vermin.

"Uhh, hey, I really like this song. What remix is it?"

The DJ scowled a scowl that Cameron would never forget. The pure disgust pierced him like a spear.

"What remix is this?" the DJ asked.

"Yeah, what remix is it," Cameron said, completely uncertain of why his question should draw such ire.

"What remix is *this*?" the DJ repeated.

"Yeah. What remix is this," Cameron answered back curtly.

"Feelin' on yo booty," the DJ whined back at him. He couldn't have pissed on Cameron's question any worse; such was his facial expression and tone of voice. He changed the song with a rip and the speakers poured out some popular EDM song that clashed with the mood and sounded awful.

Cameron recoiled in shock.

"If you ever ask me about what I play again I will fucking kill you," the DJ said.

"Wow," Cameron gasped to himself, turning and walking back to the cabana, tail between his legs. The afternoon was on the move, it was cooling off and aqua storm clouds were swelling over Uranus. The gentlemen were drunk and exhausted and giddy; the altercation with the DJ just another one of the crazy events of the day. They thanked the cocktail waitress and everyone except Cameron tipped her generously and Cameron promised everyone that he'd pay them back, but even that couldn't spoil the glorious luxury of the sparkling sky blue diamonds twinkling all around them, moving up and down at a measured thumping tempo set by the angry DJ that kept everyone at the pool in a delirious state of ecstasy…

Back in "real" time, it wasn't long before he was sleeping, arms wrapped around his body in the fetal position under the canopy. The feelings of failure and emptiness mixed with dreams of flying down a canal in a futuristic Miami, ripping through the water on a holographic See-Doo shooting lasers at enemies to the score of an unreleased track from Cut Copy.

▲

Most of the day was spent walking down the Strip toward downtown. The panorama ranged from cheap timeshares and outlet malls to the main drag and its famous casinos. The replicated monuments gleaming a dull pyrite under the dusty autumn sky. Las Vegas Boulevard shot out before him like a wormhole or a vector to the northern mountains, where the shadowplay from the clouds turned stone into illusion. Among the Grand Guignol of advertisements the masses of temporary carpetbaggers flashed by like a morning hallucination.

Once he reached downtown the quaint cottages were a stark contrast to the gaudiness of the Strip. Tiny homes with manicured front lawns and rosebushes had been converted into law offices. No other pedestrians were on the road, no cars parked next to the meters. A boarded up house on the corner advertised Office Supplies, a queer anachronism in the syphilitic museum of a neighborhood.

He walked down Bridger Avenue, past rent-controlled apartments and half-hour hotels. Art Deco government buildings sat vacant next to plots of empty desert. He couldn't see the Encore or Venetian above the houses anymore. On the other side of the quiet ghetto where he stood the concrete structures of the El Cortez and Lady Luck represented a bygone era now living in hospice.

In an empty lot of gravel there was a warning written in black letters on orange metal.

NO TRESPASSING

Someone had laid a bouquet of flowers at the base of the sign. They looked like the makeshift memorials for victims of car accidents. Hyacinth, twirled lavender and pink torpedoes shot out from bunches of leopard lilies and Brewer's lupine. Tucked into the flowers Cameron spotted a white business card. It read

FRM TLK – theVictims.co.uk.

When Cameron bent down to read the

inscription he could see the flowers were firmly rooted in the hard caliche.

As he was studying the installation two men in orange vests listlessly dragged their government-issue equipment past him on the street. One trailed a trashcan behind him in a dolly while the other walked with a broom resting on his shoulder. The squeaking wheels of the dolly stopped in front of Cameron.

"You got a cigarette, bro?" asked the man with the broom.

"Nah."

The trashman sighed. "La perra."

"What're you guys doing?" Cameron asked.

"What's it look like? Community service."

"Come on, man, we can't stand around here," urged the trashman. "They patrol the streets."

The man with the broom looked at Cameron and shrugged. "We gotta go, dude."

They started past him.

"Need some help?" Cameron called out to them.

The man with the broom faced him again and laughed. "There ain't shit to pick up. There was a dead pigeon a few blocks back but that was it."

"But you still have to keep walking up and down the street?"

"Yeah," said the trashman. "For another 96 hours or so."

"Shit."

"You can roll with us if you *want*. Anything to make the time go faster."

Cameron fell in with them as they did ladders on Bridger from Main Street to 15th. The trashman was named Miguel, he had one-hundred and forty-six hours of community service for unpaid traffic tickets. The man with the broom was Carl, serving his court appointed sentence of one-hundred hours for marijuana possession. Cameron mainly talked with Miguel, about Mexican soccer then Mexican politics. They agreed that most Americans knew too little with regard to the Mexican realpolitik. Carl walked along the street mock swinging his broom like a baseball bat. He didn't say much.

Walking past an alcove behind the Golden Nugget, a homeless man was sleeping against the wall. His trucker hat was pulled down over his face. He slept with his knees folded against his chest, arms crossed like he was trying to block out the cold. When they walked by him again, almost an hour later, the bum hadn't moved a millimeter. Further up the road an ambulance and a police squad car passed them and stopped next to the alcove. Both responders had their lights on but no siren. The next time around, the scene had been reduced to a single security guard standing serenely in front of where the bum had been sleeping.

"What happened?" Cameron asked the guard.

"Nothing."

The guard continued to stare at Cameron until he and the others walked away.

Back at the memorial again, Cameron said goodbye to Miguel and Carl. They thanked him for the company and he wished them luck as they completed their hours.

*   *   *

On Las Vegas Boulevard, buried in a cluster of pawn shops was an apartment complex called Vanguard. Cameron knew some friends that lived there and thought he'd pay them a visit. As he crossed the street the bum's image stayed with him. The sun burned warm but it was the phantom chill the bum had tried to squeeze out that he felt deep in his bones.

At Vanguard a flag flew atop the building where

his friends lived. The entrance gate had been left ajar. Inside it was quiet except for a couple arguing on a patio a few buildings away.

He climbed up the stairs to the apartment where Whinny and Snow lived. Whinny was sitting in a lawn chair on the patio. He squinted up at Cameron, peeking from under the upturned bill of his cycling cap. Smoke trailed from the wooden pipe he was holding.

"Ahoj, Whinny."

"Hey, man," Whinny answered. He always drawled and always sounded half-surprised. "What's happening?"

"Just in the neighborhood. Thought I'd come by to make sure you guys were okay."

Whinny looked around his lawn chair. "We're fine, man."

"Glad to hear it. Where's Snow?"

"On the roof as always." He toked on the wooden pipe, tapping the carb repeatedly with his index finger. "As fuckin' always," he added, exhaling.

Whinny offered Cameron the pipe. He took it and lit the greying embers in the bowl, blowing out a full cloud of blue smoke.

"That's some high-quality hashish," Whinny

told him.

Cameron nodded and coughed. His heart started speeding up and tingles went through his body.

"I'm gunna go see what Snow is up to."

"By all means."

Cameron went through the apartment and took the fire escape to the roof. Snow was sitting at one of the MacBook Air laptops he had set up on stacks of recycling crates. They were connected to each other and the tower in the middle of the roof through a series of bright colored firewire cables. A camera was set up on a tripod with its viewfinder flipped out toward Snow. Through the small screen Cameron could see a duplication of the El Cortez that lay just north of the apartment.

Cameron walked up to Snow and clapped him on the back.

"How goes it, mate?"

Snow frowned, barely turning from the screens. "Oh, hey."

"What are you doing?"

"Working."

"What's the project?"

Snow chattered on the keyboard, making a series of hieroglyphics appear on the monitor. He clicked the mouse furiously, as if the clicking brought him closer to something.

He hit enter and turned to face Cameron completely.

"I'm logging the day's film. It's part of a movie I'm working on. It should hopefully screen sometime next year if all goes well. It's really gaining momentum."

Cameron looked through the viewfinder. The American flag and the Nevada flag flapped lazily in the breeze atop the El Cortez. The neon sign looked small and old without its lights on. The Silver Slipper on Freemont Street looked like a toy.

"Some documentary about downtown?" It seemed documentaries about downtown's budding arts scene were in vogue lately.

"In a manner of speaking I suppose. It's a time lapse. I'm filming the El Cortez for an entire year. When I'm done I'm going to screen the film in its entirety, all in realtime."

Cameron blinked slowly. "Ambitious."

"Yeah, I'm excited about it. No one else is doing it."

"What inspired you to start this?"

Snow adjusted himself in his seat. "I've always

believed that the ultimate goal of film is to capture reality. In digital form a real moment can last forever. The time-lapse 'slowed down' to realtime becomes a meditation on reality. When I play it back, it will be like this year is happening, in the future, simultaneously."

He adjusted a wire and went back to entering notes into the computer. Cameron stared off, past the subject of Snow's film to the north. Las Vegas Boulevard curved into a two-lane street and disappeared. New settlements rolled toward the horizon with miles of blank desert between them and the mountains.

"Where's the connection?" Cameron asked.

Snow twitched. "What do you mean?"

"Well, you talked about the goal of film. I think, you know, the goal of art in general is to connect people – through emotions. I just wondered what you thought about that, or, where you see that connection in this project."

Snow turned back around. He was frowning as if Cameron's idea was of minor significance.

"The distance between each one of us is infinite. The closest we can ever get to any 'connection' would be like looking into a snowglobe of someone else's life.

In that respect, what I am offering fulfills the goal of art better than most."

Cameron nodded in consideration. "I like it in any event."

Whinny came onto the roof then. Some friends had called saying they were going to Fatty's for drinks and invited the three of them to join. People were meeting at Misday's house to pregame. Snow was the only one with a car, so after some cajoling they got into his Ford Focus and drove toward Misday's house in Verdant Hills.

Cameron was thankful to be leaving downtown. The image of the frozen bum hadn't gone away. Snow's attempt to recreate the present moment and make it last forever didn't help.

He kept his forehead against the cool window and watched the city slide past him as they sped down the '95. The stereo played "Panic" by The Stills from Snow's iPod. Cameron's heart raced along with it.

EIGHT

The lights shining under the eaves cast a spooky glow over Misday's house. Cardboard ghosts swayed from the branches of the pine trees. A pair of torn Burberry boxers hung limp from the flagpole in the middle of the walkway. Misday had seen them arrive from the window of his bedroom and was waiting at the door as they walked up.

After a brief hello to Misday's parents who were sitting in the living room they followed him up the stairs to his room. He had the master bedroom, consisting of a large anteroom and a smaller bedroom separated by two doors. Assembled in the anteroom were the regulars: McKiskco and Ragan were sitting on the leather couch, Harper sat at the computer while Deni lounged on the chaise longue. A bottle of Buffalo Trace sat on the coffee table next to shot glasses and a jug of orange juice. "Three Sheets" episodes looped on the TV.

Everyone slapped fives and found chairs to pull up. Cameron plopped in between McKiscko and Ragan on the couch.

"So whose shorts did I have to salute out there?"

"What do you mean?" Misday asked, looking concerned.

"There's a pair of dundies flappin' in the wind out there. You guys didn't see 'em?!"

Misday bolted to the window. Sure enough, imprinted on a pair of holey boxers was that familiar pattern so often counterfeited hanging in the place of Old Glory.

Misday aimed his accusatory grimace at Cameron. "What the hell, man. Who did it? Was it you?"

The others had gotten up to check it out. Their laughter only increased as Misday desperately tried to find the culprit.

"Wasn't me, man. You saw us get here."

"Those fucking kids. They got it coming, those disrespectful assholes."

There was a gaggle of younger blokes that lived

across from Misday. They were still in high school and prone to the mischief of boys their age. The pranks and jollies that the boys in Misday's room still engaged in.

"Don't worry, man. We'll take it down," consoled McKiscko.

"No, fuck that. That flag was a gift from our Congressman back in Pittsburgh. It's been in our family for decades."

"It's okay. We'll find it," assured McKiscko. The others bit their lips to keep from laughing.

While the seating arrangement was in flux, Cameron snagged the chair at the computer and immediately typed "thevictims.co.uk" into the Firefox toolbar. The monitor turned into a shining display of TV static. Black and white and metallic blue dots collided into each other at lightspeed while fuzz purred out of the subwoofers.

"What is that?" Ragan asked from the couch.

"A website I found today. Someone put it on a sign downtown."

The sizzle of static dissipated and the screen turned black. Then slowly in Helvetica Ultralight three words appeared:

"WHAT   IS   THERE"

"What is there," Cameron whispered.

He tried the mouse, no links. No easter eggs. He hit the refresh button. Nothing.

The group had lost interest and was busy pouring shots. Cameron joined in, cringing at the acid burning of the bourbon.

"Kara and Lizzy are coming over," Ragan said, slapping McKiscko on the arm with the back of his wrist.

"Okay."

Ragan stared at him intently.

"Who are they?" Cameron asked.

"These girls I met at Diesel."

At the mention of girls Cameron took the chance to appraise his appearance. His suit was already dirty. There were wrinkles he couldn't hide. He went to the bathroom to wet his hair and slick it to the side, clean his fingernails. He spritzed some of Misday's Acqua di Gio on his chest and came back out.

"Freshened up, huh?" asked McKiscko.

"Yep. How do I look?" He spread his arms and looked at himself again.

"You look like shit."

The girls arrived soon after. They were dressed similarly, in black tights or dark jeans, thin T-shirts and black jackets. They said hello to Ragan and shook hands with Misday as he welcomed them in. By then the room was abuzz with the clinking of shotglasses and the sounds of The Knife's *Silent Shout* coming from the computer speakers. Kara and Lizzy sat on the couch, while Ragan made room for them and poured them cocktails of bourbon and OJ.

"So, ladies. Tell us about yourselves," said Misday.

They looked at each other. "Like what do you want to know?"

"You from here?"

"Yeah. Lizzy came from LA a few years ago. I'm from here."

"What high school?"

"Bishop Gordon. Both of us."

"Oooooh, we got Gordon girls on our hands," chimed Harper.

"What's that supposed to mean?"

"Well, you know what they say about girls from Catholic schools. If they haven't had an abortion they're probably bulimic."

"Jesus Christ, who told you that?" snapped Kara.

"What a dick thing to say," echoed Lizzy.

"Hey, I don't make the rules," said Harper,

waving his hands.

"So, which one are you?" asked Misday.

"What?"

"Abortion or bulimic?"

"Uhh, neither. I could tell you some stories, though."

"Do tell."

"Nah, there were just some crazy girls at our school."

"Yeah, a lot of sluts," added Lizzy.

"We know all about it," said McKiscko. "We all went to Verdant Hills, except for Deni and Cameron. They went to Charnell. It's in the ghetto."

"Damn right," said Deni.

"You still haven't told me," said Misday. "I really wanna know."

Kara gave Misday a sour face and said, "I don't puke. That's disgusting."

Misday's eyes lit up.

It didn't take long for the whole of the pregame to center on brash comments aimed at the girls, while they sat on the couch looking blasé as they waited to be impressed. Ragan had chatted them up earlier that day at his store. He assumed that gave him dibbs on at least one of them, although Lizzy had been eyeing up McKiscko since she arrived and Misday had moved in full force with his patented brand of flirting. Harper scored points for being most abrasive while Deni made the odd comment that drew a positive reply. Snow and Whinny talked to themselves. Cameron watched the muted Premiership highlights that repeated themselves on the TV. His favorite teams were losing, bereft of all their best players due to injury or other teams' poaching. He followed the conversation, awaiting the moment to chime in with a witty comment, but his friends had cornered the market. He looked at Kara and Lizzy. Both had the faces of people who wouldn't naturally look that way; either a change of haircolor or the way they did their makeup fundamentally altered their appearance. They looked like girls with whole histories behind them they wanted to cover beneath a layer of foundation. He didn't blame them for that. He felt the uselessness of trying to penetrate that outer layer. And for what? He wasn't in love with them. He most definitely wasn't going to sleep with them. He hadn't said a word in the past twenty minutes. He'd already lost that competition. What then was the point in speaking?

"Why is he so quiet?" Lizzy asked sheepishly, looking over to Cameron.

He snapped out of the thoughts that had been boring deeper and deeper into his brain. Everyone waited for a response.

"Are we gunna do this or what? I'm tryin' to hit the bar."

He stood from his chair and walked over to the computer so they wouldn't have to all sit and stare at him like that. He changed the song to "The Prayer" by Bloc Party. The last thing he wanted to do was go to a bar and smalltalk. There was nowhere to hide in the cramped little box that was Fatty's. He listened to the music in hopes to gain some inspiration, but the group responded quickly to his rhetorical question and before his favorite part they had left.

NINE

A crunching sound woke Cameron from where he slept face down on Deni's couch. He cracked an eye open. The portable fan in the living room made half circles, fluttering the curtain as it motioned over the window. The crunching continued. He lifted himself and turned around. His hair was sticking up, the pattern of the upholstery tattooed on his face. Deni stood in the kitchen mixing a bowl of Kashi Good Friends cereal with a spoon.

"You alive?" Deni asked.

Cameron groaned a response.

Deni shook his head and went back to stirring his cereal.

"What time is it?" Cameron asked.

"Lil past one."

A loud siren was circling in Cameron's head.

"Jesus. Last night was somethin' else."

"I'll say." Deni took his cereal and walked back to his room.

Cameron looked at his suit and dress shirt crumpled in a mess on the floor. Deni must have given him the shorts he was wearing. He put a hand on his forehead and tried to remember the events of the previous night.

He didn't remember leaving Fatty's, or how they got to Deni's apartment. There was the two of them running across the hoods of cars in a parking lot. He remembered Deni kicking off the side mirrors of a truck. Then screaming at the passing cars on Whitney Ranch, daring them to stop and see what happened. And finally, the view of the moon above the streetlight from where he'd fallen into some bushes.

A pipe was sitting on the coffee table. He picked it up to take a toke but there was no lighter and only resin in the bowl.

Settling back into the folds of the thin couch Cameron closed his eyes. The rest of the night came back to him like memories of a movie he had seen a few years ago when he was high.

The dazzling faded lights of Fatty's swirled

around him while he talked with two acquaintances, Simon and Donna. They were always together, joined at the hip by some invisible linkage that also served as a formidable barrier. Most assumed that they were together, but whenever anyone asked about their relationship, one of them always answered with a laugh followed by a vague, inaudible response. It was true that they never slept with one another, although they often slept in the same bed. Their conversations never strayed from current events or the constant prompts they received on their phones.

While Cameron's friends immersed themselves in the raging party noise that filled the bar, he stood at the counter shifting his pint of Killigan's Irish Red and debated music with the unamorous duo. Despite the smoke and noise and lights Cameron was zeroed in on their conversation, as if they sat in a bubble all their own, sealed off from the cacophony and confusion.

A remix of Fall Out Boy's latest single, the inspiration for the debate, was blaring out of the jukebox. This version included a chorus voice-over by Mary J. Blige and a phoned-in verse from 50 Cent.

"You know, I don't understand it. The way a band like Fall Out Boy can be so popular these days." Cameron took a chug from the pint and explained. "I mean, it doesn't surprise me that such shitty music can be popular, but what I can't for the life of me understand, are certain *people* who are their fans. I mean, take this song that's playing now for example. I know people that like this song who only listened to Converge and Dillinger Escape Plan a mere *two years ago*."

Donna looked nervously at the vodka water she had barely sipped. Simon, someone who was always coiled into the fetal position whether standing or sitting, rotated his head to look at Cameron through lenseless ivory frames.

"What's the big deal? People have eclectic tastes," he said. "With the internet and music sharing, everything is accessible and peoples' tastes have become much more diverse. Consequently, their taste also changes much faster than before."

"You know what, Simon? I think that is total and utter bullshit."

Simon flinched and curled back into his roly-poly default posture. Donna stared wide-eyed at them, more interested in seeing what strained figments of masculinity might come out of what was surely becoming a spat. Who was going to belittle the other into submission? She watched on intently to find out.

"Why is it bullshit?" Simon almost whispered. "People can't like rap and rock at the same time?"

"Here's why it's bullshit. Two years ago, the same people who were wearing tight black Zao T-shirts – who defined themselves as hardcore and wore their favorite bands like badges of honor, the people who dyed their hair and gauged their ears – these people can tell me to my face without any shame that they like fucking Fall Out Boy? The motherfucker that kicked and flailed like an idiot in the moshpit at House of Blues so recently, has the nerve to play a Fall Out Boy duet with Mary J. Blige on the god damn jukebox?! This is unacceptable to me. Not because tastes change and people change and people like contradictory forms of music. But because the same individual will embrace the anathema of their former love, so soon, *and have no realization of it whatsoever.*"

Simon and Donna took his ranting like a personal accusation of treason; which, in a way it was, because both Simon and Donna could be lumped into the category of people Cameron just described. Cameron saw the empty holes in Simon's ears under his flat-brimmed Starter hat and worried that he had unintentionally made the argument too personal. He continued in a calmer tone.

"I grant you technology has widened peoples' tastes, but that still doesn't excuse these musical blackguards I'm talking about."

"What's your beef with Fall Out Boy, anyway?" Donna interjected.

"I'll put it to you like this: I got a word for bands that only sing about girls."

"What's that?"

"Bitchmade."

Simon jerked his attention toward Cameron then, seized by some hibernating enthusiasm. Or perhaps he sensed Cameron's conciliatory tone as an opening to strike. Donna stood close by his side.

"I'm sorry, bro, but you just sound like a hater. You see a band who works their ass off, who've been busting their ass for the better part of a decade, come into their own and find success, and just because it doesn't fit your idea of 'a perfect artsy-fartsy intellectual band' you can't stand it so you hate on them and anyone who likes them. I think what they've been able to do is impressive and I support them. If I was in their place I would do it in a second."

They both looked at Cameron like they had put

a period at the end of the argument. Cameron, with perhaps too much hesitation, still backpeddling to make sure that they weren't personally offended, replied:

"Well, it seems we share a different rubric for what 'good music' is. Success was never a factor that I looked for in the bands I like. If it was, I would only buy Celine Dion records."

The lackluster tone in which he made his final point sounded in the ears of his debaters like a concession. The near-fury he had worked himself into intensified his drunkeness so he quickly downed the rest of his beer and ordered another. Simon and Donna went back to mumbling to one another and scrolling through their phones. Cameron walked off but he didn't know where to.

Remembering the argument on Deni's couch, in Deni's borrowed clothes, he had to smile at all of his punchlines and the vehemence in which the honesty had rushed out of him. It wasn't his intention to pick a fight with the two, but rather, it was like his private feelings couldn't be contained any longer. It felt good to release them. He thought about how the wounded non-couple looked, in their ironic clothes, so easily offended. Those poor souls would never realize that it was he who was offended by their caprice.

He looked over at his suit. It lay in a pile on the floor next to the couch, wrinkled beyond what any iron could smoothen.

What about his convictions on music? His staunch patriotism for the bands he deemed worthy; what had any of that gotten him? Sooner or later even the most meaningful songs would get played out and too many evenings had been spent recycling the same old classics while he waited for his chosen artists to grace him with another release. Someone would always find the music he loved to be as petty and lowbrow as Fall Out Boy or any of the other bands he belittled. If taste could never be objective – he believed it couldn't – then he had been guilty of using his as a weapon to justify himself against those he thought vulgar. His convictions were a dull mental sword that cut nothing.

Deni walked out of the room again trailing Lizzy behind him. Her hair hung over her face, concealing the brashness she had shown to the group at Misday's house.

"I'm gunna walk her to her car," Deni said.

"Cool. Mind if I shower?"

"Go ahead."

He showered and put the suit back on. He wiped a circle out of the condensation and took a long look at himself in the bathroom mirror. The suit wasn't too messed up after all. He still looked good. Maybe that was all that mattered.

Deni came back and the two sat on the couch watching TV. After watching Divorce Court for twenty minutes Cameron felt a sudden urgent need to leave. His goodbye was brief and his exit from the apartment swift.

In the coming hours he waded deeper into Verdant Hills, taking blind alleys and hidden drives through neighborhoods where he knew no one. It had become a pastime of his to look at the houses, at the neighborhoods encased in a wash of white stucco, with their comfortable two-story domiciles, and imagine different lives to be lived in each one. He imagined back rooms where he could have an office and make fortunes off speculating with the simple click of a mouse, the proceeds of which he'd use to fund an extravagant jet-set lifestyle. Strolling down the sidewalk, the leaves of the trees were just beginning to turn, auguring a dead black winter. He loved fall but the season gave him a feeling of melancholy and dread. Bittersweet melancholy as the last rays of summer were finally expiring, and dread for the long frozen season ahead. He had grave doubts as to what he would do once the stale, frigid air of a Las Vegas winter finally set in. In the rooms of all the homes he passed, he would possess every material needed to make even the coldest season beautiful.

What a wonderful exercise for the imagination, he thought. So many scenarios hiding behind the facades, infinite possibilities happening in the backyards you can't see. Good thing you only have the time it takes to walk by to imagine, because getting any closer to reality, or the truth, would ultimately be disappointing. No, it's not about what's there, what is actually happening. It's about the façade and what that brings to mind. Somehow, that feeling inspired by the rolling homes and sprawling lawns must indicate something that truly exists. Some occult reality that far outshines anything you can see. So much can be learned from fantasy. Fantasy is more truthful, more clairvoyant certainly, than any fact. Facts are meaningless these days. Perhaps they always were. Facts with so many asterisks. So many conditions needed for any one declarative to be worth anything. Margin for error. Laboratory circumstances. No, facts mean nothing. Fantasy is where the power lies. Ask someone to describe their perfect day. Tell them that they can do whatever they want, no one will ever hear what they say, they don't have to worry about anyone finding out anything embarrassing; tell them the world is theirs for the creating and see what happens. Wouldn't their fantasy world be more indicative of who they are, on the inside, what their feelings are, what drives them, what motivates them, what scares them, than any fact? Objective reality. I don't believe in objective reality. We're all just free-associating our lives into one another, projecting our inner fantasies, whether we are aware of them or not, whether they are hideous and terrifying or achingly beautiful or hopelessly pedestrian. We're all crossing our wires so that no one is ever on the same page or talking about the same thing, even if the subject of the conversation is x, y or z. Movies we like. Records we like. People we love. Concepts we agree on. Who knows if we ever find the same wavelength. That undulating force that loops from behind the facade, the sun's rays caught in the silhouette of a cloud, the autumn breeze through a cracked window caressing your thigh. If a house burns down when no one is home, does the fire still trail sharply into the dark pink sky of twilight, puffing black clouds from burning family photos and family heirlooms into the purple night to add the perfect balance of texture and color to the evening?

By sunset he'd come to a dead end. Windmill Road terminated at a deep canon that ran between two neighborhoods. A ravine choked with sagebrush and lantana and anything that could survive on its own. It had been a happy hunting ground for teenage paintballers until an arsonist put a hex on the whole corridor. The neighborhood on the north side of the ditch was called Silver Springs. It was made up of a few clusters of homes on either side of a winding two-lane street. It had its own rec center and elementary school. Some time ago, the city had inexplicably constructed an amphitheater behind the rec center for plays that never happened. Now it stood situated in between the backyards of houses and the ditch like ruins of a Druid altar or some surviving remnant of pagan times.

Cameron remembered when those boys died on that winding road. The little brother of someone he knew, and some of his drunken friends, drove straight into a wall at ninety miles per hour. He remembered the massive memorial erected at the pulverized wall. All the bouquets and signs and letters. They were all gone now. The flowers had been blown by the breeze into the ravine where one day they might blossom into living tributes of those young boys. The roses and mums tossed by the wind onto the smooth stone of the amphitheater like ovations to the ghosts upon the stage. The ravine stayed there however, would always be there, useless except as a receptacle for the city's forgotten pain. A host to memorial flowers wilted and crumbled to dust on that burial ground in the middle of the city, forgotten yet existing all the same.

TEN

He stood long at the stoplight, looking at the crack in the earth that trailed to the swirling cosmos above the horizon. The fence that served as a barrier on the overpass was a collage of campaign posters for assemblymen and other such insignificant magisterial positions. He felt enervated as he turned around and started walking back the way he had come.

Up the hill a way he'd passed a little park that was tucked in a grove of eucalyptus trees. Chillpointe 2, they used to call it. Back in high school, when he and his friends were in Verdant Hills, they used to stop there and smoke pot, shoot hoops. He was heading toward the old park benches when he heard a strange sound coming from someone's backyard.

"C'Na."

He looked everywhere, but couldn't find the source of the sound. He shrugged and kept moving when the noise sounded again, like a mischievous loon calling out to him.

"C'Na, C'na!"

He'd heard that sound before. Someone used to address him by those truncated syllables.

"C'Na!"

When the noise sounded again he jumped quickly toward it. Above the stucco wall of a backyard were the bleached spikes of a mini-Super Sayan haircut.

"Jai Jai? Eres tu?!" Cameron called out.

The spikey afro bobbed a few times more before Jair popped his chest over the wall. He gave Cameron a devilish smile.

"Simón, C'na."

C'Na was the shortened version of Cameron's nickname. With him and his buddies, nicknames evolved fast: in the past few years Cameron had gone from Cameroon to Roony, Roons and Roon, before dovetailing into Rooniker, Roondoque and Roondoggle, then finally settling back on Roons. For Jair, a name that was uncommon and confusing enough for most people, anyway, it was Zaire followed by Jai Jai. Cameron called him Espiérnan too, but mostly just J'Na. In turn Jair called Cameron C'Na.

Cameron called out again in amazement, "No mames, cabron!"

Jair leapt over the wall and they met with high fives. He was five-foot three with a square body. He always wore baggy shorts and skateboarding tees. People gave him shit for being small, but he was fast and strong beyond his looks, as he proved time and again on the soccer field.

"What's up, mang?" he said, pinching the lapel of Cameron's blazer. "Where you goin' lookin' all fly?"

"Shit man, I was headin' toward the park. You remember Chillpointe, right?"

"Pssh, what are you doing up there?"

"I was planning on hanging out for a while. See what's crackin'."

"Fuckin' Roony."

"What're you up to? You never return my calls."

This was true. Getting Jair on the phone was like calling God himself. You could call, but most likely no one answered.

"My phone got shut off. I was in Mexico."

"Acapulco?"

"Simón, güey," Jair answered with a twinkle in his eye.

They had begun to make their way down the sidewalk. Jair's house was not far off.

"Come back to the crib and chill a while. Say what's up to Arturo. Zoom Zoom is rollin' over in a bit and we're gunna smoke a bluntsky."

Zoom Zoom, aka Richard Alvares, was Jair's friend since childhood. Needless to say, Zoom Zoom Bangarangatang had been shortened to just Zoom Zoom.

"Ha, no shit. What up with good ol' Zoomy? I forgot about that nigga."

"Well, come kick it. You'll see him."

Cameron agreed and they walked back to Jair's house. Arturo, Jair's dad, was there and happy to see him. It hadn't been since the days when Arturo had cheered on their soccer team from the sidelines, spinning and flailing with all manner of Mexican cheering contraptions, that he'd seen Cameron.

They hung out in the kitchen and listened to old stories of Arturo's pro days in the 70s. Jair's mom, who was affectionately known as Doña Pellos, had made tostadas. The TV in the living room played European sports highlights via illegal satellite.

Not long after they'd settled Jair's phone buzzed. It was Zoom Zoom. He was out front.

They hopped into Zoom Zoom's Dodge Durango and burned out of the neighborhood.

After some brief pleasantries Cameron leaned forward from the back seat and asked where they were going. Jair held an orange pill container up to Cameron's nose.

"To blaze some of this whoosh."

The smell of the marijuana hit Cameron hard in the face.

"Damn! That stuff smells potent."

"It's medical from Cali," said Zoom Zoom. "Hit the dope-scope, peep the bomb orange and purple hairs."

Jair flicked on the overhead console light, illuminating the nugs. Shining crystals covered the lush multicolored buds.

They careened through a maze of neighborhood streets, avoiding major roads until they were next to the destroyed patch of land where Cameron had seen the scarecrow. In the night the streetlights barely penetrated the darkness that lay over that harsh territory.

"Where are we going?" Cameron asked again.

"Calmate, güey. You know Cheesy's gate code?"

Cheesy (previously McCheesy and McCheeseDick) stood for McKiscko.

"I think so, unless it's changed."

"Vamos," Jair said to Zoom Zoom, pointing to the sidestreet where the gate was. When they pulled up Cameron dictated the code and Zoom Zoom punched it in. It opened.

"We'll park up against that wall and hop over to the ditch." The same drainage tunnel that ran through Groll's neighborhood extended to McKiscko's.

"Shouldn't we just blaze in the car? It seems kinda shady."

Zoom Zoom parked the car and turned to face Cameron. "And ruin this new interior? You know how long this whoosh will smell up my whip?"

"C'mon, C'na. You follow me. Es okay, güey."

Cameron followed the others as they made their way around to the gate that overlooked the ditch. If anyone was outside in their backyard, or came out of their house at that moment, the boys would be caught looking like burglars with drugs on their person. As it was, the neighborhood was deserted.

Zoom Zoom and Jair sprung over the gate. Cameron climbed after.

In the ditch they stood next to a tunnel than ran under the street. Jair produced a massive pipe from the pocket of his shorts. It was shaped like a mushroom, made of thin blown glass. Zoom Zoom broke off pieces of bud and stuffed the bowl.

They stood around smoking, passing the mushroom from person to person, refilling the bowl when needed.

Cameron's mind floated out of his head as he stared down the endless corridor of shadowy concrete that ran behind the homes. In the flat black night the houses were turned into duplicate warehouses by the dull light of streetlamps. Coming back into himself from the depths of obscurity he noticed something scurrying on the opposite ledge of the ditch. Pebbles were loosed and rolled down the sloping hill. Whatever moved remained hidden in darkness.

"Do you guys hear that? Something's moving over there."

"It's prolly just a muskrat or something," Jair said.

"Aren't those amphibious rodents?"

"Yeah, it prolly came from Lake Mead or some shit. People always be bringing things back from the lake."

"What the fuck are you talking about?" Cameron looked back to the source of the noise. The black outline of a human being was crouched and stepping toward them.

"That ain't no fucking muskrat, bro."

"Oh, shit he's right," said Zoom Zoom.

The three boys stood on guard, Jair tucking the pipe back into his pocket as they awaited the assailant's next move.

"Should we dip?" asked Zoom Zoom.

The figure finally emerged from the darkness, galloping down the slope into the ditch. From a distance it seemed to be a teenage girl dressed in an oversized letterman's jacket. She approached them on skinny, wobbly legs.

"Who is this Chalky Studebaker lookin ass," Jair whispered.

She passed through shadow and dull light on her way to them.

"Hello, boys."

Though she stood near, a cloak of shadow obscured her face. Her appearance was contradictory. She was dressed young, in a letterman's jacket bearing the letters WS on the breast. It was no high school the boys knew of. Her hair was a rat's nest and there were crows feet extending from the black eyesockets. The light caught silver wires interspersed in the matt of hair that hung over her face.

Zoom Zoom was the first to answer.

"Hey."

"What are y'all doin' down here?" She fidgeted with nervous ticks as she talked. Her fingers just bones as she swiped at her hair. Her voice trying to sound young and sweet.

"We aint doin' nothin'," Jair said, unperturbed. "What's it to you, anyway?"

She squeezed her face into a joyless smile and hugged herself. "Oh, I saw you boys down here and I had to come and say hello."

The boys balked and clucked their tongues.

"Tell me, boys. Have you taken the Lord into your heart?"

"Oh, fuck this," Jair retorted. The woman flinched and fidgeted, smiled her saccharine smile.

Jair took the pipe out of his pocket again and held it up. "You can take your bible beltin' ass the hell on outta here." He flicked the lighter ablaze, highlighting his face and his spiky hair. He looked like the demon of some foreign religion.

The woman's eyes flashed from under her filthy hair. Jair took a monster rip and blew a potent cloud right into the curdled skin of her face.

The woman squeeled with astonishment that almost sounded like joy.

"Oh, why thank you," she breathed. Her wormy smile returned and she beseeched her disgracer. "You mind if I take a little puff?"

"De hell nah," Jair barked.

"Let her hit it," Zoom Zoom said, snickering. "One hit and she'll be on her ass."

"Let's just dip," Cameron said nervously.

Jair handed over the glowing mushroom to the drainage ditch witch.

She moaned with a disgusting pleasure. She took the pipe from Jair and with a loud snarl, slammed it onto the ground, shattering it into a million pieces.

"Now you will *know* the name of the Lord!" she hissed.

"The fuck!"

"My pipe!"

"Dude, let's dip!"

Before the act could fully register the witch was on all fours, scurrying for broken bits of the pipe. She grunted and spat as she clawed for the sharp glass.

Jair took a step forward. Cameron knew this wind-up, he'd seen it countless times on the soccer field. Jair was aiming to field goal kick the woman in the face.

As his leg cocked back to strike, Cameron jumped in front of him. "Don't!"

Rebuffed, Jair's leg swung loosely and came up short.

"Fuck this bitch!" he cried out. "That was my favorite pipe!"

Again the witch shrieked her blood curdling howl. She took a larger chunk of pipe and began slashing it wildly in front of her, catching Cameron across the forearm.

It was Cameron's turn to scream as he held his arm. Flaps of torn blazer sleeve hung down, beginning to drip blood.

The woman swung wildly back and forth but

the boys were already darting up the slope. Cameron forgot his wound and jumped the wall as quickly as possible. Instead of chasing them the woman ran down the black tunnel under the street, her laughs echoing off the concrete walls.

"Is she still after us?!" yelled Zoom Zoom, who mistook the echoes for her chasing taunts.

Neither of the boys looked back until they were in the Durango. Zoom Zoom peeled out and sped forward, flying through the neighborhood and out a different gate. They drove for miles in any direction that would yield a green light.

When the blood had soaked his sleeve entirely Cameron finally forced them to drive back to Jair's house.

"What did that bitch do to you?" Jair said, looking back from the front seat with concern.

"She cut me with that fuckin pipe shard."

"You need to go to the hospital?"

"I don't think so. It just cut the skin. It isn't deep."

When they got back to Jair's house Arturo had already gone to work and Doña Pellos was asleep. They poured rubbing alcohol over the wound, which once cleaned ran a thin line down Cameron's forearm. After applying Neosporin and wrapping it with gauze they sat in front of the TV. Everyone's adrenaline still pumped hard enough to mute every show that played. No one talked.

After a while, when they had all relaxed enough, Jair piped up from where he sat on a recliner.

"You guys wanna smoke?"

Cameron and Zoom Zoom looked at each other.

"Hell yeah."

ELEVEN

Cameron ended up spending the night and the next few days at Jair's house. Zoom Zoom left and Jair's cousins came and went. They went jogging around Jair's neighborhood and Cameron played center-mid for forty-five minutes on Jair's Mexican league team. In between the exercise they smoked pot and watched soccer on TV. Cameron was sprawled out on the couch the morning Jair came to him with the news.

"Hey, man, I gotta go."

Cameron rose up quickly, rubbing the drowsiness from his eyes. "Alright, man."

"You can chill here if you want. I have to get to the airport, though."

"Where are you going, man?"

"Hertogenbosch. We leave in a couple of hours."

"Jesus, why didn't you say anything?"

Jair shrugged.

"Alright, I'm up, I'm up."

This was just like Jair, Cameron thought. Never worked a day in his life and now he was off to the Netherlands for an extended period of time. He'd probably spend a month or two traveling from beer garden to beer garden, roam the tulip fields bugged out on shrooms and tour the canals with a couple of cool locals. He'd take in exciting Eredivisie matches and cop the sickest Feyenoord away jersey. Such was the genius of Jair.

"Well, shit, man. Have a great time," Cameron said, when he was at the door to leave. "I know you will."

"Where you gunna go?"

"I'll be around."

"You going to Cheesy's party later today?"

"I hadn't heard about it."

"You didn't get the text?"

"I sold my phone."

"Oh. He's having people over later today. You should go."

Cameron nodded, "Okay."

They hugged goodbye and wished each other

luck. It had been a nice couple of days away from the streets for Cameron. He ate well and relaxed enough. Doña Pellos even mended his torn jacket sleeve.

▲

The midday sun was warm as Cameron stepped outside. Goodweather season was running long this year. It was about a mile to McKiscko's house, but he didn't walk toward it just yet. He didn't want to be early to *that* party. The rumblings of anxiousness were already brewing in the pit of his stomach.

He dawdled around the shops along Horizon Ridge for a couple of hours, stopping at Starbucks to drink a tea and read the *New York Times*. Combing through the news from the foreign correspondents, he took comfort knowing every article had been approved by the White House. The book reviews were full of slices of life and hyperbolic satire. None of the authors he knew; no books seemed interesting. He stuck around the coffeeshop much longer than he needed to, checking the clock every five minutes or so, until he finally stood to go, leaving the newspaper in disarray on the table.

As he walked to McKiscko's house, block by block his stomach tightened as the moment he'd been dreading was fast approaching. That house, the lofty two-story estate, was a pressure point to his nervous system. He'd been to that house hundreds of times since junior high but never with this sense of apprehension.

McKiscko's parents had reared what Cameron believed to be the perfect American Family. His dad owned a prominent ad agency in town that had struggled greatly during the recession but was hanging on. His mom stayed at home and took care of the house. She cooked pancakes and French toast on Saturday mornings for McKiscko and all of his friends after sleepovers, and did the same for his younger brother and sister. The kids grew up privileged but not spoiled; the parents always encouraged the kids to pursue whatever interested them. They grew to be honest and respectful of their parents. On many a night after coming home late they would recall the whole party to their mom, who'd waited up for them sometimes into the wee hours of the morning. Thus, to Cameron's mind, there was no better family in all of America than the clan McKiscko.

And he felt diametrically opposed to them – on a fundamental level. He knew at the core of his being, he would never be like them. They had followed the rules and everything had turned out as promised. Cameron on the other hand had rebuked society, and although he couldn't pinpoint any exact reason, he felt deep down that by rebuking society he was taking a stance against the McKisckos. Against the family that had treated him as one of their own. He felt like a traitor, and yet he could feel no other way.

It was true that Cameron's parents were divorced and he hadn't grown up with so many accoutrements of Americana. But it wasn't just jealousy that divided them. He often thought about what would happen should a military junta seize control of the United States. If martial law was imposed and a stark line drawn between patriot and subversive. His whole life he'd been a contrarian, prone to recognizing the seedier facts behind the facades of state and religion. In his heart he would always be a subversive, an infidel. On the other side of the line, going to church and supporting the troops, safe from harm or dishonor, were the McKisckos.

The shackles of the invisible empire slackened his pace as he approached the gate. He looked beyond the wall into the ditch and shuddered. If the gate code had changed in the few days since he was last there, he would use that as a sufficient excuse to walk away. It never occurred to him that he could just walk away, anyway.

A car pulled in and opened the gate, vaporizing his last chance at escape.

Along the McKiscko's street the sun through the clouds fell like silver and gold lace over the houses. He thought it funny how something so beautiful could cause him so much pain.

Then, as if time had stopped, as if he knew he was walking into a trap, he walked up to the door and rang the bell.

Mrs. McKiscko opened the door.

"Well, hello stranger!"

"Howdy." Cameron stretched his face into a smile.

"Come on in! Everyone's around."

"Cool, cool. How are you?"

"Another day in paradise. How about you? What's new with you? Tell me everything."

"Not much to report, really. Just finishing up school." This lie was the default response he'd use for as long as possible.

"Where are you working?"

"Nowhere right now. I might get a job with the

school newspaper." He didn't know where that came from.

"Good. That's good."

Cameron shifted his weight.

"Well, you know where everything is. Come on back."

He followed her into the kitchen. McKiscko's relatives were sitting around the kitchen table. He placated them with an awkward smile but didn't introduce himself or greet them. He spotted Misday and Harper playing ping-pong in the next room over and quickly made his exit.

The two boys were in the middle of a rally when he walked in. Each one barely nodded a hello.

"What's crackin' fellas?"

"Sup."

Through the window he could see Mr. McKiscko with his brother and some business associates around the grill. A gaggle of people were behind them sitting around the hot tub.

Cameron turned his back to the window before anyone could see him.

"When did you guys get here?"

Harper looked at him and frowned. "Twenty minutes ago."

"You don't answer your phone?" asked Misday.

"Nah, it's broke."

"Uh huh."

In between points he walked to the other side of the table and sat at the piano.

"What is it?" Harper asked.

"Point 19."

The game ended moments later.

"I need a drink," Misday said. "Let's go."

Cameron followed. It was time to face the music.

In the kitchen Misday and Harper made cocktails with silver tequila and lychee puree. They chatted with McKiscko's mom and relatives, while Cameron stood awkwardly to the side. He smiled at the jokes and pretended to look concerned at the serious talk. In truth he didn't hear a word they said. It took a while to realize that Mrs. McKiscko had been asking him a question.

"I'm sorry what?"

She laughed. "You want something to drink?"

"Uh, sure. What they're having." Misday and Harper had already slithered outside.

"There's tequila and lychee mix on the counter. Don't be shy."

He filled a red cup with equal parts lychee juice

and tequila. Before he was outside he had already taken three big gulps.

He made the perfunctory greetings to McKiscko's dad and the people at the grill. Groups of kids were scattered all over the backyard. Some girls that had recently begun to hang out with Cameron's friends pranced around in leotards. He thought that they might be going swimming but they still had their shoes on. Off to one side McKiscko's brother and a group of his younger friends sat around a table sipping diet root beers. Misday and Harper stood around the hot tub talking to some unknowns. If it wasn't for the sight of McKiscko in the pool floating toward him aboard a plastic raft, he wouldn't have known where to go.

"Boy! Where in god's name have you been?" McKiscko wore only a pair of quarter-length board shorts and sunglasses. Both cupholders were occupied by PBRs.

"I don't have my phone with me right now."

McKiscko nudged the sunglasses down the bridge of his nose to peer at him with his bright blue eyes.

"Boy, don't you ever tell me my business."

They often bantered in such non sequiturs. After

a laugh McKiscko rowed to the edge of the pool and climbed out. He took a beercan in each hand and crushed them.

"I needs a double reload. You good on drinks?"

"Just sippin' this here concoction. Lychee and tequila."

"That's my mom's favorite."

Cameron took another sip. He had almost drunk it all. "Tis delish."

In time the new girls from across town, along with Cameron and his friends, were all gathered around the steaming hot tub. Cameron stood atop the stone ledge looking into the ditch. He thought about telling the group about the witch, but couldn't find an opportunity to fit the story in. However, he did notice a streak of graffiti that he hadn't seen before. Scrawled in meticulous lines the color of neon blood was the lone word "Svadishthana."

He was transfixed upon the image until McKiscko roused him with a goose.

"Uptown!"

"Holy Jesus," Cameron yipped. "Why you sonofa…" He reached at McKiscko with both hands and plunged a finger into the soft tissue behind his collarbone. "Wally wally *downtown!*"

They continued to tussle.

"You guys are so gay," said one of the female neophytes. Her name was Olivia. She sat crosslegged in a royal red unitard and matching red keds. She looked up at the boys from underneath long black lashes. Cameron hadn't met her before.

"What, you and your friends don't downtown one another?" Cameron asked.

"Uh, no. We don't."

"What about uptown?"

"No. We don't stick our fingers up each other's asses."

"Well you should try it sometime."

"No thank you." She scoffed, tucking the bangs of her edgy haircut behind an ear. A tiny tattoo of a skull and a candy cane revealed itself half-hidden under the lobe.

Yasmeen, her best friend, initiated a roundtable discussion from the bubbly froth of the hot tub.

"The grossest thing ever! I don't want any sissy shit either!"

"Okay okay okay," answered Mia, her other best friend, from the other end of the tub. She too adorned in a royal red unitard. Cameron couldn't see if she wore shoes or not. "One time, me and my boyfriend at the time, were 69ing in my bed when I got my period!"

"Oh nooooooo."

"Yes! Yes!" screamed Yasmeen.

"And then my mom walked in on us!"

"Nooooooo."

The boys were speechless. Cameron and McKiscko nodded to each other, signaling a true winner.

"Mooore," breathed Yasmeen.

"Okay, okay, guys, I got one," chimed Misday. "One time I was fucking this girl…"

"Who?" piped Harper.

"Beth, you remember her," he answered in a quick aside. "Anyway, we were doing it and I thought she was gunna cum but instead she just started pissing. She pissed everywhere, it got all over my bed!"

"Score!" cried Yasmeen.

"Maybe she was just a squirter," commented McKiscko.

"No, this was piss. I could smell it. I know when it's a squirter, trust me."

"Mooooooore!" cried Yasmeen, her face almost

submerged in bubbles.

"One time after a night of hard drinking, I farted and a little poop came out." This anecdote came from Regan, who before then had said nothing.

"Booo this man!" yelled Yasmeen. "I shit on stories like that for breakfast."

"Who hasn't sharted?" someone passively noted.

"Seriously."

"Neeexxt."

For some reason the gaze of the entire group fell on Cameron.

"Come on, Camu, give us a story."

"Yeah and it better be more than just a couple of pebbles in your bundlewear," warned McKiscko.

"Well, let's see." Cameron wracked his brain in a panic. He took another gulp from his drink, finishing it. "This didn't happen to me, per se, but I think you'll enjoy it, anyway."

"It better be good," said Yasmeen. Mia and Olivia looked on incredulously.

"Okay, so in the 60s during the civil war in the Dominican Republic…"

People were already beginning to stare off and

lose concentration. Cameron continued anyway. "A main rebel who was fighting against the government was imprisoned by the General who ran the country at the time. The military puts him in a really shitty jail and he's in solitary confinement for weeks. They barely feed him anything and he's almost a skeleton. So after weeks of eating only slop, the main guard peaks through the tiny barred window and taunts him.

'We've got a surprise for you,' the guard says. The rebel is so gaunt and tired he can barely raise his head to await the answer.

'You've been a good captive. We don't want you to starve! So today we have cooked you a delicious bandera.' La bandera is the national dish."

More wayward glances.

"Bear with me, people. So they bring him the big bowl of steaming food and he's so hungry he gulps down the whole thing in no time. Afterwards, he's sick from so much food and all he can do is lean against the dirty wall of the cell, contemplating his certain demise at the hands of his enemies. But, what happens next? Once again the guard knocks on the door.

'Did you enjoy your meal?' the guard says. 'Was it good to eat meat again?'

'Si, socio. Muchas gracias,' replies the rebel.

'Well, then, here's a little more!' The guard then flings open the door and throws something into the cell that bounces on the floor like a basketball. He slams the door shut and all the rebel can hear is the laughing of all the guards. The rebel slowly makes his way to the object. When he picks it up he sees that it is the head of his son."

Cameron waited to see their reaction. No one moved.

"They made him eat his own son," he repeated in clarification.

The only sound was the shooting jets of the hot tub. Mia and Olivia shook their heads in indignation. Yasmeen was offended.

"Wow, you're something else," she said. The boys remained silent. The conversation was over.

Cameron wasn't proud of the story. He'd been haunted by it ever since he first heard it. But he could only smirk at their foul reactions. At least they were offended by something, he thought.

The gathering winded down and moved inside. Those that had been swimming got changed while the rest of them hung out around the TV. From the couch

Cameron could hear McKiscko's mom having a conversation with Junichi, who was more a friend of McKiscko's brother.

McKiscko's mom was fawning over him. "So you're going out of the country, I hear?"

"Only for a few weeks," said Junichi in a humble tone. "I've been made the cultural attaché for Win Resorts. They want me to go to our casino in China for training. It's really exciting."

"That *is* exciting. So impressive for someone your age."

"Yeah, I'm learning Cantonese as fast as I can. I figure it will give me great experience. This is a company I can really build a future with."

McKiscko's mom stared at Junichi for a moment. Tears almost appeared in her eyes.

"That is so wonderful, Joony."

Junichi was magnanimous. "You just have to find something that you're passionate about and pursue it with all of your strength."

McKiscko's mom pulled him in for a hug. "You're such a good kid."

Cameron winced at the results of his eavesdropping. Anyone who is passionate about sucking corporate dick for a legitimized Mafioso deserves everything they get, he bristled, bitterly. He'd refilled his cocktail cup and was almost finished again.

Junichi's story and philosophy underlined the separateness he felt toward the McKisckos. He didn't like feeling bitter, though; he knew it was a sign of weakness. Still, if being the other way meant living like Junichi then the whole world could go fuck themselves.

TWELVE

It was drawing near ten o'clock and the grown-ups had all left. The parents McKiscko waited around the kitchen while Misday and McKiscko assured them they were sober enough to drive.

"Why don't you guys just hang out here and drink?" McKiscko's mom reasoned.

"Mom, we'll be okay."

Cameron stayed as far away as possible from that conversation. He was fucked up.

Moments later they were packed into Misday's BMW.

"We got road sodas?" asked McKiscko.

Regan handed him a PBR from the back seat. "We're locked and stocked, playboy."

"Let's do this shit."

On the freeway Misday's Beamer struck lightning down the I-15. They flashed by slow moving vehicles and weaved through carpool lanes, penetrating deeper into the glowing center of the neon city. Cameron watched in a daze as the towering holographic buildings on the Strip slowly shifted on a hidden axis under the nightclouds of heaven illumined by the Luxor's beam.

Downtown they parked and marched toward Freemont Street, chugging and discarding leftover beers along the way.

Outside Ugly Bar the line to get in stretched around the block. Like factory workers desperate to clock in they lined the grimy sidewalk: the tribes of young girls with their boutique jewelry costumed as Native Americans, the greasy middle-class men with their beards and long hair that they wore like achievements. The line pulsed in copulating enthusiasm, a cacophony of neon zebra stripes and faded plaid jacks calling out to fellow streetwalkers and vigorously embracing every quasi-acquaintance that passed.

Regan knew the doorman. They shook hands and chatted while Cameron and the rest of the group shuffled past the black velvet rope that held back the salivating line and headed into the bar.

Once inside, the group immediately dispersed. Each one of Cameron's friends disappeared into the hot box of vaporized sweat and cigarette smoke until he was standing alone. Anonymous groups shifted in the dark, pushing him back and forth as he stood in the entrance. The DJ proceeded to pummel the multitudes with funk music they had heard from blocks away and now bounced off the tin-can walls with soul-crushing bombast. Under the weight of such sensory assault Cameron fled toward the bar as if it would provide some sanctuary.

On the way he slipped with almost every step on the sludgy, beer-soaked floor. The counter was barricaded with a wall four people deep of people trying to get a drink. They yelled and elbowed one another, helplessly seeking the affections of the androgynous bartenders that moped languidly from cooler to customer. Behind the unaffected bartenders the patrons' misery was doubled as their sweaty dollar bills and gleaming foreheads shined out of the dark and fog reflected in the mirror.

Cameron felt like the walls were closing in on him. He thought he was going to die in this gas chamber of foul sweat and cigarette breath.

From the swaying crowds an overweight girl was hurled from her friends and sent colliding into him. In her attempt to catch herself she threw her entire cup of beer, soaking his suit with warm PBR. The crotchet vest she wore threatened to come undone at the collarbone where the tiniest of buttons kept it together. They held each other in accidental embrace for a moment before she put both of her hands on his chest and pushed him away. He caught his balance and looked down at his soaked clothes. The girl and her friends were laughing uproariously.

Cameron thought indiscriminate, violent and hateful thoughts.

"You fat fucking cunt," he mouthed, but his insults were silenced by the blaring disco. His blood boiled under his skin. In a horror movie montage he looked from fat to disgusting to lecherous face, everyone laughing and slobbering through a fish-eye lens.

There was a tarnished couch in the corner of the room where he stole a seat and composed himself. This, he thought as he looked around. Supposedly the coolest bar in town. The only place that really spoke to his generation. He wanted to wipe out his generation.

He wanted to figure out each of the patrons' unique worst nightmares and make them all come true.

The sense of complete and utter loathing for all existence culminated when, in a burst of fog and smoke through the doorway, he saw her face.

She parted the smoke with the gait of a dominatrix, flanked on each side by two of her faggot minions. The scrap of clothing she wore sparkled like a broken chandelier scattered over her protruding breastbone. When she moved and slithered in pirouettes, leading her minions by an invisible leash, sharp scapulas jutted out from under the white naked skin of her back. Hoops of rib showed under each raised arm. He watched as her face turned in slow motion. Golden coils bounced off a skeleton's face. A kitana smile cut beneath the sharp cheekbones, the small upturned point of a nose. Two small horns marked the joining of her collarbones. This was Disco Bitch.

He didn't know her real name and never would, but at that moment he believed that love and hate was the same thing. Her slaves escorted her through the hulking masses of the dance floor and she was gone. He watched her go.

The rush from her presence was like a double

shot of Jameson, but he wanted more. He went to the bar. Twenty minutes later he had spent five of his remaining dollars on a warm can of Corona. He sipped the foamy beer and decided to find his friends.

On the back patio there was marginally more oxygen owing to the fact that it was outdoors. Despite the lack of elbow room, after a quick scan he saw Regan and Misday chatting up a couple of girls by the stage. McKiscko was with Deni; they stood with their backs to the wall, silhouetted against the projection of a Giallo nightmare.

Opposite them a group had assembled on the stage where they stood dutifully tuning their violas and mandolins, while from inside the sound of Top 40 mashups was incessant.

Cameron weighed his options. Should he stay for the competing noise of Imagine Crayons and LMAO? He saw the exit at the back of the patio. He chose to leave.

At the door a bouncer stopped him.

"I was just leaving," Cameron said.

"If you leave you can't come back."

"I know."

The bouncer begrudgingly pushed open the door and Cameron walked into the back alley. A pool of oil in the gutter reflected the dull buildings caught in the dead orange glow of the streetlamps. Barbwire ran along the fences of the nearby establishments. The quietness in the alley made it seem eerily cut off from Ugly Bar and the rest of the world.

He walked toward a side street that led away from Freemont. It wasn't but five steps down the alley that he came upon the girl squatting in an alcove. Piss splashed between her legs and flowed into the gutter. When she was finished she stood to turn. Cameron saw it was Disco Bitch.

"Oh shit," he said. In his surprise he had stopped right in front of her.

With a piercing glare she sized him up immediately. "See something you like?   Fuck off, pervert."

"I'm sorry, I didn't—"

She smiled sarcastically and brushed past him, walking back toward Ugly Bar.

"Hey, Disco Bitch!"

He called out to her automatically, surprising himself.

She turned around abruptly.

"What did you call me?"

He walked a few feet over to her.

"I said, 'Hey. Disco Bitch.'"

"Fuck you, asshole."

"Wait. Wait. I didn't mean to see you pissing, really. I was just leaving. And Disco Bitch is just what I call you."

"Do you *know* me?"

"No. We've never met. I've seen you before, though. Downtown, in the scene. I don't know your name so I call you Disco Bitch."

She fingered the plastic fork she kept tucked into her bodice. She used it to defend herself. If anyone got too fresh, she found plastic forks cut skin expertly. Sometimes they broke off underneath the skin. It sent creepers running.

He continued quickly so she wouldn't leave. "We've never met but I've always admired you. You intrigue me."

She watched him carefully, studying his clothes and hair, his posture. She was mildly impressed with his audacity, but had judged him overall to be harmless.

"Faggot, huh?"

"What?"

"You're a faggot that likes to watch girls pee."

"What?! No." he stammered. "It's totally

random, us meeting here, seriously."

"Yeah. Okay, buddy." She made to go.

"I had to tell you," he said. "That I respect you."

"Respect me? Why?"

"You're one of the few people I've seen downtown that really doesn't give a fuck. Everyone else is so bitchmade. Wannabes and cool kids. All that shit sucks. You seem like you can rage."

She walked up to him and put her face very close to his.

"Good," she said.

"Good what?" He didn't move and didn't blink.

"Good thing you weren't hitting on me. Cuz I'd cut your dick off."

Cameron exhaled and took a step back. "Yeah. That is good."

Her eyes continued to scan him incredulously. "You seem like a real nice guy," she said. "But I don't know what the hell I'm doing talking to you back here." Again she turned to go.

"Wait!"

She turned her head. "Better be good, sunshine."

"You ever see yourself with a nice guy like me?" He was throwing it all out there. Throwing it all away.

She laughed. "Oh, sweety. I usually don't go for

nice little boys. I like *men*."

"What, like tough guys.? Assholes? Guys that treat you like shit?"

When she laughed at these assumptions it sounded like the laughter of a child. She looked at him and there was a twinkle in her eye.

"I need someone who can really *hurt me*."

He stood, nodding his head slowly. An intense feeling was building in his gut. "I don't understand chicks like you. Always in these abusive relationships. It's such bullshit."

"You just don't get it," she said with a belittling chuckle. "I don't mind the pain."

"Why don't you just kill yourself, then?" he grunted behind clenched teeth.

She half-whispered her response. Her voice sounded like velvet and honey. "What's the slowest way to commit suicide?"

Without thinking Cameron answered.

"To live."

"Now you're getting it."

She ran the sharp bones of her hand across his soaked lapel. "Have a good life."

She turned and walked back to the bar. The

bouncer opened the door for her. Once again she was gone.

Cameron stood in the piss-stained alley. He did nothing to stop her.

THIRTEEN

He walked the deserted streets of downtown alone but for the spirits of the dead vagrants invisible beside him. Trees shook in the wind and their leaves, still yet to fall, carved up the black street with shadows.

He thought about what an accomplishment the conversation had been. He had stepped up to her and bared his soul. That meant he wasn't a coward. He'd been completely honest with her even if it was hard or put him at a disadvantage. And she had engaged him back. He thought he saw something like a mutual respect in her demeanor. Could that be something like attraction? He wasn't overconfident. He had a suspicion the conversation didn't mean the same thing to her as it did to him. How would he know? He was being truthful when he said he would probably never see her again. It was a chance taken and a chance lost nonetheless. He didn't feel any better for not having chickened out. She called him "nice." A nice boy. The world is no place for nice people. Nice is not enough.

Drunk and dirty he stumbled through the abandoned streets. He kicked over trashcans in fury, threw glass bottles as far as he could. Remembering every moment from the conversation, he winced at the parts that made him most proud.

In the barren frontyard of a foreclosed home, he dropped to his knees and tore at the hard earth.

"Urghhhh! Rip me from this fucking city! Rip me from it!"

He moaned guttural wails of hatred and despair at the night sky. He pounded the mud and the gravel until his knuckles were raw.

"I HOPE THERE IS NEVER ANY PEACE ON EARTH!" he screamed. "I WANT NO MORE JOY AND NO MORE PAIN!"

Rolling onto his back, a cadaver unto a shallow grave, he pinched his eyes closed to block out the dull black sky. One with the discarded refuse, amongst the rubble, he whispered:

"And every victory is a defeat."

FOURTEEN

Sometime the next morning Cameron rolled out the front door of the Cross & Sword. His clothes and hair were in filthy tatters and the sun was a heatlamp two inches away from his face.

After a brutal ten mile hike from downtown, he'd arrived at the pub a few hours before dawn. A friends of his, Set, was behind the bar working the graveyard shift. He'd tried to level Cameron out with a few pints of Pilsner, but Cameron could barely stand. Set let him go up to one of the lofts that was closed off to the public and rest; Cameron ended up sleeping under a table using his blazer for a blanket and his shoes for a pillow. The next morning, when it was time for Set to get off, he woke Cameron and ordered him a fry-up breakfast.

The sleep and food was a life saver, but now it was time to go.

In the morning heat Cameron felt like his body was floating away, rising above the parking lot and the pub to see the city from an aerial view. Pit dead center in nightmare valley the mountains rose directly behind the buildings at the horizon, forming tiers of blank cement followed by line after line of ochre and blue terraces that led to even higher summits of skymountains, their ice blue cumulous cliffs stretching into the atmosphere, deflecting the sun in a sharp halo that hung over the city its sickle shadows.

At a torn opening in the fence behind the pub he crawled under and snuck into the adjacent neighborhood. The rows of condos were mainly inhabited by college students or the drug dealers that supplied them. He sat at a concrete bench in the center of the neighborhood for a while before remembering he knew someone that lived nearby. Joe, another old buddy from soccer, lived in a condo by himself just a block over.

He walked toward Joe's house, on the way basking in the warm sun of the third season. Halloween was coming. Sunlight didn't stop the skeleton from waving in the breeze. Lynched goblins and ghosts were strung up in trees and windows every few houses or so. He could smell the candy in the air. He caught a glimpse of himself in the reflection of a car window – that of a zombie, an unfed werewolf; it was as good a costume as any. The season was calling. He was ready.

From the outside, Joe's house looked ominous. Whereas other houses had decorations or fecund gardens, Joe's house stood blank. The lawn had turned to gravel, the paint was dry and lined with cracks, the windows completely covered with dirty old curtains. He rang the doorbell and waited, taking the intermittent time to recall his memories of Joe.

Joseph K. Moran was born in 1985, the same year as Cameron, to parents whom never really liked each other. His dad was one of the most successful real estate developers in the city. Since Las Vegas had been the fastest growing city in America for nearly two decades, that meant he was one of the wealthiest developers in the country. Sometime before the bubble burst he sold his company and was rumored to live on a yacht outside Seattle. Joe's mom was a New Age freak that despised money (although she accepted every alimony check sent her way). She had raised Joe in a liberal manner that called for little discipline. By seventh grade Joe was already dealing marijuana to a network that encompassed six junior highs and two high schools. Between soccer practice (Joe was a tremendous athlete), he lost his virginity at the age of eleven and had tried coke and hippy flipped before he was a teenager. He was always light years ahead of the game in terms of experience. He quit soccer before the end of high school and Cameron only saw him sporadically after that. He'd lived by himself in the condo since the tenth grade.

A noise snapped Cameron out of his recollections. In the window beside the door, the curtain was suddenly thrust aside. An emaciated face adorned with a thick beard peered through the crack at Cameron. The eyes darted around quickly, at Cameron, behind him, from side to side. Joe cracked the door open a second later.

"Who is it?"

"Yo man, it's Cameron. From soccer."

Joe pulled the door open a bit more and bore into Cameron with his piercing eyes. He didn't trust the figure before him.

"Cameron."

"Yeah, Cameron. From Premier. C'mon man, you know me."

The face squeezed into a smile. Even with the

beard and sunken cheeks, there was no mistaking it for Joe's.

"Roony. What the fuck are you doing here? Come in, come in." He opened the door just enough for Cameron to slip through. Inside the house it was completely dark. The only light came from the cracks under the doors. Joe shuffled in his expensive silk bathrobe and slippers back to the couch.

Cameron took a seat in a recliner. "I was over at the Cross for breakfast. Thought I'd come by to check up on ya."

Joe leaned over the coffee table and poured out a little mound of coke onto a magazine. A razorblade appeared in his hand and in two seconds the coke was divided into four long rails. Joe made two of the lines disappear with half a sniff.

"You're up," he said to Cameron, handing him a chrome straw.

"Starting early, huh?"

Joe stared at him and said nothing. Cameron saw that look in his eyes before, usually after he had just destroyed someone on the other team.

"Well, what the hell, right?" Cameron took the straw and snorted the leftover lines. He sat back in the recliner and looked around the room. A squiggly line started to twang from inside his body. Reality seemed like someone else's joke.

Joe tapped his feet rapidly, but his face looked calm. "What's new, Roon?"

"Nothing really, man. I've been just roaming around lately. I don't work. Haven't been to school in weeks. I guess I have no idea what I'm doing right now."

He took a deep breath to accommodate the thumping of his heart.

"Really," Joe replied. "So you don't do anything?"

"No. I guess not. Not anything that moves me forward in life that is. I can't be bothered with that shit right now, y'know? None of it feels right. It feels like I'm being dragged down this path against my will, to a place I don't want to go. Everyone has deemed it the Correct Way or The Source of all that is Good and to be Honored, but it makes me sick when I think about it. I have this violent backlash against it." He took a moment to catch his breath. "I don't know, man. I'm in a weird place right now."

Joe kept his tiny black pupils fixed on Cameron but didn't move. Didn't nod.

"What are you doing now?" Cameron asked. Immediately he regretted it. He hated this question more than any other. It was so generic. The Mother of All Cop Outs. The only thing that this question stated was that the current conversation was going nowhere. No one ever cares about the answer either, and people just have an answer so they don't feel awkward. The Mother of All Sellouts.

Joe seemed to feel the same way. "You're lookin' at it."

Cameron couldn't feel his face. He thought his teeth had all fallen out. "This is some good coke," he said. He couldn't help fidgeting. His mind was going a million miles an hour. He hated doing drugs and then doing nothing. He could just sit and do nothing, anyway, why did he need to do something that gave him the exact symptoms of anxiety?!

"C'mon, man. You know me," Joe replied, and it was true. Joe never bothered with anything that wasn't of the finest quality. Drugs, cars, girls. But he wasn't the average spoiled rich kid. He had unwavering standards. If he didn't have the best he had nothing. And judging by the looks of the house, these days he had a whole lot of nothing.

"I have a shipment of acid coming in," he added. He glared at Cameron intensely.

"Really?" Cameron had never done acid. He was positive it would make him go crazy.

"Pure LSD-25. I take ten hits at a time."

The backs of Cameron's ears became hot. "Ten hits? That's absurd."

"What's the point of doing it unless you go all the way?"

"I guess... you're right."

Joe broke up two more lines and zapped one of them. "Hey mother, you want another?"

"Nah, man. I'm feelin' it pretty good already."

Joe zapped the other. He turned on the TV and they watched PCU on Comedy Central. They didn't talk much. At one of the commercial breaks Cameron said he had to get going.

"Got somewhere to be?" Joe asked.

"Hah. Always somewhere to be."

Joe walked him to the door.

"Good seeing you, man," Cameron said.

"You too, buddy. Take care of yourself." The door shut like a vice.

Cameron walked down Joe's street unsure of

where he was going or what he was doing. He was completely freaked out.

Seething and dehydrated he made his way to Maryland Parkway, that festering suture of a street that ran along the middle of the city. Two different vagrants solicited him before he'd walked a single block, one of them asking to use his cellphone. Kids walked to and from the university across the street. *His* university. Already it had become a place to which he had no connection.

It was another block or so before he realized he was being followed. He'd first seen the man somewhere around the Starbucks and thought he was just another hobo. But each time he looked back the man was still there, walking with a slow, painful limp. Cameron looked again. They made eye contact.

"Shit." Cameron quickened his pace. The man's face was pitilessly sunburnt. His hair hung like frayed ropes from a balding, pink scalp. Everything about him was in tatters, his shredded clothes, the flaps of skin that hung from his open wounds. From around the corner more ghosts joined him. One was very tall and hadn't eaten in centuries. Others wore bandanas made from the human skin of their enemies. They trailed behind Cameron slowly, tired from their endless journey through the world's most horrible places.

They were gaining on him when a Volkswagen Bunny pulled up to a stop sign and blocked their path. The vehicle was filled with freshman college students merrily on their way to the Coffee Bean. The sounds of their laughing and "You Drive Me Crazy" by Britney Spears sparkled out of the open windows.

The ghosts groaned and banged on the sides of the Bunny. One of the zombie's eyes popped out and fell into the car through the sun roof. The children screamed and sped off, almost causing an accident in the intersection.

When the car was gone more evil spirits had joined their ranks to pursue Cameron. They puked thick ectoplasm onto the cement full of skull shards and bits of bone. An evil dark blue light shined from their eyes and sockets. They were coming for him.

His quickened pace turned to an all-out sprint. He kept his head on a swivel: the ghosts were receding further into the distance but their moaning was still loud in his ears. He pushed past the pedestrians that crowded the sidewalk. Another bum, with green track marks spotting his arms, tried to step in front of him and demand fifty cents. Cameron pushed him with both hands into a bramble of thorn bushes and kept running. At full stride he booked across the busy intersection at Flamingo, just missing a wave of oncoming traffic.

Caught on the other side of the street the dark blue light was fading. He doubled over to catch his breath. Filthy newspaper stands with broken windows were plastered with stickers for *Gay Vegas* and *Le Vegas Gazette*. The headline on the latter rag read, "MORE EVIDENCE OF NIGHTCLAW." In a black and white picture, the brick wall next to the university soccer fields had deep rivets scratched into it with black skid marks slashed over them. The caption read "Two more bums were found behind the dumpster, split from groin to sternum."

He looked down the road in front of him. Mary Land Parkway. What a carnival of death. Who were those ghosts? Who were these living people that walked around him? Where were they all going? He turned one last time to see the progress of his chasers but the blue light had been smothered by the crowds.

He hugged his blazer around himself as his sweat turned cold and he continued north. Past signs that read HIDDEN DRIVE AHEAD and DEAD END. Before entering downtown Maryland Parkway split into a roundabout at Huntridge Circle Park. Exhausted, Cameron fell onto a park bench and without trying or wanting to, quickly fell asleep.

His dreams took on the colors of a slow burning sunset mixed with the smell of fried food cooking on asphalt that wafted through the trees. He rolled off the air mattress in McKiscko's room and onto the blank wooden floor. "McKiscko doesn't have wooden floors," he said, but it didn't bother him. He floated out of the empty room. The whole house was empty. Through the loft window the neighborhood was miles and miles of smoldering coal plants that turned the sky into a fireplace. He bounced down the stairs, merrily merrily merrily, feet never touching the floor.

Downstairs the dark blue light was blinding through the bay window. The pictures of family vacations and graduations that usually adorned the hallway wall were replaced by three giant claw marks scratched into the wood. The white paint on the walls turned sooty from smoke. He parted the French doors and into the backyard, over the aqua pool and steaming jaccuzi, over the wall and into the ditch where he settled lightly onto a pillowed surface of dandelions. He felt happy and safe until he saw the scrawled chakra on the cement slope of the ditch. The intricate hieroglyphics moved and stayed stationary. The blood red neon letters more vibrant than possible.

SVADISHTHANA

Seeing the tag instantly kicked in his memory of the witch that haunted the area and with a sweeping fear he turned to face the tunnel just as it was shooting toward him to encompass him completely -

And he woke up on the park bench with a violent jolt. The black leaves were waving at him. The sky was the same color as it had been in his dream. All around him the noise of confused cars bisecting the roundabout. Cameron left the park as the lights of office buildings came on and the neon signs of downtown fizzed and came to light.

He got off Maryland at Sahara and took backroads heading south, back toward the Cross.

He came to Commercial Center, a vast expanse of tremored asphalt overgrown with wild tufts of grass. The Stratosphere injected the dusk with its sinister red syringe and the Western mountains of Mordor loomed just beyond the shady pool halls and swinger's clubs.

The cespitose parking lot and nefarious vendors fenced in a land that looked like some excavation site.

He'd found a broken piece of clove and gotten matches from a 7-11. On an electrical box next to the road he sat and smoked.

Through the clouds of spicy smoke an apparition.

The smoke dissipated and there stood the Black Lion.

"You got another one of those?" His voice was surprisingly high. He had a long sinewy body. A salt and pepper beard thick but becoming on his ascertaining face. The acute eyes of an animal.

"Nah. Found this bit on the ground. You're welcome to it if you can get anything."

Cameron handed the man what he thought was only filter. The man took it between fingernails that had turned to claw. He took a series of short puffs and amassed an unbelievable amount of smoke from the remnant.

"Thank ye," he said.

"De nada."

"You got any money?"

"Some."

"Gimme some."

Cameron looked at him. The Lion's eyes betrayed neither politeness nor malice, just pure unprejudiced efficiency.

"I got about ten bucks, and I was hopin' to get something to eat. You hungry?"

"Hell yes."

"Let's go to Subway, I'll buy you a sandwich."

"Well, Y'see, I don't got any teeth so I cain't really eat no sammiches."

"What do you eat then?"

"'Ever I can."

Cameron slid off the electrical box. "Come on. Let's go to Subway. I'll get you some soup and a couple bags of chips."

"Now you're talkin, sonny."

They went to the sandwich shop. Cameron bought a six-inch steak and cheese, two bags of chips and a cup of chicken noodle. They sat at a table and ate.

"You live around here?" Cameron asked.

"Yeah, I stay 'round here. 'Cross the street a'ways I got a spot. All those buildings closed down now."

"By the old Scientology building?"

"Yeah 'round thataway."

He poured the chips into the soup and waited for them to turn to mush, then slurped the gruel slowly.

"How is that?" Cameron asked.

"Oh, it's good."

Cameron chewed his sandwich.

"I ain't never seen you before," the man said. "You fixin' to stay 'round here?"

"Dunno," Cameron replied.

The man studied him closely. "Ain't real safe in this hood."

"Yeah? Tell me a place that is."

"I'm not fuckin' witchya. There's some bad characters hang around here. Hos and drug dillahs. Worst kinda people." The lines on the thick ebony skin of the man's face told a story of survival.

"Well, I wasn't planning on sticking around."

"That's probably good."

When they had finished eating they walked outside and parted ways. The man thanked Cameron for the food and walked back toward Commercial Center, under the black and green leaves and into the night.

In the end he got back on Maryland Parkway because it had the most light. Of all the tall buildings lining the street the only ones with business were the hospitals. None of the old business complexes had managed to remain solvent. Even so, some still kept the lights on in the top floors for appearance's sake. Cameron imagined a lone worker staffing the evacuated offices, looking out from the glowing yellow square at the city around him, at all the dim lanterns that lit the desolate dark. In the highest floors of seedy apartment buildings he imagined a life behind the curtains. A clean life filled with modern furniture and vibrant green plants growing under crisp halogen lamps. A life he could lead together with her. He could hear the sweet music of pianos and violins drizzle out of the windows into the night that celebrated their coming together. But he could not see her face.

By the time he'd reached the university he walked through the parking lot a deranged wanderer. His path was sideways and aimless. Up ahead he saw Misday walking out of the athletic complex, at first thinking him to be a hallucination or worse, a fantasm. Hurriedly he began jogging to overtake him.

"Hey, mate!" he called out, when he had gotten

from behind a row of vehicles.

"Whoa, shit!" Misday turned with a fright, hands by his face in ready position.

"It's me, man. It's Cameron."

Misday remained tense for a moment longer before dropping his guard. "Jesus Christ, I had my keys ready to stab you, bro. What the hell are you doing here?"

"You'll never believe it. I was just passing through."

Misday was still breathing hard.

"You mind if I roll with you?"

"Sure, I guess. I was just heading home."

"That's cool."

Cameron got in and they drove off. At Misday's he showered and borrowed some new clothes. Misday's mom had made ziti. Cameron ate seconds and thirds. They watched movies and played Fifa. That night Cameron slept on the couch comfortable and warm, barely believing the day he'd just lived.

FIFTEEN

The next morning when Misday rolled out of bed for school Cameron was already awake watching EPL highlights.

"Ahoj-hoj, mate!" Cameron called out to him.

"Chow, vole," Misday responded in a hoarse morning rasp.

After a prolonged stay in the bathroom Misday was at his closet dressing for the day.

"Punished the shelf, huh?"

Misday groaned.

"What's the matter?"

"Don't wanna go to school."

Cameron thought on how this conversation could be held at any point in their lives thus far and be as equally apposite.

"Then don't," he said, smacking his lips after a sip from a freshly opened Carlsberg. "Stay home, we get some bomb grub and watch Champions League, baby!"

"Oh, that sounds glorious."

"Then let's do it, mate!"

"I have to go to school, man."

"What classes you got?"

"COM 102 and Math 260."

"Math 260, what is that, anyway?"

"Pre-algebra."

"What? Are you gunna be a fuckin' math teacher some day? That shit is absolutely pointless. I mean, that is unless they make you differentiate equations to determine the price of bottle service. Even then you have about a degree's worth of classes before you'd even learn how."

Misday looked like he had just smelled shit.

"And COM 102, that's where you gotta make all the speeches?"

"No, that was 101. 102 is Interpersonal Communication."

"You do plenty of that downtown, bro. And by the stories you tell it seems to pay off fine."

A smile started to creep onto Misday's face.

"Huh? Huuuhhh? That's more like it, huh?!"

Cameron popped off the couch and ran over to Misday, immediately peppering him with jabs and hooks.

"I should still go, I think," he said, batting away Cameron's slapboxing.

"C'mon, man. We got Arsenal, Champions League, and Carlsberg, the official beer of Arsenal!" He punctuated his appeal with a left hook to the body.

Misday made a choked sound and dropped to a knee.

"Shit, man, you alright?"

"Damn you and your fucking jiujitsu."

"Muay thai, bro. Learn it." He feinted a teep to Misday's chin but stopped short of connecting.

"Stop, man. Seriously."

"Seriously, we have an awesome day ahead of us."

Misday rose to his feet, standing in a loose pair of Calvin Klein underwear and an undershirt. He checked his phone. Cameron bounced on his feet, shot jabs and right hands in the air.

"Lemme text this chick to see if she can get the notes for me."

"Which class?"

"COM."

"Perfect, bro! You can meet up later and get the notes! Do a little 'interpersonal communicating,' huh?"

"Pssh, she's not even that hot."

"1-10."

"About a six."

"Good enough! It's final. No school for you."

"I'll send the text."

He sent the text and while they awaited the answer they watched Sky Sports News. Misday's classmate actually called him back to inform him that she would take the notes, and to offer to give them to him over coffee, but by then they were both so enamored in the sporting day ahead of them that Misday cleared the call.

Misday had coupons upon coupons for a local pizza shop and they ordered in two pizzas, wings, meatball sandwiches and a two-liter of coke. During the game (Arsenal vs. Bayern Munich, Knockout Round, ECL) they finished the rest of the Carlsbergs that crowded Misday's mini-fridge.

At halftime Misday got a call. The more he talked the more animated he became, but held a finger to Cameron's inquiries until he was off the phone.

"Who the fuck was that?"

"You'll never fuckin' guess."

"Oh, I'll fuckin' guess."

"You can't."

"Who was it then?"

"Justin."

"Fuck you."

"I'm serious. It was."

"Heff?!"

"Yeah, Justin. He goes by Justin now."

"No *fucking* way!"

"Yeah, man. He's coming through."

"Well, slap me and call me Susan. If this day isn't getting better by the minute!"

And as forewarned, right before the second half Justin "Heff" Heffringer burst through the door.

"Who saved me some gabagool?!"

Cameron could barely recognize his old friend, the man he had called his best friend back during those crazy days at Charnell High School. Heff really had become Justin. No longer pudgy and pale, the man before him stood bronze and svelte. He had grown his hair long and bleached it platinum blonde, which he slicked back in a ponytail. He also wore a beard of blonde hairs, with only slight telltale streaks of ginger to imply what the rest of the head had once looked like. He stood before them clad in fitted white Diesel jeans and a Marc Jacobs plaid flannel shirt. More stylish than ever.

"Hey, Misday. Who the fuck is this?" Cameron joked.

'You sonofa bitch! Get over here!" Justin grabbed Cameron and pressed his gruff face to Cameron's cheek.

"We got a meatball sandwich and one more Carlsberg if you want," said Misday.

"No eggplant parm?"

"Nah, man."

"Fuck it, gimme the sandwich. It's so good to see you guys!"

"You too, brother. How was Australia?"

"Oh my god, bro. The pussy." Justin smacked his lips. "Unbelievable."

"They got all those hot blondes down there, right?" Cameron asked.

"No. Not at all. Dark pussy. It's all about that dark pussy down there."

"Like African?"

"The darker the better, bro."

Misday tossed him a sandwich and slapped the beer down in front of him.

"Oh fuck yeah." Justin smashed a quarter of the sandwich in one bite.

They buzzed around while the game raged on, reminiscing on old times and hearing all the lurid tales Justin had to tell. His stepdad owned a company that did a lot of work in Melbourne. Justin had left Vegas after high school to work down there instead of going to college. In that time he said he had made and spent roughly two-hundred thousand dollars, but still had enough to put a down payment on a three-story house in Vegas he found for dirt cheap.

"So, you're gunna live here now?"

"Nope. Renting it out, playboy."

"Then back to Australia?"

"Uh-uh, my little whoa'deh."

"Then where?!"

"Miami, baby. Home of the darkest poon and the clearest lagoons."

"That sounds fuckin' tits," said Misday.

"You don't get it. Tits are done, man. Small tits, dark pussy. That's hot now."

"What the fuck are you talking about?" Misday

balked. "It's just an expression."

Justin couldn't answer. He was shoving the rest of the twelve-inch sub entirely into his mouth.

Cameron finished a beer and belched. "Well, fuck me."

Misday took another call. "McKiscko's comin' over!"

"McKiscko?!" screamed Justin.

"Tootle-oo!" cheered Cameron. All of his friends were gathering, from the corners of the globe, as if by his summoning. A Supernatural Friendship Alliance was forming. Together they would fight the evil that had seized the city. Just in time for Halloween.

*   *   *

By sunset they had blazed through Verdant Hills like a seven year fire. The sky turned to permutations of soft pinks and shades of red, overlapping one another while to the north deep clouds the color of stone groaned and growled. Justin had said that he wanted to smoke (the weed in Australia was all schwag) so they went to pick up from Jordan, an old friend who lived in a gated community on a golf course.

Inside Jordan's mansion the evening burned bright through the massive windows that overlooked the course.

"Where's a good place to blaze?" Cameron asked. They couldn't go to Misday's or McKiscko's house; their parents were home.

"I always go to this one spot on the ninth hole," said Jordan.

"Anyone playing still?"

"Hell nah."

At the ninth hole they sat upon a hill of grass carpet and watched as the world stretched down into the valley and away to the horizon, where cracks of lightning soundlessly streaked across the sky and highlighted massive towers of clouds previously invisible. The city was a blanket of twinkling lights scattered across the desert before reaching the Strip. Next to the digital skyscrapers and lit up replicas the imposing gold towers of the main casinos loomed like fortresses signifying the very seat of The Empire.

The boys lay sprawled out on the lawn passing a blunt from hand to hand and watching the lightning like a firework show. Not a soul to come stop them.

"This is really beautiful," McKiscko said.

"You sure picked the right spot," said Justin.

Before the dark had taken the last bits of scarlet from the sky, McKiscko got a call from Yasmeen. She was hosting a party at her house, which was in a different golf course community in the northwest part of town. Since Justin had just come back they said it was his choice. The idea of new chicks made it an easy one.

*   *   *

Yasmeen's house was huge and brightly lit. When she opened the front door Thom Yorke's remix of "Proud Evolution" was blasting from the top floor. Young girls, still teenagers, were chasing each other down stairs shooting crazy string and popping off confetti canisters. Yasmeen's younger sister Evita was sloshing around with a few other boys and girls in a portable pool they'd brought into the living room. The water and dish soap solution made their bodies and the floor outside the pool slick and slippery.

"Hey guys," Yasmeen said, with a bright smile and big shining eyes.

Justin walked in like he owned the place and

one of the teenage girls there immediately asked if he was a celebrity.

"Down under I am," he said with a wink. "If you know what I mean." The girl ran away giggling.

Cameron stood frozen in the foyer. "I have fallen into a place that is better than heaven." Above him two more girls peered through the railing at him and tickled one another. He walked through the house in a daze, past the pool and into the kitchen.

McKiscko had his arm around Yasmeen. "What do ya got to drink, good lookin'?"

"Mmmm... I got Jaeger."

"Jaeger!" exclaimed the boys.

She handed McKiscko a .75 liter bottle. The top cracked like knuckles as he spun it off. Pull to pull, from McKiscko to Misday to Justin to Cameron to Jordan to Yasmeen, it didn't touch the granite counter top until it was empty.

Through the kitchen window Cameron saw Regan standing on a concrete ledge over the pool finger tapping on a Gibson SG.

"What's Ragu doing here?!"

"You know Ragu?"

Cameron looked over to a skinny boy their age in extremely low cut jeans and a tank top. He had

Olivia under one bony arm as they made their way over.

"Yeah I know Ragu," Cameron said. "Do you?"

"Course, brother. We're in the same band."

"Oh, shit! I forgot the rest of his band lived up here."

The young man brushed a length of long hair behind an ear and extended a hand. "Rhett."

Cameron shook his hand. "Cameron. Pleased to meet ya."

"Likewise."

Olivia batted her sharp eyelashes as she looked up at Rhett. She didn't see anyone else.

"You guys down to party tonight?" Rhett said, arching his brows.

"We just smashed a bottle of Jaeger in twenty minutes, of course we're down to party!" Justin cheered.

Rhett looked at Justin. "Have I seen you somewhere? E! Network?"

Justin blushed.

Rhett took a baggy of pink powder from his pocket and wagged it in front of them. "Well if you guys are, then I have just the thing."

"What is this?" perked up McKiscko.

"Tokyo Dream. Got it on our last tour."

"They love these guys in Japan," said Olivia.

"Finest molly in the world."

Justin's jugular vein began pulsing under his bronzed skin. "I tried molly in Australia. My dick was hard for a month."

"Itssssss… the best," whispered Mia, who'd appeared from thin air.

They moved to the highest floor of Yasmeen's mansion. The loft window overlooked the entire city where the Strip sparkled in all of its crystalline splendor like a video game. They placed the pixie dust under their tongue and the fog rolled in. The cars speeding on the highway became streaks of light while up above the stars multiplied against a backdrop of celestial clouds.

Everyone splayed out on deconstructed couches and bean bags strewn across the wooden floor. Infinite numbers of blankets and pillows were added to the mix. Yasmeen's younger brother was sober and served as the DJ, mixing the tracks from long heavy beats by M83 to the tranced out fantasy bliss of unknown European deep house.

Regan and the bandmates, along with the rest of the guests joined them. When songs came on that everyone knew they all sang along, grasping each other by the limbs and squeezing to show their connection. "Martynas M Sleepless Mix" of Avril 14th by Aphex Twin came on and Cameron looked over to Yasmeen's brother who was in deep concentration as he twiddled the nobs on his massive mixing station. Tears pooled in Cameron's eyes.

"Better than heaven," he whispered.

A hand reached through the fog, caressed his face. Through the covers and between the lights that danced across the ceiling while the rest of the house had gone dark all the girls were smiling and all his friends were happy.

SIXTEEN

It is morning. The kitchen shows the disarray from the night before. The silly string hanging from the ceiling fan spinning slowly over the island. The granite counter top covered with bottles and cups and torn open bags of cookies. All set in the frame as if on purpose, as if each individual piece of garbage had been placed by a film crew. In the living room the pool is crumpled on one side, a little soapy water pooled up in the folds. An oily streak is on the wood floor and there is a stain on the carpet that has dried and crusted over. Amongst the entertainment system and photos on the mantle, of Yasmeen with her brother and sister in Hawaii and at the Golden Gate Bridge on a foggy day with her mother, red beer cups are tipped over and there are cigarette butts stubbed out in pots of flowers. Streamers in every color of the rainbow hang from the TV and protrude from the couch cushions. Confetti is everywhere.

Cameron was the first to wake. He walked slowly through the hallways of the mansion, past the paintings and pictures and the various rooms where his friends were still sleeping. McKiscko and Yasmeen were in the master bedroom with the double doors closed. Misday slept with an open mouth and half-open eyes, one hairy thigh over Mia who slept on her stomach tucked under covers and pillows. Some kids were sleeping in the backyard on the trampoline, immune to the morning sun.

He stepped out the front door and shielded his eyes from the brightness. He thought about heading into the city. Back inside, the house was submerged in morning shadow.

From Yasmeen's porch he could see the golf course. A foursome was already playing; they stood at their golf carts putting on their gloves. He decided to walk around the neighborhood until everyone else woke up.

The homes inside the complex varied from arcane duplexes that shared large common areas to custom mansions like Yasmeen's. He took a curving road that followed the wall that surrounded the complex. Pieces of glass and wrought iron spikes had been embedded in the cement ledge of the wall to keep out pigeons and thieves. Rising above the wall on the other side were nondescript office buildings, to the east he could see the Strip under a fog of dust and pollution.

Then a street of miniature brownstones. Little two-story homes made of brick or painted in outdated pastel colors. Trimmed hedges and rosebushes lined the porch steps. An American flag hung next to a door. He stopped in front of a house that caught his fancy; it was painted lime green and had a greenhouse annexed to one side.

"Excuse me, sonny. Excuse me?"

Oh no, I'm caught, he thought.

"Sonny?"

Behind him, parked along the wall was a pea-green SUV. An old man was at the back rummaging through the open trunk. He peeked around the car and called to Cameron.

"I say, excuse me, sonny!"

Cameron approached the man with caution.

In the trunk of the SUV there was a large rectangular box. The man hung halfway inside, trying to shift it.

"Need some help there, mister?"

The man stumbled back out and faced Cameron. He was hunchbacked and wore leg braces around his calves below his khaki shorts. He shifted his weight nervously, not looking Cameron in the face.

"Oh, good. You're here," he muttered. "Can you help me please?"

"Sure," Cameron replied. "You want me to get that box for ya?"

"Oh yes. I was just at K Mart and I picked it up. For the life of me I don't even know what it is!"

Cameron studied the man with a growing sense of suspicion. On the outside of the box was a picture of an electrical fireplace housed in a thin bookcase. A flatscreen TV was mounted on top.

"Looks pretty cool."

"I tried to get someone to tell me what it is," the man went on. "No one in the whole store knew anything." His face shifted from excited to forlorn to frightened as he spoke.

"Well, lead the way, sir. I'll bring it in for ya." He reached under the box and felt it wasn't too heavy.

"That would be wonderful," said the man.

He led Cameron back to the lime green house. After fumbling with four different locks and opening two doors they walked in. The thought flashed across Cameron's mind: What if this is a trap? What if he's some kind of serial killer or something? He looked at the man's hobbled legs and figured if push came to shove he could probably escape.

Inside the house was all lime green and shadow. The curtains were drawn on all the windows and the walls were painted the same color as the outside. Green shag carpet lined the floor, where Kleenex and other rubbish lay around, like the man never bothered to throw anything away in a waste-basket. The furniture in the living room was assembled just as carelessly; the couch wasn't pushed up against the wall, and a coffee table and recliner had been plopped down willy-nilly.

"Just set it down right here," the man said, pointing in front of the coffee table.

"You sure? I can set it up wherever you want."

The man shook his head like it made no difference. "Right there's fine."

"As you wish."

The man flinched but didn't say anything.

I gotta get outta here ASAP, Cameron thought.

"You want some tea? I have jasmine tea."

Cameron hesitated. "Sure, I love jasmine tea."

"Oh, you do? Good, good. Why don't you go sit outside in the garden. I'll bring it out." He limped off into the kitchen and disappeared. Cameron looked around the house some more. Pictures hung crookedly on the walls. A dining room area was completely empty. In the corner of the living room the bust of a mannequin stood perched on a stainless steel pole. Sewing needles stuck out in twos and threes over the canvass.

He could hear the man making a racket in the kitchen and thought to ask him if he needed help. He thought it more prudent though to get outside and wait, lest he be trapped inside this weird house forever.

He went out the side door and sat at a table next to the greenhouse. The patio area was surrounded with spikey cactuses shaded by a gangly Palo Verde tree.

It wasn't long before the clanking of china could be heard as the man struggled through the side door. Cameron held the door open as the man labored to set the tray on the table. The smell of jasmine filled the air.

"My name is Cameron, by the way," he said

when they were both seated.

"I'm Norm." Norm didn't offer his hand.

"Nice to meet ya, Norm."

"I used to work for Lazzarini, you know."

"Excuse me?"

"Lucas Lazzarini. I worked under him for many years."

"I'm sorry, I don't know who that is," Cameron replied.

Norm's face became grave. "That's a shame. Lucas Lazzarini was the most talented tailor in the world. The man was brilliant."

"Ah, so that explains the mannequin in there. I thought maybe you were into voodoo or something."

Cameron's chuckles didn't translate the joke. Norm waved Cameron off, dismissing whatever the comment was. He hadn't heard it, anyway. Instead he went on with his story.

"Lazzo, as he was affectionately called, mastered the art of tailoring before he was a teenager. He grew up in his father's shop, which had been his grandfather's and great-grandfather's before him. He helped his father with the measurements and so forth. The shop was famous. We made clothes for footballers and mafiosi, moviestars and businessmen. Everyone came to Lazzarini's. Even middle-class bureaucrats would come to get their dress shirts and ties. You always got a fair price at Lazzarini's."

He wagged a bony finger at Cameron.

"So, the young Lazzo. At an early age he's already copying his dad's work perfectly. Not long after he begins making suggestions. Take it in a little here, adjust the lapel there. Client after client couldn't stop raving about how good this kid was. Back then they called him Bambino D'oro.

By the time he was a young man in his twenties, tailoring was no longer his main concern. He would often say, 'If you have the perfect fit anything can look good.'

From then on he became obsessed with color combinations and different patterns, different textures and fabrics. He used to spend days holed up in the warehouse looking for the perfect match. Track suits were very popular in that day, everyone made them, but he was the first to make them in Cola Stain and Crimson. That combination became extremely successful. He next did a series of trenchcoats in a pattern he called Treeshade & Grass that sold out in minutes. Its counterpart, the limited edition Nightshade jacket, is literally impossible to find."

Cameron sipped his tea and listened.

"After so much success so quickly he basically stopped making clothes shortly after. We in the shop continued with his designs - he had hundreds of prototypes that were amazing in themselves - but he wasn't interested anymore. His horizons were expanding too fast. I remember him saying that he didn't need the confines of clothing anymore. He would remark that he had begun to hear music in terms of colors and patterns. His favorite songs were Cherry Cola or Acquafresca. He never did say what musicians played music like that, though."

"So where is this Lazzo now?"

"He disappeared. We inquired all over. No one could find him. The shop fell into disrepair and disorganization without him. It was a scandal." Norm exhaled and shifted in his seat uncomfortably, placing one leg brace over the other.

"Really. You never saw him again?"

"I did, yes. I did see him one last time. It was on my way to work. I was feeling a bit sad, the shop was closing soon and I felt a time in my life was ending. As I turned the corner, the same as every day, who do I see but Lazzo, sitting upon a broken brick wall on the side of the road. I'll never forget the smile on his face. The happiest smile I'd ever see.

So I go to him and I say, 'Lazzo, where have you been? The shop is nothing without you! Please come back.' I beseech him with tears in my eyes. And Lazzo, he just smiles that beautiful smile and says, 'Normando, we don't need the shop anymore. Everything we need is here all the time.' And I tell him, pleading to him, 'But Lazzo, it is your family's shop! It's been in the family for generations!' He is unperturbed. He tells me that his family is happy and at peace. He tells me God is the most elite of all tailors and that his work is everywhere. Existence itself is perfect. Be it eucalyptus on brick, cumulonimbus on skymetal, gumstain on asphalt. The combinations are infinite. Before I could press him further he clapped me on the back, still smiling, and told me all I have to do is look around, that I'd see. Then he walked away, as easy as if he were heading toward a friend's house or a stroll in the park."

"And that was it? He was gone?"

"Gone. After some months we went to his house but he wasn't there. We found only old paperbacks and strips of different colored linen strewn about. He was gone."

"Just like that, huh. He just disappeared? Where you think he went?"

"I don't think he disappeared at all. I believe he became the scenery all around us. That was his ultimate goal. To be free from the constraints of his art. To be free of all constraints. He believed the world to be endlessly beautiful and wanted to become a part of it completely."

Cameron sipped his tea and thought. Norm was staring off into space; after a while he didn't even realize Cameron was still there.

"So you gunna be okay setting up that fireplace thing?" he asked.

Norm squinted at him and made a face as he came out of contemplation like someone jerked out of a trance. "Huh?"

"I should probably get going. I have friends waiting for me."

Norm stared at him while he stood from the table.

"Well, thanks for the tea." Cameron slowly began making his way toward the street. Norm called him back.

"Hey, sonny."

"Yeah?"

"Come 'ere and let me give you some bucks." He had pulled a wad of crumpled hundreds from the pocket of his shorts.

"No, no. It's okay. It was nothing."

"Well, let me get your address, I'll come by and repay you later."

The same fear from before, the fear of being in the lair of some nefarious killer, returned.

"I'm kind of in between places right now." They stared at one another. "I'll be around."

He began once more to walk away, hoping Norm wouldn't call him again. He didn't. The old man sat in frozen dementia under the Palo Verde tree with the steaming jasmine billowing from the teapot past his face. He watched Cameron go and didn't say anything.

*   *   *

When Cameron got back to Yasmeen's the gang was in the driveway getting into Misday's BMW.

"Better hurry up, Roony. We're outta here," said McKiscko.

"I'm comin'."

"Where did you go?" asked Misday from the driver's seat.

"Just for a walk."

They were all quiet.

"How 'bout last night, huh?" Cameron interjected.

Everyone chuckled.

"I thought I was in heaven. Better than heaven, in fact."

The rest of the car stared straight out the windows with blank faces of weary satisfaction. They went to Denny's and ate breakfast in the same state of harmonious stupor. Every once in a while someone would recall something from the previous night and everyone would laugh until the exertion became too much, their hearts beating too fast, and they'd take a deep breath and retire back to their coffees and sodas. Before they ordered Cameron asked Misday to spot him so as to avoid any awkward scenes when the bill came. Misday had agreed without hesitation.

Sitting there in the diner the magnificence of their adventure washed over Cameron in a stern realization. It was over now. He saw himself as a patron of two worlds: the world of last night, the social realm, the one he shared with others and the world at large, a life of endless tasks needed to be done and parties and events to take part in. In that sense, the party at Yasmeen's represented a culmination of what his life could be if he lived in that world always. No shyness, no cynicism; with such a combination of setting and company, real life really could be like his dreams. And yet, that's what it was: Fantasy. True he had no regrets about the party and he could in no way blame felicity for conspiring against him, quite the opposite in fact, but it was for this reason that something inside him felt defeated. The party had changed nothing. All it proved was that he was incapable of controlling those moments when serendipity shined upon him, no matter what world he decided to take part in. And that other world, that ethereal land of his dreams where transcendental beauty was God, the world invaded and eviscerated by the boorishness of heathens, debased by the constant trampling of the uninitiated who cared nothing at all for what he held sacred, the gleam of The Feeling that showed him things he couldn't describe, always pushing him toward further battles, further glories, the world he associated with death which could only be ruled by the Reaper... The party had done nothing to reconcile him with this Sisterworld. Connection to his fellow man was not enough to keep him from dreaming, of feeling this place.

Before leaving Denny's he looked out the window one last time, filled with the sense that he was saying goodbye to something. A new responsibility had taken ahold of him: He must pursue that spiritual world with all of his strength. He must submit completely to it. Believe in it wholeheartedly. He looked to Sean, then McKiscko, Jordan, Justin. If he didn't give everything then he'd be turning his back on them. On all of them.

SEVENTEEN

They got back to Misday's house around noon. Everyone got in their cars and drove home, no one felt like hanging out any longer. Cameron stayed behind to get his stuff. When he got upstairs his suit was waiting for him, washed and pressed by Misday's mom, hanging on the shower pole.

"Oh, fantastic," Cameron said, taking it by the hanger and draping it over his forearm. The red stitching where Jair's mom had repaired the sleeve was still intact. The stitches ran along the inseam surrounded by dark brown spots where the real blood had dried into stains. Cameron thought the modifications made the ensemble look even cooler.

Misday flopped on the couch. Cameron changed back into the suit and set the clothes he'd borrowed on the bed. He went downstairs and ate another helping of ziti even though he wasn't hungry and grabbed two water bottles from the refrigerator.

He called goodbye up the stairs but Misday was already sleeping.

It was a beautiful day outside. He walked through Misday's neighborhood to Warm Springs Parkway and followed it to the top of its steep hill. The wall of sound from the rushing cars passing him on the street buzzed in his ears like a manmade eternal ohm.

"I haven't had it so rough lately," he said to himself. He waved and said hello to an old lady that walked past him trailing a basket on wheels. He felt happy.

As he continued down the hill the panoramic view of the eastern mountains opened up before him. First the brick-colored terraces and sharp fissures that separated the spiny peaks, then the summit of Sunrise Mountain and the rounded black and green cousins to the left and right respectively, until the diameter of the city's eastern edge could be seen. The clouds turned the summits into a kaleidoscope of stone and shadow, molding the range into some gothic architecture that far predated man. This spawn of countless battles between Quetzalcoatl and Tezcatlipoca was the only barrier between the city and the abyss.

Furthest away, just outside the shadow of Sunrise Mountain, loomed the dormant desert volcano. Black Mountain. At its mouth with two separate mountains rising like horned vectors on either side it gleamed in the afternoon moisture a castle of terra begotten from the impenetrable depths. The crown jewel in the dirt of Death Valley. Mineral veins trickled over the polished surface like spiderwebs on anthracite.

It was the throne of Valhalla. It had been calling him. From his vantage it looked only a skip away, but Cameron knew the mileage was deceptive. He'd have to wait until next morning to begin the trip. He was close. Close to realizing the ultimate reason for his journey. Past the city, past society, far out there in the desert and among those mountains lay the answer to questions he couldn't yet articulate.

Walking around town admiring faded brick walls wasn't going to cut it. He needed to go to the source. He was going to force a climax and face the essence of his conceit. His destiny swirled inside him and he clenched his gut to harness the hurricane spirit. Tomorrow at the eye of Black Mountain he would join the righteous or meet his demise.

EIGHTEEN

At dawn an orange line burned across the horizon and spread away from the black mountains like a planet slowly orbiting away from eclipse. The city shuddered to life in a sickening homage to the first single-celled organism escaping the primordial stew.

By afternoon he was in the valley filling up his water bottles in the park where he used to play soccer tournaments as a child. The giant wooden soccer ball sat atop its pole, looking like a tee shot set up for a giant. His battered Diadoras sifted through the overgrown grass across the endless stretch of the complex. No painted lines survived to demarcate where he'd once played. On the far end of the fields little black dots ran back and forth. The players in a weekend Mexican League soundlessly chanting and running, pantomimes in the mirage of a memory.

The university football stadium next to the fields

was completely empty. The roar of ten thousand screaming fans was just the wind ripping through the empty bleachers. He passed into the desert beyond, a foppish cultural exile banished from the city of his birth into the barren expanse of Golgotha.

After a stretch of flat gravel he came to the first of the mountains. Steam sizzled off the bodies of rock and blew past his face smelling of sulfur. He stopped to catch his breath and drank the last drops of his water, discarding the bottles into the crushed garnet where they became indistinguishable. A fighter jet materialized out of nowhere, blazing a dark chemtrail over the peaks toward some secret base. Moments later the sound of a shrieking pterodactyl suspended in the empty sky.

He climbed over sharp ridges of rock until he was navigating a ravine of sand that ran narrowly through the crags to where the obsidian temple of Black Mountain's pulsing veins stretched black bloodshot cracks from underneath its skin of stone. His feet sunk a foot deep in the dense pebbles and the rocks burnt his hands to the touch as he squeezed between mountains that threatened to trap him forever. He couldn't tell if the sounds he heard were vultures crowing or the wind through the ravine. He couldn't see the stadium anymore behind him.

At the entrance to the cave entering Black Mountain he slumped over exhausted, a gaunt dehydrated animal. Covered in a sweat that had begun to chill in the coming sunset he waited for the emissary of Beelzebub to emerge from the throat of the mountain and strike him down. Streaks of cathode aurora spiraled from within the black tunnel out into the bluish evening in an irregular frequency, beckoning. When the demon didn't come he hitched himself up and passed through the jaws of the dragon's mouth and descended deep into the cave.

In the hall his eyes darted like a frightened reptile's. Across the shining of electric green over the stalactites were painted ambiguous scenes, untold futures described in the brief flashes. He didn't know where he was going so he followed the scrambled radio whispers as they led him deeper into the mountain.

His pupils had taken up the whole of his iris but he still had no grasp on the visions before him. Brief twinkles and shadows against complete darkness lit the way until he bumped into something and stopped cold. He reached out frantically to feel what he'd come to. It felt like cloth. There was some padding and a wooden beam. He jumped back in a fright and scurried against the rock wall. From the center of the blackness a swirling light rippled and died away like electronic fire, illuminating the couch he'd bumped into, sitting amongst coffee tables and stacks and stacks of books.

Light shadowed his sunken face as he stepped forward, feet crunching loudly on the gravel until he could see the room more clearly. The light came from a smashed open television set propped on a couple of stones in front of the couch. Its diffracted rays cascaded over the ridges of the cave ceiling, showing what looked like the roof of a mouth. He nestled himself next to a stack of books and tried to control his breathing. Beside him stood a dusty life-size skeleton, a castaway cadaver from some forgotten science experiment. The plastic bones hung from a pole among the pots and pans and other detritus, the remains of an old miner or an effigy used by a sadistic biology teacher in a midnight ritual. Amongst the hoarder's flotsam Cameron stood there another piece of refuse. Then his eyes fully adjusted and he saw the man.

Sitting on the couch at such an angle that his

face was always obscured the man sat straight up against the broken couch without making an indentation in the cushions. He sat like he was watching the TV. A hat cast further shadow over his features and he looked to be wearing an unfinished suit like one would find at a tailor shop, with chalk marks outlining where pockets and alterations would be made. He still hadn't turned to regard the newcomer, but Cameron could feel his penetrating stare.

Cameron shielded himself with the skeleton and peeked out from behind the skull.

"Who are you?" he asked.

The man didn't move. He continued to sit and watch the TV while his whole essence stared at Cameron.

"Who are you?" Cameron asked again with more urgency.

The man turned slowly to face Cameron, his face still covered in a veil of shadow. The vision of the man was occluded, as if to look upon him was always out of the corner of an eye.

A humming in the tunnel made the whole cave vibrate. The tables and tin cookware trembled against the rocks.

"I am the idea of Man," said the voice.

The vibrating shook Cameron's bones into a numb and delirious acceptance.

"Whose idea?"

"Yours."

The answer came out in a sigh that dissipated into the cavernous black.

In the shattered glass of the TV screen there was no reflection. The vibrating caused the books to open and their pages to flutter. In horror Cameron saw that they were all blank.

"Am I dead?" he asked. He tried to remember the name of the boatman on the River Styx, but couldn't.

The man was right. He was an idea. Reality had a consistency as irregular and static as the multiplying canine teeth that bubbled in the rock above him, or the wavy lines of light and dark emanating from the television.

"What do you think?" the man replied.

"I think this is a place outside of time. You're some spirit of the Mountain my mind can comprehend. "

"There is no such place. We've always been

here."

The shadows over his face continued to swirl as he turned back to face the TV.

"So time doesn't exist. Or time exists all the time. Every moment is always happening."

The figure didn't answer.

"We're stuck," Cameron said.

"And yet the feeling that we are racing toward it."

"Toward what?"

"The life we have always been living. This very moment."

The humming settled into a steady drone.

"We're stuck in this hamster-wheel of a world," Cameron said, almost to himself. "Never going anywhere. Doomed to repeat the same life over and over? What a hell."

"You find ways of forgetting," said the man.

"Nostalgia," Cameron whispered. Remembering those best-nights-ever. The good times that memory has a way of turning into legend. Our own personal mythology to retreat to when the present day isn't to our liking.

"Do you ever feel nostalgia for something that

hasn't happened yet?" asked the man.

"Yes."

The droning hum was a minor key held down in his heart.

The voice returned.

"Do you ever feel that you are the only one to walk this Earth? That everyone else has disappeared?"

"Yes."

"Victim."

"What?" Cameron whispered.

"You are a victim of your own destiny," said the man. Strobe flashes in the cave revealed snippets of the skull, Cameron's face, the outline of the man's hat, the silhouette of his jawline. The frequency of light and sound was intensifying by the second.

"Denial does nothing to impede the onslaught of fate. All of your attempts at escaping will fail. Until you love your own lot you will be in hell. You will want impossible outcomes."

The swirling cathode light and the roar of the cave's vibration all came to a sudden halt.

"You will always long for what doesn't exist."

ΠΙΠΕΤΕΕΠ

The colors and textures of temporal reality continued to flicker in the strokes of an expressionist's painting. The leaves of books tore from their spines and danced across the streaks of light in a frenzied puppet show. Cameron floated like in his dream back out of the cave and over the treacherous terrain with energy he didn't have.

Outside in the desert the sun was setting across town, settling just above the western mountains, and everything was covered in a cold blue light.

As he trekked from the desert back onto the main road that eventually took him to the outskirts of Verdant Hills, he constantly remarked on what a ridiculous figure he made. He was battered by the wind of passing cars as he swayed and stumbled in his tattered suit, not having eaten all day with his heart palpitating, talking to himself and high fiving branches. He dribbled an imaginary basketball, juking the runners and mothers that walked their dogs that passed him. To the passersby and cars that all ignored him and drove off as fast as possible he was an unleashed urban psycho. He yelled questions and demands for confrontations, but they failed to respond, averting their eyes as if he wasn't there.

On Horizon Ridge again, where it was still a ragged strip of two-lane road a few miles away from his friends' houses, he became extremely dizzy and had to stop. He took refuge under the porch of a church building that never got started and had already been foreclosed. The skeleton of the cathedral had remained standing by some unholy purpose, the stain from where the gilded cross had been removed a sunburned stigmata on its façade.

Just beyond the church a complex of futuristic modern apartments sat on the gravel like an alien starship crash landed on Earth and abandoned. Rebar and dusty trapezoidal flats against the purple sky, the tinted windows of the empty apartments reflected the mountains and radio towers in ghostly duplications against the twinkling mirage of the city. Cameron giggled nervously.

On the side of the church he climbed in through a broken window. Inside the pews were all askew, missing their cushions; some had broken kneelers where people had stamped them. Hiding under the seats and covering themselves with strips of wall insulation, lonely goths from the city had come to the abandoned church to deny existence. Curled into postures of agony, black eyes bleeding from corpsepaint, the wretches squeezed as hard as they could under their broken wooden covers, desperately trying to concentrate themselves into oblivion.

He walked past the broken altar out into the gravel parking lot outside the church. Behind him the unpainted buttresses rose to the starlit night like hands beseeching a dead god. In the warmth of a fire someone had set inside a rusted trashcan Cameron sat and looked at Las Vegas. He couldn't stop laughing.

Sitting in front of the TV tapping his foot incessantly. The games or shows or commercials on TV just as ceaseless. Talking talking talking and everything drowned out. What time is it?   The fucking sun is burning a hole in the living room it's so goddamn bright. The clock reads 11:01. Only. He tried to sleep the entire day, refusing to get up. He fought not to get up for as long as he could until he was bored in his dreams waiting for the subway in some foreign hostile land. He couldn't get it out of his head. The endless questioning circled and circled and circled. I'm sure if I start from the beginning something will happen that will make sense, give me a reason. The night started out just like any other these days, standing in the bathroom reluctantly getting ready, dreading the night ahead of him. I didn't have to go, no one was forcing me. That was probably it. The anxiety. You're not yourself when you're consumed with anxiety. It almost made him smile. Then the rest of it played out in his mind. Heart backfiring. What the fuck. The truth really was that he didn't like her, didn't know her besides exchanging a few remarks. He didn't find her all that attractive. The truth was that he never turned down a dare. You fucking put me on the spot and I'll fucking call you on it. He called her on it. It didn't work out. He failed. Was he more pissed at not coming through or for taking her on in the first place? Questions that never matter in the morning after success. You win, you get the results. That's all there is. The questioning is a sign of failure. Oh, the torment. It would almost numb itself out for a while, staring in the face of your worst nightmare. It doesn't have a continuously wrenching effect. It waits for the split second you've begun to think about something else, then you remember and it's the memory that gets you. Short Term Memory Spike. I'll buy every ounce of marijuana in the fucking city to blaze away this trait. The dull blades moving in his blood, I'd do anything to burn it down and walk away. It was all wrong from the beginning. From the way we kept getting walked in on, before that leaning against the soiled fence with all those people walking by. Fuck, if I would have seen me there I woulda shook my head with disgust. I walked down the road willingly though, no one calls my fucking bluff. Her skin felt like thick plastic. Weren't women supposed to be soft? Jesus, I never really noticed. It should be one of those things you don't have to notice. This wasn't for love. I was doing this to make myself relevant. The reasons going through my head while I'm trying to get hard. Squeezing her floppy, mushy tits. No fucking wonder. What the fuck am I doing? The television goes on and on, the cell phone rings. Backfire, sizzle in the veins. Do they know? Eyes dart everywhere, outside, the hallway, the refrigerator. Someone's ready to bust in. Fuck it, I'm ready for whatever they come at me with. Accuse me of anything. She's on her back with her eyes closed tight as we make out. I know this because I open my eyes, sometimes for stretches that seem like at least half an hour. I move my tongue in circles on purpose because there *is no reason for my kiss, she fights back with her lips moving around my lower lip, then upper. "Do what you were doing before." My hands had completely forgotten they were there. No more inner thigh squeezing from before, when I thought I had the juice. "I paaaaaanic… / I panic." The song I remember at the most inopportune time. Fuck. Stop thinking stop thinking. "What's wrong?" The question is snide. She was waiting for this. I don't answer. Once more our naked bodies dry humping harder. She's into it. She wraps her legs around me and squeezes, makes me want to puke. Wilted fucking penis. Fucking babydick. You can't be serious. "Where's Your Girlfriend" comes on my head radio and turns something once admired into disgust. Disgusted with myself. Her head hits the pillow with a sigh of frustration. The party outside is loud as fuck I can hear them talking about us. Going back out now would only mean one thing. Way too early. What do I do. I panic. Have you ever tried to get dressed before she figures out what is going on? Let's just say slow motion gets you there faster, and I couldn't move slow enough. The jig was up. The bluff had been called, one way or another. Cellphone keeps ringing. Who the shit would be calling right now all my friends are still fucking asleep god fucking damn it. It's McKiscko calling to give me a heads up about what everyone is saying. The ringleader of the rumors will have to be called out. Fuck it I'm ready to fight. It's her, she left something and wants to know if I have it. No, she wouldn't call. We would never speak again. Who the fuck could it be?!*

Hey mom. What's up. Uh-huh. Huh? No, honey, I won't be back this week. I'm staying here in Arizona for a while longer, but I have good news? What news. We're getting married! It's kind of sudden I know but I couldn't be happier! What. I need to stay down here to sort out some details but you should be fine with groceries and I drop the phone to the couch where it rattles with excited language until I throw it into the hallway against the wall so hard it leaves a divot in the walling and clacks on the tile and breaks finally silencing that incessant talking. Floating upstairs to my room. This is where I've lived, since we left the other house and came here in high school, after the 'rents got divorced. The medals lining the wall under the ceiling the pictures of backyards and notes gotten from girls with drawings on them hearts and trophies and quotes I'd liked and tacked up there for inspiration the bands all broken up or sold out the friends I'd let down or stopped liking or never hung out with anymore the girls notes pitiful scribbles of juvenilia I put so much stock in and the television keeps talking and talking my mom calls the house phone leaves a message something must have happened I get really bad connection here but I'm excited to start this new chapter there's a lot to build on a good relationship. Back down the stairs, the phone battery on the ground don't slide it back in don't turn it on. It's been meaning to happen for a while now. Face the music. The front door opens and it is hideously bright outside. Flat heat, still air, the sun a lightbulb in the sky at two-hundred feet. Close the door, just like you would when you leave each day for school or to hang out with your friends. Past the truck, no keys, no clothes, no medals, no numbers, no memories. No, the memories are still there. There is no weed that will take them away.

TWENTY

He sat on the mildewed couch with a feeling of triumph. It had been a long day, one that hadn't gone as smoothly as he expected. Through it all though, having beaten back every obstacle, every sidetrack that threatened to sap his will, he had seen his mission through to the very end. He was victorious.

He stared up at the high ceilings of his new home. Thick beams of sunlight angled in through the loft windows on the second floor. The blinds behind him over the living room windows stayed closed so no one would see him. That is, if anyone was around in the first place. He had come to the neighborhood like a post-apocalyptic survivor finding one last safe house in an otherwise deserted land. Rebar spiked out from abandoned foundations of the houses next door. The house he'd taken for his new abode was the only one on the street that was completely built. An enclave of plaster houses sat a street over riddled with for sale signs. The neighborhood was basically a wasteland.

He remembered the fifth of fütyülős; took it from his jacket pocket and unscrewed the gold lid. It looked like water in the thick glass bottle. He lifted the bottle to his nose and sniffed. Fire water. As soon as the liquid touched his tongue his whole mouth was enflamed with an intense rush of grape and effervescent gasoline. "So bomb," he breathed.

The couch creaked when he laid his head back to rest. When he adjusted himself the soggy wooden skeleton made squishing sounds. It had once been a fine divan, upholstered in fancy emerald satin. Pieces of insulation and frayed strings of wood burst forth from the armrest like someone had set off a firecracker in between the seams. Aside from that, and the fact that it was obviously very old, it was in perfect condition. He didn't understand why it had been left behind.

He sighed as the light from the top floor changed inflections, growing dimmer, streaked with rainbow hues of neon shadow. There were a great many things he didn't understand.

After Valhalla something changed in Cameron.

Before the encounter in the volcano he had walked the streets with a vague sense of ambition. He was out looking for something, some trace of beauty hiding behind the clouds, an essence within the shifting mountains that surrounded the valley. But the conversation with the mountain spirit had enervated his searches. If the future was already foretold, what was sought had already been found. Whatever pain he would feel was already felt. After that realization he traversed the city like an animal. His sole purpose on earth was finding the means for survival, and even that he attended to with a growing apathy. He had become a stray dog. Anyone that tried to own or feed him would be bitten.

The moonshine was making him emotional. He thought about the previous week, all the events leading up to this relaxing moment at his new house. He knew the details in and out, having just lived them, but the reminiscing gratified him anew, anyway:

TWENTY-ONE

It started with a mercurial morning. A shopping cart had been following him around the city for some time. Just when he thought he had lost it, he would turn a corner, into an alley behind the Best Buy, and stuck to a felled tree, two wheels off the ground over a dead branch, there the shopping cart would be. Before that, he saw it in the parking lot of a Target, propped up on a cement curb in between parking spaces.

That morning when he came upon it yet again, a solitary basket-on-wheels reined to the skeleton of a tree, these anomalous objects alone in a vast sea of asphalt, he decided not to try and evade it any longer. Instead he'd use the vehicle for transportation. And thus in those dreary days of mid-October, he could be seen, a wiry miscreant riding push mongo on a rickety old shopping cart stolen from some distant Seafood City.

He kept to sidestreets and backroads. Places where traffic didn't congregate. Straightaways where he could hit full stride on his new wheels.

If it wasn't too cold, he'd crash in vacant lots of desert, sometimes finding destroyed bits of foam mattress to sleep on, using torn rags for blankets. In a cluster of custom homes, somewhere in a part of town that used to be an outskirt, he found a row of shacks that had been abandoned some years prior. The neighborhood had no streetlights. At night it was dark enough to sneak in through the window of one of the shacks where the wooden board had been broken. Inside the shack he'd sleep in the corner with the cobwebs, placing his shirt over his nose so as not to breathe in pure dust, and listen as the horses from nearby ranches bayed at the moon and whatever banshees kept those unholy hours.

He'd rise before dawn – he never slept well – and roll off down the road on his shopping cart before the world woke up and ascertained his quarters.

It got so he'd have to travel further and further during the day to reach new places he could steal from. He had grown paranoid of all the closest grocery stores. Every time he went in for a Gatorade or an apple, he swore that everyone, employees and customers both, was looking at him. He still wore his dandy suit, and had added a thick cotton Damani Dada sweatshirt and a waterproof North Face jacket, both stolen from Ross. Still, his lifestyle couldn't avoid filth. He hadn't showered in at least two weeks. His hair was matted and long, the scraggly stray hairs that grew on his face in patches looked like dirt. He was running out of options.

In what became a two-day trek, he made his way back downtown. He went past the bars and apartments to where Las Vegas Boulevard dissolved into a curving two lane road. Riding the cart was unfeasible for most of the trip so he mainly walked it, picking up bottles he could refill or any other stray objects that caught his fancy.

When he reached Catholic Charities all that was left of the Strip had joined the city limits of North Las Vegas. The aid compound sat past the strip clubs with their all-Spanish advertising and the graveyards that housed not only the old neon signs but all the old generations of Las Vegas humans as well. It was the only soup kitchen he knew of.

It was before lunchtime when he arrived. He left his shopping cart outside the gate and walked in. Groups of people were waiting outside a set of double doors, in line for immigration help. More of the unemployed milled around the bus stop. He maneuvered through them and around back to the soup kitchen. Three times a day Catholic Charities served a free meal to the population of vagrants that hung around downtown.

He waited in line for an hour, standing listlessly against the wall. In front of him two bums conversed in some secret language, mumbling unintelligible thoughts to one another with a fractured vocabulary. Behind him a man breathed heavily; it seemed to take all of his body's energy just to keep him alive enough to wait in line. Cameron said nothing and stared straight ahead.

In the cafeteria he got his food, a turkey sandwich on white with potato wedges, a salad and a cup of fruit punch. He hadn't eaten in two days. He'd gone past the point of hunger and only had a dead feeling in his stomach when he sat down to eat. It was only after he had scarfed the entire meal that he felt hungry.

Looking around the room, at the homeless and the drug addicts and the needy and disadvantaged, at the workers in cheap suits and crooked ties, at the Monsignor with his fly unzipped that moved through the cafeteria greeting those he passed with senile salutations, Cameron only felt disgust. He felt no confederacy to this example of humanity. Most people there, including the workers on lunchbreak from their desk jobs, all ate their turkey sandwiches numbly like inmates at a prison mess hall. No populist emotions stirred inside him. No feelings of benevolent altruism warmed his heart. The bored workers served the disadvantaged. Everyone went through the motions and played their part. He could have been back at school or at his own desk job. Even in the fringes of society nothing was different.

He threw the empty plate away and walked outside. The shopping cart was gone, off to chase some other vagabond. He thought about the distance to his shacks, now even further away without transportation.

He walked up the hill toward the mortuary and the kid's museum, trying not to panic as he thought about the night ahead of him. Attached to the museum was a library he hadn't known about. This is good, he thought. He had an idea.

Inside the library, hordes of bored bums watched TV in what looked like a holding cell. The rows of tables in the magazine section were filled with people scanning the periodicals with forlorn looks on their faces. He went straight to the computers.

On the internet he could get enough information to pick his next residence. It was his plan to look up, via the county assessor's website, a list of foreclosed homes in the area. He would cross-reference the list with google images and any listings or advertisements he could access and find a house that was safe. Of course it would have to fit his taste as well. He preferred something modern and spacious, in an area that was not too congested. If all went according to plan, finding a new place would be a cinch.

As soon as the screen saver disappeared he was thwarted.

Please enter your login information. He tried his name, his old four-digit pin number. Denied. He didn't remember the barcode of his library card. After a few more useless shots in the dark he gave up.

He went to the help desk and waited in line. When he reached the counter an exasperated young woman stared at him, waiting impatiently to hear what his problem was.

"Hey, how's it going."

She continued to stare.

"Good, that's good. I was having trouble

logging on to the computer. I need to access to the internet."

"You can't look at porn here," she sneered.

"Huh?!"

"I said, do you have your library card."

"No, not on me. I do have one, though."

She got his name and information and looked him up. "Okay, here are the forms you need to fill out." She handed him a stapled stack of papers, then went back to staring at the social media profile on her monitor.

He looked them over briefly. "Um, excuse me. This is a library card renewal form."

She looked up from her computer, squinting behind cheap plastic frames. "Yes."

"I already have a library card. I need to use the internet."

"You have to have a library card first."

Cameron's blood began to simmer. "Am I missing something here?"

"If you lost your card, you need to renew it."

"You have my information in the computer."

"You still need a physical card. Once the forms are processed and you've paid the fee, then you can create an account and use the internet."

He looked over the forms again. A one dollar fee was due with the forms for a new card. Thirty day processing time.

"Is there anything else I can help you with, sir?" she asked with an ingratiating tone.

He considered cussing her out, but couldn't think of anything clever. After sharing a final dirty look he walked away without saying anything.

He didn't know what to do. He didn't exactly have anywhere to go. A two-day expedition back to those rickety shacks sounded like a death wish.

To cool off, he browsed the fiction section. In the aisles he went to his old standards: McCarthy and Bolaño, an adult-fiction book by Christopher Pike. He looked for *House of Leaves* but they didn't have it. In the large-print section he found *Harvest on the Don* by Sholokhov, which he didn't even know existed. He took it, along with *Letters to a Young Poet* by Rilke, and sat at a table in between two bums.

He flipped through the pages of the books and set them down. The words were all jumbled. He couldn't concentrate until he knew what he was going to do for the night. The bums next to him shifted uncomfortably in their puffy plastic jackets. One wiped his nose with a dirt-brown finger. Luckily for Cameron he was too used to his own stink to notice the stench coming from his neighbors.

With a nervous tick he peeled off the barcode on the back of the Rilke book. Just to spite the bitch at the help desk, he was going to steal it. Meanwhile at the computer where he'd first been blocked, an old woman was fussing with the mouse and keyboard. She gasped and groaned after each heavy keystoke and errant click.

This was his chance.

"You look like you need some help," he said when he got to the computer stand.

She didn't notice him approach and looked at him with confusion. Her eyes were extremely large from under the bifocals she wore.

"Oh, this confounded thing," she griped. She punched a few keys again and sighed when they didn't do what she wanted.

"What are you trying to do? I might be able to help you."

"Well that's very kind of you, but I don't think there is any hope."

"Let's give it a try, huh?"

"Well, ok…"

Apparently a new recipe for fat burning red velvet enchiladas had just been released by Dr. Phil, and she was eager to get it. The browser she kept using needed an update and wouldn't let her navigate without installing it first. Every time she got the prompt she kept pressing cancel. Then she would repeat the steps again and again.

Cameron used Firefox instead and had the recipe up in thirty seconds. She looked at him like he was a computer genius. He printed copies and took a few dollar bills to collect them from the printer.

"Bring my change, sir," the woman reminded.

He brought back the copies and gave them to the woman, along with the extra dime and nickel.

"There ya go, ma'am. You'll be grubbing on healthy Mexican in no time."

"Mm, yes, well. No thanks to this darned machine."

"Yeah, tell me about it."

"Well, I thank you, young man."

"Glad I could help."

The woman shuffled off with her recipes,

trailing a backpack on wheels behind her. She hadn't thought to log off. Probably didn't even know the term.

"Booya, grandma," Cameron said, and seized control of the computer.

He went to the Clark County Assessor's website and began searching parcels for foreclosed units. The map of Las Vegas was bloody with red squares, indicating foreclosures. Whole neighborhoods were listed as bank owned. In this sea of red he saw one thing: Opportunity. From the glittering display of the 1024 x 600 pixel monitor, the city's depression was his oyster.

Moments later he had found what he believed a suitable domicile: 3500 SF 5 BDR 5 BA / 2 story w/ guesthouse / pool. It was in a neighborhood desolated by urban flight. Judging by the GPS map it was the only one built on its street. A rickety gate, unmanned, stood outside the small subdivision. It was situated against the mountains that curved around Anthem, a part of town that lay to the south of Verdant Hills.

Having no change to spare he wrote the pertinent details on a small square of scrap paper and tucked it into his jacket, next to the book by Rilke. He left the computer idling on livescores.com and exited the library without so much of a turn of the head to see what the bitch librarian or the ragged bums were up to.

He was pretty happy with himself as he left the library. He had a new book and directions to a new house. Living outside the confines of the modern economy made him feel good. He wanted to be outside of everything: outside of society to roam the outskirts of the city, outside the expectations of a normal person, outside the boundaries of a friend, and most importantly and hardest of all, outside of his mind.

The warm sun shined off the empty parking lot outside the mortuary, the desert sky inconceivably massive above him, the hot grass dotted with headstones across the street, all these things inspired him. He didn't see the mentally ill milling around the bus stop. He didn't see the government building next to the graveyard where the officials made decisions. He didn't realize that it was too late in the day and he'd never make it to the house before tomorrow. He could have sat around the library and read until the dinner session at Catholic Charities, but he was too energized by what preoccupied him to think about his best interest.

Without thinking he had set to walking with

pace toward North Las Vegas, going the opposite direction of where his new home lay. He wasn't paying attention to where he was going because he was caught in the grip of an active daydream.

Active daydreaming was a term he used when referring to the forceful act of imagining. Daydreaming usually happens when one was bored, when the mind wanders. Not so with these kind of thoughts. Active daydreaming was a concerted effort to remove himself from the present reality and transport to a made-up world by sheer brainpower.

This often took the form of what-ifs. If he had been recruited by a visiting scout from Europe then he would be playing in a home game for PSV Eindhoven, decked out in their teal and black away kits, playing in an attacking center-mid role against the heathens of Rotterdam.

If he'd been more concerned with his studies in high school and the grades would have flowed to him as they seemed to do for the valedictorians and salutatorians, then he would have been in Berkley right now double-majoring in botany and film. He'd have spent the lazy summers during the offseason learning how to play guitar and program electronic music on dual MacBook Airs. Making movies from there would be easy, he had plenty of ideas.

Sometimes though, he would venture into territory even he didn't recognize. He'd take a side-road, a small two-lane alley that dead-ended somewhere in Northtown. It would lead into a dense thicket of fir trees, some forest not native to the Mojave Desert, and zigzag downward past switchback after switchback until he reached the front steps of the doorless mansion. A massive plantation house looming high into the growing sunset.

Pillars wound with ivy mirrored each other on either side of the porch steps, white lace curtains were drawn in every window. Standing in the front yard, staked into the trampled, damp grass, a statue of Cassandra tore out her hair. She screamed at him warnings that couldn't breach the stone. He thought she was beautiful and kept going. The mansion, as aforementioned, didn't have a door. Curious, but this whole situation was, he thought. Plus none of this even exists. He went in through a window and into a foyer lined with black wooden floors. The inside was barely lit from what light remained outside; the hallways were blanketed in shadow. In the center of twin winding staircases, placed upon a polished slab of marble sat a bust of Veerappan carved out of sandalwood, his Kattobomon mustache pointing up each set of steps. When he went upstairs he found rooms furnished but covered in old linens. Dusty volumes of ancient Greek philosophers lined the immense library, a rocking chair in the bedroom creaked although it was empty. He was too afraid to venture far, but in one of the rooms, the one with the mirror outlined in black iron, he found the diary of someone who must have once lived there. He opened the tarnished compendium and sifted through the moth-eaten leaves. The writings made up an epistolary novel, a correspondence that was never sent nor received. There was a certain letter that struck him in particular. It was addressed to no one and consisted of only a single poem:

Dear _____,

Awake in the rain
In the field where I'd slept,
Eyes shut so tight to forget all the pain,
And still it was your voice
That woke me from my grave.
I looked through the trees,

Frantically, in vain, for your face,
While I clutched my collar,
Pulled my jacket as tight as I could around me,
Clenched my jaw til there were cracks
And I could feel your hand softly.
I knew why I'd come here.
To confront death
And demand of it what life had denied me.
The sky, the field,
Mirrored themselves in infinity.
Yet, I could still look into your eyes
And know that you loved me.
Even if my grasps were like claws
Tearing at the roots, grasping nothing,
The wind blew calm and steady
And brought your song sweetly to me.

I was sightless when you vanished.

Your ghost was already haunting,
Your embrace moving through me,
I could only perish in the ecstasy
Of your lips' sweet melody

He would've have read further but he was disturbed. The house creaked and groaned. Angry spirits whistled down the hallways. He snatched the leaf with the poem from the book and quickly descended the staircase then back out the window he'd come in from. Danger would befall the mansion ere nightfall. Running back through the forest, past a decaying Cortezar with maggots copulating in his mouth, he reached the city limits again. Traffic on the street was heavy. The wind blew harshly in his face.

Whenever he awoke from these active satanic daymares it would be the world around him that seemed counterfeit. Every ounce of beauty squeezed from the gland in his brain that controlled happiness. All he could see was the solidness of stone. The concrete ground and the brick building that formed this corporeal reality. And he hated it.

Miles away from anything or anyone he knew, the sky turning black against the lights of the barrio, he had a terrible feeling that he was at the mercy of the night's prowlers. Across the street, black figures moved in the shadows and he never met their gaze. He held suspicion for every soul out there. A stranger, everyone would see him as a potential victim. He put his head down and headed toward civilization. He walked. He would walk with folded arms, cradling his stolen literature and the scrap of paper that held his future, until the sun rose over those dreadful pitch-black mountains and he could find safety.

"Will I ever find security? Are the keys to these mysteries even in existence?" he asked himself, then dismissed the notion altogether. The street held no opinion of such abstractions.

He plodded the northern sidewalks, alongside the parlous audacity of every man thankfully hidden. The capacity for violence that gleams from within each of us like a shameful totem. There will be no trust on the streets tonight. There would be no peace.

*   *   *

Strange mists came in and hovered over the frozen grass in the netherdawn. Out of similar black clouds in his mind he emerged from dreamravaged halfsleep. A conversation replayed itself entirely before he realized it had happened, a nonsensical colloquy with a neighborhood vagrant, talks of cell phones and ATM machines, comments on the cast of vampires that shared the streets, all in a tone of hyperventilated jollity undulating in and out of consciousness.

Snow on the northern mountains. Streaks of cloud running under the peaks. Whether sky or stone, he couldn't tell the difference.

A white fifteen-passenger van pulled into the parking lot in front of the gazebo he sat under. The troupe of convicts shuffled out in ones and twos, pushing each other and playing grab-ass while the marshal watched with bored misanthropy and ordered the foreman to divvy out trashcans and picks.

He thought of the frozen bum downtown swaddled in the pose of death. The security guard telling him to move along with the same face the marshal had.

The convicts paired off, one holding a pick while the other rolled the trashcan, and commenced to take laps around the park. The otherworldly marine layer had burned off and it was morning.

TWENTY-TWO

He got his bearings by following street signs until he knew where he was again. The walk to his final destination was considerable. It would take him easily the rest of the day to get there. For a moment his resolve was tempted. Go there tomorrow, it said. It's really far, fuck it, it complained. You're hungry, you're thirsty, you're tired. Go back to Catholic Charities and have a good meal. Stay at the library and read all the books you should have read. It went on and on. Like the previous day had never happened. Every excuse imaginable tested his will, but he would not be courted by negativity. He outsmarted the devil of laziness that sat perched constantly upon his shoulder by flicking it away with an idea: he'd stop by Deni's work and pick up some provisions.

Deni worked at a liquor store by the university, which was about halfway between where he was and his new house. The promise of a treat, alcohol and possibly something to eat (although that was unlikely considering all the shop had was alcoholic chocolates which he thought were disgusting) gave him a little burst of excitement and steeled his nerves for the long trek. It might take him until dark to get there, but what did he care? He had nothing else to do.

When he got close to campus it was almost midday. Crossing the busy intersection at Flamingo he recognized the homeless woman that always hung around outside the nearby Del Taco. She was sleeping face first in the crosswalk next to the median, in the middle of the road. The sound of car horns screaming was like that of tortured animals trying to escape. No one knew what was going on, everyone's sight was occluded. The angry mob of cars sat on their horns in frustration.

Last time he saw her, the old black lady was camped out on the corner across from the university. From her stoop she'd yell at the kids and the people that walked by. She was a humongous woman, always clad in a filthy dress and tattered rags. It was not uncommon for her to shit black liquid from where she stood, paying no mind to the splattering filth at her feet. Her home was a shopping cart so dirty it bore the color of no known grocery store. It carried everything she owned. While she sat and cooked in the sun, the cart sat unattended on the curb, overflowing with the superfluities of a street hoarder.

Now she slumbered with her face buried in the asphalt next to the median and didn't move. No one dared touch her, and it would take four strong firemen arriving half an hour later to lift her from where she slept so that traffic could resume its normal course. Cameron never saw her again and never found out if she was dead.

By the time she was taken away he was already up the street, an anonymous figure intermixed with the drunken tourists that had ventured off the Strip for cheaper alcohol. A few wizened crackheads chatted with the out-of-towners, trying to hustle the gullible gamblers while the tourists looked at them as if they were zoo animals. The vision of the woman sleeping on the road was stuck in his head along with the worrying thought that it had been an omen.

Inside the liquor store Deni was yelling at a customer to get the fuck out. The vagrant pretended not to understand. He pleaded with Deni for another pint of wine. The store manager, a giant bearded man that looked like a bouncer, came from out back and helped the wine-o to understand.

The drunk waddled outside where he immediately began to chat up a trio of overweight bleach-blondes in bikinis. Cameron slid up to the counter and shook his head.

"How's business, Denzo?"

Deni shook his head too. "Motherfuckers," he said.

"What's crackin'?"

"Besides dealing with the scum of the earth every five seconds?"

"Yeah, besides that?"

"Same shit."

"I hear ya."

"What are you doing?"

"On my way up to my new place."

Deni narrowed his eyes. "You moving to a new place?"

Cameron put on a cheeky smile. "Yep. Nice big house over in Anthem."

"No shit. With who?"

"Just me."

Deni laughed at the nonsense. "Okay," he said. "What're you drinkin'?"

"Dunno yet. Thought I'd take a look around first."

Deni pointed to the rows of liquor behind him. "Look away."

Cameron walked by the shelves of tequila and brandy and whiskey. The amount of alcohol made him nauseous. Cinnamon flavored rums and orange infused vodka. Saliva accumulated spontaneously at the corners of his jaws, the foretaste of vomit.

He came to a small section of spirits. When he saw the bottle he almost cried out.

"Holy shit!" he whisper-shouted instead, looking side to side to see if anyone else had realized the treasure that was in stock.

A clear bottle with a long neck sat on the shelf gathering dust. Fütyülős. Hungarian grape snaps. 70% alcohol. It was his favorite.

Deni soon joined him in the aisle.

"Dude, I didn't know you had this!" Cameron said.

"What is it?"

"Fütyülős!"

"Foot you what?"

"Fütyülős!"

Deni snickered. "What the fuck is that?"

Cameron took hold of the bottle by the neck and showed it to Deni. "Remember when Laz brought that shit back from Europe in the canola oil bottle, the shit that looked like Crisco but tasted like fire water? Remember how after one shot and a Davidoff we were all fucked?"

Deni snickered some more and slapped his leg. "Holy shit I do remember that stuff. It was fucking terrible."

"No, man. It was fantastic. I didn't think I'd see it again."

"Fuck that."

"I gotta have it, bro."

"Take it. No one drinks that shit."

"It's cool with the boss?"

"I don't think he'll worry about it too much. I don't even know how we got that stuff."

"Sweet," Cameron said, genuinely pleased.

Deni walked with him toward the door.

"When do you get off?"

"Couple of hours."

"Why don't you stop by the new crib."

"Seriously?"

"Yeah, come check it out, we'll sip on this fire."

"You're fuckin' crazy, man."

"You gunna come?"

Deni looked around. "Yeah, I'll stop by." He put the bottle in a paper bag while Cameron copied the directions on the back of a receipt.

"Hey, man. I hate to ask, but," he said, handing Deni the directions.

"What is it?"

"You got a couple bucks I could borrow? I haven't eaten today. I…"

"Yeah, man. For sure, I got you." He pulled a thin fold of bills from his pocket and peeled off a five.

"Dude, I appreciate it, really. I'll pay you back."

Deni waved him off.

"So come by later, yeah?"

"Yeah, sure man. See ya in a bit."

They slapped fives and Cameron walked back out into the street. A bustling group of drunken Americans in lederhosen moved past him, leaving Hoenschoenhaus and singing Journey songs at the tops of their lungs.

In a shopping center nearby he stopped at a Vietnamese restaurant and bought two sardine sandwiches. A dollar bill and some coins was all the money he had left. He ate one slowly and put the second one in his jacket. When he was finished he walked outside and shivered, more from the thought of what lay ahead than the slight chill that had gathered in the air. Surveying the expanse of faded parking lot and the beat up cars that huddled in clumps across it, the skittering of the poor crowded on the sidewalks and the massive new building of the Journalism school across the street that had already faded in the sun, he was filled with an oppressive uncertainty that made him feel scared, unsafe. There was no sign of the ghosts he had seen earlier, but they could be anywhere, he thought. He couldn't wait to get away from there and back into Verdant Hills but he still had many miles to go yet before he could roam the suburban streets alone.

TWENTY-THREE

The gate shielding the neighborhood from the outside world was made of thin iron bars painted light blue. He'd walked by it a few times before realizing it was the one; the computer map or the map in his brain being wrong, or both, and anyway, the directions always got jumbled up along the way. Now, after miles of walking, the frail gate was all that stood between him and his home, provided he had no trouble breaking in. No cars drove down the curved avenue where the entrance was. A good sign to begin with. He peered between the bars of the gate to get a glimpse of the streets beyond: a random car here and there looked like they'd been empty a long time. The neighborhood was a cluster of paper-mache homes with chunks of cement foundation in between where the developers had given up. The crushed gravel lay in front of him like a field. Against the close horizon a row of houses the same skin-color as the gravel blended upwards, the terrestrial objects soaked in the dusk colors, the deep blues and soft pinks all refracting as shadows, giving off the smell of autumn chill on stone.

He was skinny enough that he could have squeezed between the bars but he slid underneath the gate instead just to be safe. He checked his paper for the exact address. Around a corner in a forlorn section of the neighborhood the single house stood amongst a metallic garden of rebar.

He walked with his back upright and chest puffed out. If anyone asked, he was meeting his flaky real estate agent here to take a look at the place.

Who is your real estate agent?   asked the suspicious neighbor.

He scanned the area for a name on a sign. There were many to choose from.

Uhh, Benny Paul. Yes, old Benny. He's always late.

Mmhm, The suspicious neighbor would say, shaking its head before walking back slowly to their house, the one that was supposed to be a new beginning in a new town, a nice neighborhood judging by all the photographs online, New and Affordable Luxury Living! This is the New Las Vegas! but was more like making payments on a tombstone. And the interest was rising. The amortization negative.

No one came to press him for details. It didn't look possible that anyone could care. The windows of the houses were all shuttered with wooden blinds. KEEP OUT and BEWARE signs were posted at the backyard gates. The residents kept to themselves. If it wasn't a bill collector it was a bank representative or developer foreman or construction crew eyeing your lady or some sniveling disabled person selling you politics. So they hunkered in like recluses, locked in under the imposition of an un-mandatory twenty-four hour curfew.

At the front door Cameron lifted the dusty lock-box by the padlock that hung from the doorknob. He dropped it absentmindedly and began to turn toward the backyard when he heard the unmistakable sound of keys tinkling on cement.

"No fucking way," he gasped, turning back around lightning fast. A set of two keys on a ring of thin wire lay on the complimentary welcome mat. "No fucking way!" he cheered, too loudly, which he followed immediately with another scan of the premises to see if he had alerted any of the neighbors.

"Now just wait until neither one fits," he grumbled, fumbling with the keys and fitting the first one into the lock. Turn, click, bang. The door opened.

It creaked on its hinges and Cameron was blasted in the face with the smell of dank emptiness. Squares of light leaned against the wall of the second floor, half-visible above the balustrade. The living room was a giant blank space of concrete, either not yet carpeted or the flooring had been ripped out. A fireplace stood against the wall with a plastered chimney rising to the ceiling. A black stain came out where no fire had been made and onto the floor like it had been vomited. He attached the padlock back together sans keys, then entered the house and closed the door quietly behind him.

"Well," he told someone imaginary, "is it everything you've hoped for?"

He walked through a corridor that led into the kitchen and an adjacent dining room area. Leaning against the wall lengthwise was a divan upholstered in dark green. He went over and inspected it: the seats

still had cushion, it didn't collapse on itself when he set
it back down.

The view from the dining room was of a gravel
backyard and a brown cinderblock wall. The sky was
barely visible above it and darkening fast. Before
moving the divan to the living room he checked the
cupboards and the fridge. Only a white box of maggot
pad thai. The thought that someone had been there and
might be coming back was one Cameron didn't linger
on. Something about the whole place exuded
abandonment. No one was coming back for this.

He dragged the green divan into the living
room, clacking it against the walls on either side in the
corridor, listening to the soggy wood flex and sag. He
placed it next to the fireplace and sat down very
carefully, one leg crossed over the other. He imagined a
great fiery hearth blazing, ornate figurines from the Far
East on the mantle, above the hearth a framed Rothko
original.

He took out the book by Rilke and ran his hand
over the grey canvass cover. He checked the back
where the barcode used to be. The inside-flap once full
of stamped dates removed. It was his book now. No,
rather, books don't belong to anyone. They belong to
everyone. That's why it isn't a crime to steal them.

When he was finished he would leave it on an electrical box where someone was sure to find it.

While the soft piano notes of Satie's *Gnossiennes* floated around the house he sat reading the consoling letters. The fire burned in the hearth. His tender psyche was soothed by the gentle encouragement.

This is pretty class, he thought. What could make it classier? Ah, yes! The fine brandy! He took out the bottle and sniffed, took a sip. He set the book down for a moment and drifted into the land of comfortable memories.

It only took a few sips until he was suddenly ripped from his reverie by a loud bang on the door.

"I can hear you in there, motherfucker!"

His teeth clamped vice shut; eyes pulled wide. Visceral survival instinct instantly kicked in. He tried to move into a ready position but every slight movement issued a loud creaking noise. Whoever was outside could hear it. A tremble beneath his ribcage. He'd been caught.

Boom. Boom. BOOM.

"K'monnn, brah, I aint tryin' to wait outside all night, niggy."

He knew that voice.

Another series of loud booms. "If you don't

open up I'm gunna blast my way in, motherfucker!"

Deni. That son of a bitch.

Cameron jumped off the divan and leaped to the front door. He peered through the keyhole, staring directly down Deni's throat as it mouthed obscenities. Cameron turned the knob and slid the door back slightly.

"Get in man," he hissed. "And shut the fuck up, someone will hear you."

"Heeeey, brother, what you doin' leavin me out there to freeze." Deni was piss drunk. His orange 1985 Saab Aero was parked at the end of the walkway.

"Dude, just get inside." Cameron shut the door behind him. "You shouldn't have parked so close man, you'll give us up."

"What the fuck are you talking about? I talked to the security guard already, how do you think I found this place, anyway?"

"You what?"

"You live out in the fucking sticks, bro." Deni looked around. "Nice decorating."

"The security guard let you come here?"

Deni shrugged. "It's your place right?"

Cameron narrowed his eyes. "I'm squatting,

bro."

"Hah! No wonder this place is such a shithole."

"Yeah, you gotta make do," Cameron grumbled. He plopped back onto the divan causing a cloud of dust and straw wood to puff into the air. "Welcome to my humble abode," he said in between coughs.

Deni sat tentatively on the other side.

"So you're what, on the lam or something?"

"On the lam from life."

Deni giggled. "Alright, then."

"I was just enjoying some of the fruits of my labor," Cameron said, holding out the bottle of fütyülős like a sommelier. He unscrewed the lid and held it to Deni's nose. "Rip ehhhhhhh."

Deni recoiled immediately. "My god that stuff is strong."

"So bomb," Cameron replied, taking a sizable pull.

"You've obviously had a couple," he told Deni when he had recovered from the burning in his mouth.

"I work at a liquor store, man. Of course I had a couple."

"What did you bring then, mate?"

Deni reached into the sidepockets of his jacket

and produced two fifths of Jim Beam in glass bottles.

"Nice," Cameron commented.

"I'll take this any day over that shit."

"Suit yourself."

They settled in, and before long they couldn't talk about drinking anymore or else they'd finish all the liquor and then they'd be really fucked up. Cameron took out the sandwich and handed half to Deni. He was drunk too by now and cut the silence with a story.

"So get this, you'll never believe the shit that happened the other night."

Deni perked up out of his drunken loll. "Ooo, what?"

"I come across Jair, you know Jair right? Played soccer with him, funny Mexican dude? Yeah? Well I come across him randomly, Oh! After I left your house after Fatty's that night. Man that night was a whole 'nother story…"

They stopped to move upstairs where an outside streetlight made things more visible. Downstairs had become near pitchblack. On the second floor they sat with their backs against opposite walls, astride the squares of light carved into the shadow.

Deni sipped his whiskey while Cameron continued. "So I randomly come across Jair, who I haven't seen in years, I thought he had moved to Acapulco or Germany or some shit, and he asks if I'm down to blaze. So of course I say I'm down and I follow him to the ditch outside McKiscko's house. You know where that is? Outside his backyard wall?"

Deni nodded to go on. "Lord knows why the fuck we were going there, but Jair said we had to meet up with his homie, this dude Zoom Zoom, who went to Verdant Hills."

"Okay."

"So we meet up with Zoom Zoom and we spark the pipe and we're passing it back and forth when out of nowhere this creepy ass lady enters our conversation."

"Whaaaaat."

"No one saw her coming! We were all talking, in turns kinda, and then she just butted in with a 'Hello, boys,' all evil sounding and shit I swear."

Deni guffawed. The story was too outlandish to question.

"We're all creeped out, obviously, and Zoom Zoom and Jair immediately start clowning on her ass, saying she looks like, who was it, B.B. Bluff! You know, from *Doug*?"

"Yeah, okay, so what happened?"

"Eventually she asks if she can rip the pipe, so I kind of reluctantly hand it over to her. As soon as she takes it though I know I shouldn't have done it."

"Uh huh?"

"She takes it and a second later that pipe is shattered on the cement. Without hesitation she spiked that bad boy down like she'd just scored a touchdown at Lambo."

"No!"

"Get this. Before doing it she says, 'In the Name of Jesus, I pray!' and fucking tomahawk dunked Jair's sick ass pipe onto the ground."

"What did you guys do? Was Jair pissed?"

"Hell yeah, he was. Everyone was cussing her out. I think Jair is about to drop kick her in the face when she grabs a chunk of the broken pipe and starts swinging it wildly at everyone. In no time Jair and Zoom Zoom are out of the ditch and gone. I stayed back to try and calm her down, I don't know why."

"So what did *she* do?"

Cameron stood and took off his jacket. He pulled up the sleeve of his shirt and showed Deni the long scars of various thicknesses that crisscrossed his forearm.

"Oh, shit, man. That looks bad."

"I put up my hands like this to calm her down," Cameron continued, raising his hands in a stop motion. "And she fucking swung at me. It was just instinct to block with my forearm."

"How did she not kill you?"

"It seemed like as soon as the glass met flesh it freaked even her out. She stood looking at me with fear in her eyes like she expected me to kill her. I was fuming mad but more scared. My arm was gushing blood. I thought she had cut a major vein like the one people cut when they want to kill themselves."

"Did you fuck her up at least?"

"Nah, man. I gave her a look that kept her standing in place, turned and hightailed it the fuck out of there."

"Jesus, man. Let me see those cuts? Those things are brutal."

"Not too deep, really. A little Neosporin, a day off the street, it was manageable."

"Manageable. I'll say."

"Yeah."

"That when you came here? You couldn't go

home or something, your mom would freak out?"

After a moment's pause Cameron answered. "No, not like that. I stayed at Jair's house a few days, though."

"So you just walk around VH and stay at friends' houses?"

"Pretty much. I've only stayed at Jair's and Misday's, though. When I can't find a place like this."

"What about McKiscko's?"

"I can't show up to his parents' house in this state. High as fuck or bleeding. No way. I stopped by Groll's a few times, pounded on the garage, threw pebbles at his window and shit. No dice with that motherfucker."

"He didn't let you in."

"No, he didn't. He simply refuses to answer." Cameron shook his head and looked at the ground. "I guess I should have expected it."

"Jesus. Why do you say that?"

Cameron took another pull from the fütyülős. His drunkenness was like a car speeding on a rollercoaster of emotions.

"I guess I can't really blame him," Cameron

mumbled.

"Why not?"

"I dunno. I have been fucked up to Groll in the past. I used to treat him like shit in high school."

"Dude we all treated him like shit. We used to call him Dave Groll, or Grill then Grilldo, remember?"

"Yeah, I coined that nickname actually. I regret that."

The sound of a car driving in the street outside came into the house. A spotlight shot through the cracks and crossed the entire house, drawing a blinding line on the back wall while in the window's range.

"Fuck. Security guard." Cameron ducked under the beam of the light.

They waited until the guard passed. The spotlight, like that of an army patrol, made them feel like fugitives. Cameron went on in a hushed tone. "So I don't really blame him."

"Yeah, but dude, you were outside waiting. What if it would have been after that witch attacked you? No one should let someone be stranded outside."

"It wasn't. And how would he know, anyway?"

"Regardless. We're all still homies, no matter

what we've done to each other. I mean I wouldn't let someone I know just stand outside, what if they were in trouble?"

"I don't know," Cameron said shaking his head. "I don't even think he knew it was me. I'm just saying it doesn't matter because of all the bad I've done him. It works out, anyway."

"Works out? That doesn't work out. You think you deserved it?"

"Yeah, I guess that's what I'm saying."

"I dunno, man. I don't think that."

"I hooked up with girls he was in love with. I knew he liked them and I did it, anyway."

"Who? Like Carey and Nicole and them?"

"Carey, yeah."

"Give me a break, man, who hasn't hooked up with her?" Deni had propelled himself into the lower quadrant of light to ask this question, his face illuminated.

"I know but that's not the point. She didn't mean anything to me but she meant something to him, and he was my friend. It was fucked up."

"That's nonsense, man." Deni recoiled back into the darkness of the shadow, with only faint glints of light shining off his forehead and his eyes, to think about the treacheries committed against friends to which everyone he knew was guilty. It didn't justify a lack of help in time of physical peril but it didn't change the nature of the transgression, either.

It was dark now. The streetlight shining into the house was too bright. The buzz they both felt had crashed, taking their energy along with it. They stayed like that, silent in the dark for a while.

Blinking his eyes awake, Deni managed to ask one last question.

"Why're you doing this?"

Cameron, still awake as he sat upright against the opposite wall, knew exactly what he was talking about. Almost as if he'd been expecting the question all along.

"I don't believe in anything anymore," he said.

Deni frowned, curling into a ball as he tried to force the drunkenness to push him to sleep. Cameron looked at him and the empty room and the tops of empty houses through the window and his dreams of beauty all seemed like a series of empty, inanimate objects. He lay on his back and stared at the popcorn ceiling, trying to ascribe names to the mountain ridges that swirled and disappeared within the jagged topography. Blanketed over him was a feeling of utter defeat.

Across from him Deni pinched his eyes shut and tried not to think about Cameron's answer. The line between belief and the abyss came dangerously into perspective. The blackness beyond the stack of cards that held it all together threatened to envelope him like the jaws of Hell.

It was like this, in a rage of half-dreams and discomfort that the two spent the night in the empty house.

TWENTY-FOUR

The sun wasn't up long before they woke. Neither had slept well. The brightness coming through the windows was more than enough excuse for them to leave. They groaned as they stood and walked out the front door, holding their heads like the sun was a sledgehammer. The bottles lay knocked over upstairs with only swallows left, the Rilke book sat dog-eared next to the divan.

Outside they got into Deni's orange Saab without so much as a look in either direction. The weather was brisk, colder than it had been lately.

"You got work today?" Cameron said, frowning into the sun.

"Nope."

Deni punched the face of the deck. "El Caminos in the West" by Grandaddy came on. Driving toward the freeway the city looked frozen in dust. Cameron looked out his window. The drab buildings and the endless desert all reflected the sun in a way that made him nauseous. He didn't squint, nor did he shield his eyes from the piercing light of the sun. His head was already throbbing with a nascent hangover, and he did nothing to abate it. Driving into the city they sang along with the bittersweet melody:

> *"El caminos in the west,*
> *We're all collapsed and futureless.*
> *I'll paint the words a simple wish*
> *For peace of mind and happiness."*

That evening saw the boys grouped around a table in László's kitchen. They rummaged through the fridge and cupboards, assortments of chips and trail mixes and plates of leftover goulash were scattered everywhere. László was squeezing salmon roe out of a tube onto a gluten-free cracker. A giant plastic bottle of Canadian Mist was diminishing quickly.

Cameron had a reckless streak brimming within him. He'd showered and changed back into his suit. He bunched up the crusty sweater and the dirty jacket he'd stolen and stuffed them in a laundry hamper. László gave him a thick woolen cardigan to wear instead. After changing, he spent the next couple of hours relaxing on the comfortable couch and eating his stomach full with homemade Hungarian delicacies. He took shot after shot, snaps and whiskey, his tolerance undaunted. He was positive he could have drunk a whole bottle and still function.

Sitting at the table, as the rest of his friends flurried around him, making jokes and yelling at the TV, he didn't say much. He watched the proceedings with a calm reserve that was like a thin layer of rock over violent magma.

"Where's Antonio?" he asked out of the blue. The question was absurd, Antonio hadn't been around for some time.

"Antonio? Why? That motherfucker disappeared. He went to Mexico."

"Back to Las Altas?"

"I dunno."

"What about Robertstein?"

"He left home. People think he's homeless."

"What's the plan tonight?" someone asked.

"Downtown," answered Misday, like clockwork.

Beneath the table Cameron squeezed his fist.

TWENTY-FIVE

Downtown. Freemont street teemed with Las Vegas' worthless unwashed. The group made their way to Ugly Bar moving by program alone and took turns slapping five with the doorman as the cries from the proles waiting in line competed with the blasting music coming from inside.

As soon as they walked in, Regan ushered everyone to the bar. As if he had called ahead, an old friend of his was already pouring cheap tequila into tiny plastic shot glasses. The boys yelled cheers and clinked their thimbles, swallowing the tequila and throwing the glasses behind them into the indiscriminate darkness of the bar.

The dancefloor shifted in opaque scarlet and black shapes. A cobwebbing of smoke and dry ice fog suspended above the moving figures. Into the thick of the swaying crowd Cameron descended with his elbows. He attempted to start an impromptu mosh pit, but it didn't catch. For some reason the rest of the floor didn't think moshing was an appropriate way to show their affection for the house remixes of The Who Anthology that the DJ was playing. Cameron shrieked at the people he bumped into, asking why they weren't moshing but his screams got drowned out by the combination of Pete Townsend and smooth jazz Reason synth pads.

He continued to gallop in a circle swinging his arm violently, ignoring the crowd's apathy. People thought he was crazy and drunk. He was crazy, and drunk, but completely in control. And he was going to make them pay. He threw a no-look elbow which sent the beercup flying out the hands of an innocent bystander. McKiscko appeared from the fog. Cameron asked for a sip of his beer then downed the entire can in one gulp. At the DJ booth he waited patiently for the selector's attention and then told him if he didn't play Depeche Mode in the next fifteen minutes he would strangle him with his own bowels. The DJ, with one hand to the headphone that covered his ear, nodded and gave him a thumbs-up.

He didn't know where his friends were and he

didn't care. Misday emerged from the stalks of human bodies and said, "Let's get a shot," and he followed. They pounded the Jameson and then another. Justin joined them at the counter and they did another. With narrowed eyes, Cameron scanned the crowded barroom. This, the Ugly Bar, the alternative to the high price posturing of the Strip with its long lines and fifteen dollar drinks, this, the home of the scumbags and misfits, Vegas' alternative scene, all standing in comfortable groups of twos and threes, laughing with acquaintances and nodding their heads to the beat whether it was fast or slow. The middleclass doing everything they can to live up to their mediocre expectations of Friday night. Pudgy twenty-year-olds bumping baby fat in their skin tight clothes. Girls staring with bored, heavily mascaraed eyes at the huddled idiots whose job it was to perpetually impress them. Cameron hoped these people cared about something, because once he found out what it was, he was going to destroy it forever.

He started by pushing Justin to buy a couple more shots. Justin protested, saying he almost threw up after the last one.

"Come on, man. Don't be a little bitch,"

Cameron demanded.

Justin bought two more and choked his down, tears welling up in the corner of his eyes and drool falling from his mouth in thick strings. Cameron pounded it like nothing. In the crosshairs of his gaze he caught a group of girls sitting around a table lit only by the tiny flame of a single candle. Most of them were on their phones checking text messages that had yet to arrive; others looked at the ceiling or the back wall. Cameron swiped a beer from someone at the bar standing next to him who had their back turned. As he pounded it the foam spilt out the corners of his mouth and drenched László's cardigan. He crushed the can in his hand and threw like a sidewinding fastball at the DJ, barely missing his head. From the counter of the bar he took off toward the girls' table. When he was a few feet away he jumped in an extended head first dive, crashing into the table and sliding across its entirety, knocking over the candle and all the drinks assembled there.

Justin looked on from the bar in disbelief. The girls didn't even regard Cameron, who was wedged head over heels in between two hair-drying stations. With bored expressions perfectly in-tact they calmly stood and walked away.

This made Cameron furious. No reaction? No indignation?! He promised himself that the next person he talked to was going to get fucked up.

Back at the bar Justin tried to ask him what he was doing. Cameron ignored him and instead again swiped another beer from an unsuspecting patron.

"Hey, man, what the fuck are you doing?" the man protested.

"I'm drinking a fucking beer, what does it look like?"

"Are you kidding me bro? That was my beer!"

"Okay, you want it? Here!" Cameron faked like he was going to douse the man in the face but instead plunged the liquid into the face of the man's friend who stood beside him, completely blindsiding the unsuspecting friend with a blast of beer to the eyes. While the surprise was still fresh, Cameron plunged the beercan in an open-palm uppercut into the first man's face, cutting him on the upper lip and nose with the tab.

A melee ensued. It seemed the whole bar turned into a wave of people swept up in the fight. Justin landed an overhand right directly on the chin of the friend who was still dazed and blinded by the beer, indeed the most innocent bystander of all, crumpling him to the ground to get trampled by the crowds who tried to get out of the way while security pounced like hyenas. Cameron was ducking and moving, a fist caught him square on his nose. When his vision came back he was being flung outside the bar; when he wiped his face it came back all bloody. Someone speared him from behind, thrusting him face first into the cement while a security guard handcuffed him. They strung him up and placed him against the bar's facade, in front of the line of people waiting to get in and passersby all commenting with jolly remarks and witty put-downs at his ruffled disposition.

In the days and years that passed, Cameron never remembered what he had said to the guards while waiting outside in handcuffs. Metro was never called and he wasn't sent to jail for being a violent danger to society. All he knew was that that night had been the most fun he'd ever had downtown.

Whatever he said to the guards, in even and thoughtful remarks, worked because they let him go fifteen minutes later. They also told him if he ever came back he would be escorted out in a stretcher.

He wasn't done. He ran off the little street of hip bars, fleeing under the holographic miasma of the Freemont Street Experience, past the lecherous fortune teller's wagon and the live band shredding Bon Jovi, through the endless crowds of raging tourists, the inbred vacationers and the robots encased in copper.

The adrenaline running through his veins would not stop. Outside Cannons, a local strip club, he jockeyed with the doorman for entrance. The owner of the club was the father of an old high school buddy. He dropped his friend's name but the doorman wouldn't let him in and threatened to call security.

Down the street again he fled. Slapping beers out of the hands of tourists and kicking over signs. Sprinting, sprinting, endlessly down Main Street and cutting in and out of 3rd and 4th Street, zigzagging to lose the police who were surely on his tail.

His running woke the bums that slept on the benches outside the courthouse. Others popped their heads out of the bail bondsmen shops and 24 Hour adult arcades to see what the commotion was.

Then long stretches of dead quiet downtown night. Sprinting.

After Charleston there were no more busy

streets. The neighborhood of weekly hotels behind the Stratosphere glowed sickly yellow, the only bright spot amongst the black of the apartment complexes.

Once he arrived at Commercial Center he stopped along a chain link fence and exhaled fire. The fence sectioned off a giant plot of destroyed asphalt. From the fit of exertion he kneeled on the gravel and blasted the pavement with whiskey flavored water. Bits of fruit skins and grains of rice were mixed in with the vomit. He collapsed against the sagging fence. His eyes struggled to stay open. His head pounded. He only wanted to sleep for hours and hours. Sleep forever.

Closing his eyes caused a ringing in his head so great that he puked again and was forced to watch.

From the black abyss of Karen Avenue the train scuttled toward him in disjointed unity, the ranks of transvestite teenage hookers moving like frightened cattle, powdered faces motionless behind white lace. Bedecked in tight leather minishorts for the boys and ill-fitting fetish regalia, some yet to see their thirteenth year, the prostitutes winced under the invisible shackles of their master who walked confidently behind them, Nymphomatriarch to these unhallowed walkways. Cameron flinched at each clink of her stiletto heels against the sidewalk. In black stockings over bulging calves, a tight black dress and velvet overcoat, the slumlord Devil moved her troupe shuffling onward in a parody of a funeral procession.

The train stopped in front of Cameron, bringing a sickening realness to the dead concrete landscape that surrounded him.

The slavemaster looked down. Her face was pinched at the cheek and orbital bones, a plastic skin pulled tight over the skull and riveted with pock marks, she carried the botoxed default expression of a smile. Teeth sharp when her mouth opened, the voice like a female's pitched down to unnatural depths.

"You should stay awake and join the piercing of the night."

Shivers ran through the cold blood of her slaves. A young boy hideously emaciated in belly shirt and miniskirt, bones protruding at the knobby knees and elbows, walked toward Cameron. His face shuddered behind the throwaway bride's veil. Black lips parted. He reached out a trembling hand that was covered in a thin film of slime. Behind him amongst her fiends the grin of Trollface promised sadistic torture.

All went black.

TWENTY-SIX

The hand that eventually grasped him by the arm and pulled him to his feet was that of the Black Lion. When Cameron came to, Trollface and her forsaken subordinates were skittering back into the cracks and tunnels of the drug dens from whence they issued.

Cameron wiped at the flecks of vomit stuck to his sweater. The Lion looked on stoically.

"Come on now. Can't stay around here. Let's go, let's go."

Cameron followed dumbly, sober neither in mind or step.

They crossed the street and walked to the canopied staircase of an abandoned business park. In the crook under the mezzanine it was pitch-black.

"You kin take the bag," the Lion said.

Cameron felt around in the dark until he slid

over the nylon sleeping bag in the corner. His eyes adjusted and he shifted into the sleeping bag, then forced his eyes shut. The Lion stood just within the shadow of the first flight of stairs, his eyes shining like green coins, on lookout for any coming of Trollface's nefarious emissaries.

TWENTY-SEVEN

He woke before dawn. The sky a heavy midnight blue streaked with black clouds. Streetlights made dim by the smattering of orange coming from the horizon.

"You up now?"

The Lion was still standing at his post watching the street.

"Yeah," Cameron mumbled. The degree of physical despair he felt was incalculable.

"Alright, then. I reckon you're safe for the time bein'."

Cameron labored out of the sleeping bag and stood up. His muscles felt like pieces of wood that broke with each movement.

"Told you not to hang around here. Now you believe me? That old witch. You're lucky I seen ya from my perch down on Karen. She wouldn'ta been easy on ya."

Cameron, a sallow sunken skeleton huddled in the corner, nodded.

"Now get on," the Lion said. "Don't come back here."

Cameron nodded again.

"I mean it."

Cameron passed from the black corner out from under the stairs and onto the sidewalk. He took a few steps, the walk of an ashamed man not yet fully acquainted with his guilt. He turned back. The Lion stood an ebony statue. He had put on his sunglasses. He looked dignified. Cameron never saw another bum with that look.

"Thank you," Cameron called back to him.

The head of the ebony statue rotated vertically, up and down, up and down.

Cameron headed west.

TWENTY-EIGHT

At midmorning he was a black speck coming out of the wobbly mirage of the desert. He traipsed over the detritus of a bygone era's trash until he came to the sidewalk again. In front of him the mountains shone like red and blue streaked glaciers. He walked the sidewalk while in his mind he walked an endless path, a figure-eight of questions and answers that brought him to the original questions.

In his spiraling self-pity he was struck with the sudden urgency to be productive. He reasoned his guilt was coming from him trying to game the system. He'd lived for free these past weeks and it was the filching that had caught up to him. He didn't have the morale to steal today but he was hungry, starving actually, and possessed by a terrible thirst.

The fact was too, that he felt guilty about

something else; he just didn't want to think about it. The episode with Trollface had been the culmination of a deeper canker that had been festering on his soul for too long. His fantasies were whimsical and rebellious; everything was going fine until he came into real danger. Lord knows he'd been stoking the flames and tempting fate long enough now. And when it came down to it, what had he done? How had he stood up for himself? He fainted. If it wasn't for the noble bum saving him he could have woken up a sex slave in some depraved dungeon. This regret, this silent subterfuge, touched upon much larger issues. Sushumna raised inside him a frail obelisk. Masculinity. The Fear. In his present state he couldn't deal with it. Instead he did what he thought any normal person would do when they needed money and some quick confidence. He got a job.

TWENTY-NINE

The midday sun was an authoritarian God that allowed no shadow. Even the blue of the cloudless sky burned, bereft of all moisture. Out of the bubbling mirage in a desert lot his figure shuffled onward against the heat. He walked to the next intersection that didn't have any pedestrians. Without pausing to look around he stopped next to the yellow pole of the stoplight and stuck out his hand, palm facing up. And with that he had begun his new job. He was timid and the rapid beating of his heart made him feel awkward, but this would pass. It was never easy on the first day.

The light was green and the cars passed him without notice. He continued to stand in supplication until it turned red and the cars began to line up in front of him. After a few moments when he'd had no takers he took to walking toward the back of the line, looking into each passenger window for a client.

Most didn't look his way, knowingly or not. A man with a mustache in a Dodge pickup smushed his face together in rejection. Some made eye contact involuntarily, looking at Cameron with confused faces, like they didn't want to know what he was. The light turned green and the cars passed. He stood empty-handed on the sidewalk and watched them drive away.

Dreams of orange Gatorade and melted popsicles taunted him. Nowhere did he see an opportunity to slake his thirst. He smacked his sandpaper tongue around his lips, only the feint trace of vomit and whiskey.

When the next round of cars stopped at the light he was more forward. He held out his hand and shook it, mouthing silently the words, "Come on man, I need some money," or lifting the fingers to his mouth in a mock munch. He'd seen an old meth addict do the same motion by his mom's house. By all accounts the strategy had worked for her because she was at the same corner every morning demanding her wages, and she must have made money because he could tell her meth addiction was being fed, so black and mushy were her teeth, so sore-ridden her skin. Meth addicts weren't the type of mentors they had told him about in school, but in his condition he had to make do.

He was rejected and ignored over and over. A man sitting in his Corola with the windows down audibly clucked his tongue when Cameron bent down and held out his hand. He was laughed at, honked at, spat at. More than once tough looking customers kept their eyes trained on him, checking the light every couple of seconds, questioning if they had enough time to waste this motherfucker or not.

Playing defense, Cameron ignored them back. The light was going to turn green again and they would have no choice but to get going to where they were off to, to their own jobs they hated or back to the homes of their nagging wives. Their anger wouldn't outlast the honking of the cars behind them.

After three more cycles Cameron didn't give two shits what people thought about him anymore. He laughed when they thought up creative ways to insult him. He had made thirty-six cents. His hand shook as he looked at the copper and silver in his crusty palm. It wasn't enough. He couldn't even get a small cup at 7-11. He looked desperately in the empty lot for a bottle; there were water dispensers where he could get a half-gallon for a quarter. But where?   Walking far and aimless was becoming less and less of an option.

He thought by now he'd have at least a couple of dollars. In the neighborhoods beyond the busy intersection the rooftops of mid-century modern homes rose above the brick walls in between pine trees. Maybe I'll stay in one of those tonight he said to himself in a slow, delirious voice. All his schemes and tricks came back to him in the voice of teasing children. It isn't gunna work! It's not gunna woooork! With every car that whizzed past him he felt his grip on reality quiver. His will to find a solution loosening, threatening to jettison completely. Enchiladas. Pizza.

While he was struggling to hold onto the last remnants of composure he was visited upon by a fellow tradesman. A nameless vagabond covered in a thick crust of dirt. Patches of skin on the man's face were savagely burnt from the sun, his eyes a fiery red.

Cameron's alarm bells were ringing as his colleague approached. Hopefully he'll just be passin' through, he told himself knowing it to be untrue.

The man stopped in front of Cameron a couple of sidewalk squares away, blinking his terrible red eyes in their tiny sockets. The lines of his face looked to be from butterknives stomped into leather. He didn't say anything so neither did Cameron. The light turned red and Cameron began to move past him, back to work.

"Now just wait here a minute," the man said. A twang in his voice that sounded Southern, or Texan.

"Alright then," Cameron mumbled and tried to move past. The man put a black fingernailed hand on Cameron's stomach.

"Yeah?" Cameron asked.

The man shot air out of his nostrils, confounded. He looked at Cameron with an uncertainty tainted with anger that hid behind his eyes and crept through in thin red cracks.

"You were *told* to come here?" the man asked.

Cameron frowned but kept his face straight. "Yeah."

"Now, see I don't know about that. God 'ammit, then." He slapped the leg of his cargo pants and dust puffed into the air. "You tellin' me they fuckin' doublebooked on me?" He looked at Cameron with a visceral need for explanation.

"I don't know what to say, brother. I been here all day."

"Who was it, then?"

"Who was it what?"

"Who *told* you? Who told you to report here then, heh?"

Cameron hesitated. "I don't know what you're talking about," he said and immediately knew it was the wrong thing to say.

The man studied Cameron before relaxing into his spite. He licked the small black stubs he used as teeth.

"You mean you doan even know what yer doin here?"

He said it with a visible anxiousness while licking his broken lips, like he couldn't wait for the answer.

"Yeah, whatever man," Cameron retorted, ignoring him. The seconds counted down from twenty-four and it seemed like an entire day before the light turned red and he would be able to cross the street. This corner was compromised.

"Now wait here a god damned minute I'm getting to the bottom of this," the man said gruffly, grabbing a fistful of Cameron's sweater to keep him from crossing the street. Cameron spun and whacked the man's hand away with a twirling backhand.

"Don't fuckin' touch me," he said, flashing

serious eyes at the man. The fear was at bay but constantly threatened to boil over. Don't show anything to this cocksucker, he told himself.

"Ewwwoooo," the man crooned, like a goblin spitting up blood. "Sermen gunna lahhhk you." He licked the broken skin of his lips, covering them with the balm of his sticky saliva. "You know what Sermen done with lil scabs like you?" He moved closer to Cameron, forcing him to backpeddle. "He fucks em in the ass and keeps em in chains at the bottom of his house. Use em for slaves and meat." He hickled a piercing repetition of demonic laughs that landed like razors in Cameron's ears.

The man enveloped Cameron with his rapist's gaze. Doubt twinkled in Cameron's eyes on its own; when he tried to block it out with a frown it only made the man smile. Cameron prepped himself for combat.

He glanced at the intersection. The light was still green. The nearest cluster of cars was still a couple of hundred yards off, speeding fast.

The man lunged for Cameron again with both hands. Cameron was quick off the mark, bolting off the sidewalk. The man got only air.

He made it to the middle of the street to the barrage of horns. Cars had blazed by him deadly close.

A threesome of cars had to pass before he could make it to the other side. At the corner the crazed bum was hooting like a gorilla, waving his arms and yelling something to the corner diagonal from him. Cattycorner one of the man's cohorts waved back and started to cross the street to cut Cameron off. He knew if he got caught in the pickle he'd be fucked. The threesome whizzed past. Cameron didn't stop running.

His shoes slapped the concrete, his sides bit with cramps, in his throat he tasted blood from scathed lungs. Behind him, the two bums had met and were talking and pointing in his direction.

He cut through a shopping center and down a narrow avenue. No matter where he went he always seemed exposed. There was nowhere to hide.

At a stop sign he turned west, away from the street he'd been working and jogged down the street against the pain in his knees and chest. He was soaked in sweat. It was a long intricate neighborhood and when he got out on the other side, on Jones Boulevard, he was even more unclear of where he was. At the nearest stoplight he saw another bum was working the corner. Cameron held his breath as he walked by the bum, doing his best impression of a regular pedestrian, hoping to god these madmen didn't carry cellphones.

THIRTY

The sun and the moon were both in the sky but it was too early for sleep. He wasn't tired. He was scared. He worried someone might have followed him or that the cops would soon be called. Getting into the house had been too easy. He had hopped the wall into the backyard where he sat drinking from the hose spigot until he almost puked, then came in through a side door, through the garage to where he now sat in the dank, empty living room. At least it had carpet, he thought.

Time passed. He couldn't rest. He forced his eyes closed, vainly trying to active daydream. All hope of escapism vanished with the slamming of a car door.

He parted the thin blinds and looked out the window. Four men in various ensembles of military surplus fatigues and wrap around glasses were coming toward the front door. One of them was carrying a baseball bat.

In a panic he pressed his back against the wall. It was ridiculous; he was still in the middle of the living room. The sun burst through every window in the house mockingly bright. No shadows offered themselves to hide within. No leftover furniture to hide behind.

The jangle of the door knob was like prickles along his spine. It was locked. Immediately the jangle was replaced with the jarring sound of the lock-pick's teethe tearing into the keyhole.

He forced his body out of its inertia. He had milliseconds to figure something out.

When the lock was picked and the door kicked open the mercenaries walked into an empty living room. Cameron was ducked in the corner of the bathroom by the toilet. He wasn't hidden at all. There was no shower curtain hanging over the bathtub. The opaque window above the toilet was mercilessly thin and didn't open.

Below the sink he reached for the cupboard doors even though he knew he wouldn't be able to fit inside. They were sealed shut, just for show.

BAM!

The sound came accompanied by the crunch of splintered wood. A horrible confusion of thoughts paralyzed him as he speculated about what was happening on the other side of the door.

In broken thoughts he tried to remember if the houses next door were vacant or not. Maybe someone would hear the noise and call the police. It didn't matter. The crashing sounds coming from within the house bore no sign of mitigation.

He stood, saw his terrified face in the mirror above the sink.

"If you're gunna run you have to do it now. You have to do it now."

Soul crushing hesitation.

Behind the door brutal crushing sounds. Laughing.

Cameron squeezed his eyes shut, clenched his fists, tightened his anus.

The sounds of footsteps were loud in the tile corridor. The mercenaries exchanged jovial banter.

"They won't look in here they won't look in here please please they won't look in here."

Unrepentant footsteps marching down the hall. Just outside the bathroom.

Cameron tightened even further.

WHACK!

The bathroom door opened with such force it slapped the wall. The first man to enter was so surprised when he saw Cameron he jumped with fright.

"Holy shit you scared me!" the man said.

Cameron tried not to shake, shrugging as if they were both in on the same joke.

"Hey fellas, we got a live one!" the man called out behind him in a high pitched cackle.

He wore black tactical fatigues and steel toed military boots. A TruSpec vest and utility belt equipped with pepper spray and handcuffs. Tucked into a holster on the front of his pants was a Sig Sauer P226 Combat 9mm.

He looked at Cameron from behind his black Oakley Monster Dogs.

"Look, man," Cameron tried to reason. "I don't live here, I won't say anything."

"Shut the fuck up you little bitch," the man interrupted, shooting a huge hand directly at Cameron's throat. He latched his thick, strong fingers around Cameron's neck and squeezed only slightly, but it was already crushing Cameron's windpipe.

The man squeezed a little tighter until Cameron's eyes were popping out of his head. This amused the man.

"Hey fellas!" He yelled out. "Hurry up I got a beaner!"

"Woohooo!"

"Fuck yeah!"

The celebratory exclamations poured in from around the house.

The man let go of Cameron's throat and he collapsed onto the floor, choking as he tried not to cough.

The man put his boot on Cameron's sternum and pinned him against the bathtub.

"I'm just squatting here, I'll leave," Cameron said. His voice cracked when he tried to sound stern.

The man snickered. "You ain't leavin.' We just got here."

The other three men crowded into the doorway, piling on top one another like in a cartoon.

"Hey guys, he said he's just squatting here," the first man said.

They were all so muscled they couldn't fit in the doorway. Two of them were pushed into the bathroom and with all of them in, there was no space left.

The one left outside grabbed another by the arm and switched places with him. He had close-cropped blonde hair.

"Remy, Julio, go finish the house. Dex and I will take care of this beaner. I wanna be outta here in fifteen minutes, no exceptions."

The man with the baseball bat and Remy disappeared down the hall. The blonde took off his silver Oakley Crosshairs and looked at Cameron with his bright blue eyes. Dex still kept Cameron fixed to the ground with his boot.

"What do we have here," said the blonde. The freckles on his cheeks seemed to shine with excitement.

"He said he doesn't live here," Dex answered dumbly.

"Really? I never would have guessed." He slapped Dex in the back of the head and ordered him to pull Cameron up. "Let's take him out to the living room where there's more space."

They dragged Cameron like a mute rag doll into the living room and pushed him against the wall.

"Hey jackasses! Prep the sinks and walls for copper extract!" the blonde yelled upstairs, where booming sounds continued to explode like bombs. Then he turned his attention back to Cameron.

"Cuff him," he said to Dex.

Cameron tried to resist but Dex was easily too strong. He secured one elbow around Cameron's back while cuffing one wrist then yanked his other arm around and cuffed the wrists together in a reverse prayer pose. Cameron thought his arms were going to be ripped off at the shoulders.

"What the hell you guys," Cameron said pathetically.

"Man, shut the fuck up!" said the first man, returning his boot just below Cameron's sternum with a vicious front-kick.

Cameron retched as he slammed into the wall, crumpling again to the floor.

Dex laughed at this but not like it was a joke. The blonde one checked his cellphone.

"Let's do this beaner and scram. I gotta get back, Sandra is on my ass."

"The old ball and chain hangin' from your nuts is sure getting heavy."

The blonde clicked his tongue and complained. "I told you man, she gets pissed when I'm not there for Sofia's practice."

"You sound like a bitch sometimes you know that?"

"You try having kids."

"I do, somewheres."

With the sudden turn of light conversing Cameron allowed himself to think the danger had subsided.

"Alright, honey, time to get fucked," said Dex. The disgusted look stayed on his face as he lifted Cameron up by the scruff of the neck and pulled him to his feet.

He kept Cameron pinned to the wall with a baseball-gloved hand, then gestured to the blonde.

"You want this one, Ben?"

Ben the Blonde scoffed. "Of course I fucking want this one. Whattaya think you fuckin' wiseguy?"

Dex shrugged.

"Just hold him up for me," Ben commanded.

One of the other men looked over the balustrade. "You guys need help with that beaner?"

"Shut the fuck up and prep the walls!" Ben

yelled back.

By now sweat was dripping from Cameron's face and soaking his clothes. He looked from Dex to Ben. A lump so thick was in his throat he thought he might choke. When he couldn't breathe he coughed and hocked up some phlegm, causing the Dex to laugh.

"We haven't even done anything yet!"

"Shut up and go finish the rest of the house!"

"You don't need help?" whimpered Dex.

"Just do it! This shithole won't take much to ruin. Even a god damned retard like you could finish the job."

"Geeze, alright," mumbled Dex. He sulked away, grabbing an aluminum baseball bat that lay against the wall by the staircase. Cameron watched him disappear up the stairs.

Ben reached into a compartment on his belt and pulled out a roll of duct tape, stretching a length of it with a violent ripping sound. He spread the tape over Cameron's mouth and ripped it from the roll. Cameron's eyes rolled back and forth in his head.

"First, we need music."

Ben took his iPhone which was also connected

to his belt and shifted a few screens. He connected it to a mini "bomb" bluetooth stereo and set the device on the ground, then tapped the screen a few more times. "Dust to Dust" by the Misfits filled the room with its opening riffs.

"This is what I'm talking about!" Ben yelled. His face brightened. His blonde hair sharpened at the tiny gelled spikes.

Cameron tried to mumble an exhausted protest through the duct tape but Ben punched him in the stomach.

"Shut the *fuck* up." Cameron gargled and wretched. "Hold still, you fucking Mexican."

He grabbed Cameron at the button fly of his trousers and ripped down violently, tearing them at the crotch. One of the metal buttons shot off and rolled over the tile by the front door.

Cameron's eyes went white with terror. He'd expected pain. He hadn't expected this.

"Let's see what you got you little fag boy," Ben said. There was a definite joy in his tone. Ben then yanked Cameron's tattered boxer briefs down around his ankles.

"Ha!" he squeeled. "Look at that bush! I can

barely see his cock!"

Cameron's legs buckled and folded inward at the knees.

"Guys! Come down and look at this!"

The trio came booming down the stairs.

"Holy shit, man, what are you doing?" one asked.

"Fuck it look like? We're gunna make this cocksucker pay. Hold him steady."

Dex and Remy came back downstairs and kept him upright while Ben slammed a steel-toed boot right into his pubic mound.

Muffled from the thick tape, Cameron's agony couldn't be fully expressed.

Ben screamed out in laughter.

"How was that on your little baby cock?" He said, bending his face disturbingly close to Cameron's red, shriveled penis.

"Did you like that?" Ben asked the penis, then flicked the head as hard as possible. Cameron had gone numb after the kick, the rest of the gang stood around as if even they were disturbed by this brand of torture.

Cameron's eyes were fluttering and rolling back in his head again. Ben steadied his lolling head and slapped him hard across the face. He took Cameron by the cardigan and ripped it open at the chest. Then the same with the blazer. Cameron's chin fell back against his sternum.

Ben took a serrated bowie knife from a hip-holster and held its point up close to his face, admiring the shine of the stainless steel.

"How does this look to you?" He asked rhetorically, licking the long smooth side, opposite the sharp ridged edge. Then he split open Cameron's blouse lengthwise, exposing his naked chest completely.

Cameron wasn't looking. He was in and out of consciousness.

Shattering glass and deep thudding sounds of plaster and walling being destroyed sounded from the kitchen, where Julio was going wild with the baseball bat. The Misfit's song on repeat a savage dance anthem to extreme pain.

"Make him look!" Ben thundered. Dex held Cameron's head up by the chin.

Cameron's squinted bug eyes looked at Ben. A profound energy spiraled out from the center of his being. He watched Ben come closer with the knife with eyes that expected death, his breath held as the blade pierced the skin.

In the kitchen a glass shower rained down onto the floor after a crushing blow.

The knife dug into the flesh where the two collarbones met at the apex of the sternum and dragged slowly to the right nipple, bouncing over the steppe of ribcage. Then straight across to the left nipple, tearing over what little muscle that existed of Cameron's pectoral. Then, lifting the blade he pressed it back to the first incision point and Ben pressed harder, bringing the blade down in a straight line to the center of the abdomen. Vomit water dribbled from beneath the duct tape.

Ben stood back to look at his handiwork. Blood was trickling from the incisions, white spongy tissue visible under the flaps of skin. The bloody 4 would be forever carved into Cameron's body.

"We got a buzz," Dex said, looking down at his utility belt. The police scanner at his hip croaked in a forlorn siren. "They're approaching the neighborhood."

"They comin' for us?" Ben grunted.

"I dunno man but they're close."

Ben was still reluctant. He was just getting into the groove.

"We should go, bro," Dex said.

Julio came back from the kitchen. "We really gotta go, Ben!" Indecipherable chatter made static noises on his intercom.

"What we gunna do with him?" Remy asked apologetically.

"Gas him and leave him. He'll be gone before anyone comes."

Ben gathered his phone and joined the group at the front door, as did Remy. Julio took a small can of black spraypaint and blasted Cameron point blank in the face.

THIRTY-ONE

He wandered out of the hospital like an escapee from the psychic ward for MK-ULTRA rejects. The pain medication was designed not to affect the opiate receptors or the serotonin uninhibitors so it only filled his guts with sickness to distract from the sutures that pussed and oozed instead of making him feel good. The black spray paint couldn't be completely removed from his face, but it had faded, so his permanently blood-red eyes shown brighter and more sinister. Stumbling out onto the street he was the perverse blackface gutter punk nigger.

The nurses had spongebathed him while he was still comatose but he was dirtier now than he had been when the neighbors of that haunted house heard him moaning and called for paramedics. He felt worse, too. He'd been given new clothes that walked on their own. They hadn't been washed in centuries.

The swollen digit on his chest itched. Your whole life has been the diagnosis. Now, The Surgery.

Their questions had all gone unanswered. He only mouthed mumbled nothings with a useless tongue scorched and devoid of papillae.

They thought he was an insane drug addict and treated him thus. The nurse jabbed the syringe into the pit of his elbow to take the blood. When it came back clean of drugs they were angry. Now he was an unknown, they didn't know where to put him. Do you have ID? No. Do you have *insurance?* Nuhhh. "God damn it," they hissed under their breath. "Sew him up and get his ass the FUCK out of here."

And so he was, booted right out of the inner city hospital onto the most hostile of streets. Deranged and psychotic, with no reference to anything anymore. He didn't even know what part of town he was in. He asked people walking by, crackheads and scumbags, for any clue as to what he was doing there. What had happened to him? They skittered out of his way immediately. He was abhorrent to them.

As he got closer to the university he stopped near a cluster of apartments that housed students living off-campus. A tennis court faced the street, lined with black sun-screens. A sign on the outside of the fence read "Wimbleton" [sic] in white cursive letters. He looked at the misspelling and tried to laugh, felt a crack along the roof of his mouth and tasted blood. Up the street a ways he saw a bald man with a sun-splotched face in a full UniQlo track suit coming toward him. It was Bjorn. He had stopped some kids coming from the apartments and seemed to be soliciting them for money, or possibly a pick-up game. Cameron walked up to the group.

"Bjorn!"

The sunburnt Serbian turned his steely blue eyes from the students, who at the sight of another street freak looked even more confused. Their eyes searched desperately for an opportunity to escape, and his unforgiving gaze fell upon Cameron.

"Ta je," he grunted.

"Dude, what's up?! It's been a while huh?" Cameron tried to move in for a handshake-hug but was rebuffed as Bjorn pushed him away.

"You don't remember? We played tennis before. At Paradise Park."

"We gotta go, mister. We have to get to class," said one of the kids and the two of them skittered off.

Bjorn's gaze turned malevolent. "What you do here? Huh?!" he barked at Cameron. In the blue astigmatisms there was no recognition of who Cameron was.

"Remember?" Cameron, wild eyed and black faced, asked in one last attempt to rouse his memory. The question came out in an obtuse mumble from the cut in his mouth.

"E'edee uewe lepu pichku mate, rinuewe!" Bjorn yelled. His face came so close to Cameron's nose he thought Bjorn was going to head butt him. He pushed past Cameron and walked briskly down the street in the opposite direction, throwing his hands in the air and yelling out further obscenities.

Deflated and delirious Cameron turned back south and shuffled onward.

"Dust to Dust" was stuck in his head, only this version was slowed down, played by a masked monster at a cobwebbed piano. The image pleased him. The song was beautiful, slow and evil, hanging in the afternoon air. He smiled his black lips as wide as he could, horrifying his fellow pedestrians on the street. In a dead mass of purple snapdragon on the side of the road he collapsed, laughing to himself. He'd become the monster he'd always wanted to be.

He lay there until a security guard buzzed up to him on a Segway and made him leave. No one was going to give his humanity the benefit of the doubt. He was a floating demon of human indignity. His mouth burned. It couldn't produce saliva anymore. Ashes to ashes. Dust to dust.

The mutilation had ushered forth a promise that all his darkest dreams would come true. If reality threatened to unmask this feeling, he'd resist. Pain had given him a twisted purpose; it was the soothsayer's human bone pointing the direction of his destiny. He knew where to go. Tonight there would be sacrifice. By the fall of the Blood Moon his journey would culminate in shining visceral immolation.

South toward the Druid Altar. It was in Verdant Hills, tucked in the graveyard behind the Recreation Center. Eleven miles by the raven's flight from where he was now. He would traverse the distance without thought of food or water. Ritual fasting was needed in order to obtain the rites from the spirit world. He was determined. He was going to meet the forces that he'd been seeking all along. He would force a confrontation.

Halfway there he came upon a vast shopping center where beyond the asphalt lay an organic-only WalMart. Zombies with sunken jaws and dangling flesh shuffled up and down the sidewalk holding picket signs that cursed corporate America. They held banners aimed at the speeding traffic and mumbled chants about the need to overthrow hegemonic regimes.

Cameron leaned against the fence and caught his breath. He felt akin to these zombies and was curious to their cause. The absurd incantations from the protesters were whispered like prayers for a Black Emperor, beseeching the Dark Cloud to begin Armageddon.

An old man, skinny and tall, shuffled past him, pigeon-toed in Velcro shoes.

"What's all this, then?" Cameron asked. He leaned into the fence and flashed his blood eyes at the man.

The man frowned back at him from behind wrap-around specs.

"Protestin'," said the man.

"Protesting what?"

"Organic WalMart, can't you read the sign?"

"Why you protesting against them? They do something to you personally?"

"Hell yes they did. They refuse to pay us a decent living wage."

Cameron's gas tank dipped below empty. His eyes watched the man, two red marbles inside a spraypainted skull. "So you worked for them?"

"You're damned right. Well *they* did." He pointed to a vague nobody. "We're Union. 333 Grocers."

"Haven't heard of that one."

"Well, we're here, all day and all night. Until WalMart changes its ways."

"Think they'll budge?"

"They haven't recognized us yet, but our Lieutenant says it's any day now."

"That they repay you?"

"Well, negotiations have to begin first. But any day now. Says our Lieutenant."

Cameron lost all respect for this zombie. The chanters at their blank mass, sitting in the heat waiting to die, pretending to fight a behemoth with useless weapons. They'd all given in to their defeat. They weren't even trying.

"Well, good luck," Cameron told the man, pushing off the fence.

"Yeah, my shift's about done, anyhow. Gotta get over to Sunset Medical. Those bastards make WalMart look like Catholic Charities."

"So you guys just go from place to place,

fighting tyranny wherever you see it, huh?"

The man shrugged. "I just go where the Union tells me to go, brother."

"Hah."

*   *   *

the witChing hOur, tHE palo VerDes have aLl turned to black smiles yawNing toward sunset. Hhe crEpt UNderneath the blacktop of the abandoned schoolyard, through the waving headstones in the playGRound, between the shredded fence links and into the Druid Altar. a noise, a scurry, children were running from the entrance of the public auditORIUm just across the STReeT, dressed as muRDerous ravens and oWl-brothers of molokh. their cries were candy corn laughter bleeding from their mouths into the EVEning sky. "for sure i have found the valLey of ShhhhaytOon.." it was his hope, his fear. for the moment it was allayed; just kids running to their eager parents, away in SUVs and shiny mercedes, to their mansions and safe bourgeoisie dreams. he laughed, his walking FALTered, swaying with the darkened breeze, thinKING of the cozy family halloween. The AltAr was directLy behind the auditorium building, DANGerously close. anyone with half a mind for iNstinct would knOW sOmeOne crept nearby. anyone with a soul must feel the hallowed earth upon which they stood, must tAsTe the blood that forEVER STAINED the sharp cLAW bRANches of every MEsquite tree. they didn't know, comforted as they were, clutching their children for dear life. the sky was darkest directly above his head, thinning as it spREaD centrifugally until it reached the flAmes of the demOnic horizOn. eVERYthing circled this moment. the telephone rang in the red booth that was his tomBstone, the girl from the ditch, the ghost that didn't exist, was calling him. "HellOo?" The very center of the altar. He could hear the gods of Valhalla screEaming. The blood in the mountains, he could hear their AGONy. "Please answer, I know you're there." The smooth stone of the circular alTar gathereD every bit of light that was left. the conductor. a monument to eternal emotions staked into the heathen earth, forgotten behind the theatre. What lurks behind the curtAin. What monster sways? He fell to his knees knowing no one was looking. He shrieked in a torment that could only be conjured by ancestors. The breeze moaned, the pine trees waved. Wind through the nEEDLes and the sun raging at the world's end. I in the calm purple descENDing, an enDLESS sleep covered him, the fOreveR blanket of graSs and dirt. To becOMe the earth, the moNUMENt himself, in fraGiLe bone. Behind the mountain the sun was smiling, full of bleeding TEeth. The golden fury of the crimSON sky. He was the trees, the grass, the air, the cloudszzz. The eviL creSted and swirLed withIN the typhoon of his spirit, taking with it every human emotion, inhaling the PSYchotic scream of the city and making it a bEaUtiful swan song, a blissful call from the living spirits of the world's past lives, returning to the atmosphere the most vivid green and purple lights that shot off like stars toward the distant heavens. ThunDer cracked. All scars ceased to be, as did his skin, as the air passed through him and took him away to become the distant voice beyond the lightning.

Far away, a place he would never find even given thousands of years of searching, the red booth's wooden frame cracked and crumbled, its telephone still ringing. "hELloO?"

THIRTY-TWO

He went back to his mother's house. Delirious as he was, plodding the sidewalk of his complex and up the oil-stained driveway in soggy donated shoes, he didn't even notice the FOR SALE sign newly erected in the front lawn. When his mother opened the door he all but collapsed in her arms.

Her expression went from fright to shock as she realized it was her son. She said, "*Cameron?*" and there were tears behind her voice already. The question was a manifestation of her initial confusion, but it also summed up everything she wanted to know about the creature before her. He didn't elaborate; a shake of the head to let her know he understood her confusion was all he could muster before stumbling into her embrace. He leaned on her to support his weak limbs. She hugged him tight to her body with pure maternal instinct.

They ambled up the stairs slowly; she carried him like he was a drunk that needed to be lain down. In the bathroom she helped him to undress. He winced as he took off the dirty sweatshirt from the hospital. Every movement seemed to reopen a tender suture. His mother helped pull the rest of it over his head and raised arms, just like when he was a kid, and shrieked when she saw the jagged numeral plastered over his sternum. Blood soaked through the gauze in places, making the "4" look like a toddler had written it in red crayon.

"Oh, what happened?" she whispered.

"Vandals. Broke into a house. Attacked me," he mumbled back.

He put his hand on her shoulder and stepped out of the shoes, then took off his pants and underwear. His mother gasped again when she saw how skinny he'd become. She drew a hot bath then stepped out to get fresh gauze. When she got back he was sitting in the tub with his arms wrapped around his shins, adding hot tears to the bathwater. The hot water sent pain through his body in a constant arpeggio. She ran a loofa gently over his back, up and down.

They sat like that a while, both crying.

THIRTY-THREE

For the next week he laid on the couch recovering. He watched whatever was on TV no matter how stupid he thought it was. His mom flitted around the adjacent kitchen, sometimes leaving to go to work or run errands. She kept an up-to-date account of how he was feeling, and brought him soup and tea.

By Halloween, he could move freely again. That night he sat on the futon in the upstairs loft and looked out the window. Beyond the neighborhood the black streets trailed up the hill toward the black sky, outlined in the orange glow of streetlights. He thought about all the neighborhoods hidden by the giant trees, all the vampires and werewolves stalking the streets, the ghosts carrying their pillow cases, the teenagers with jack-o-lanterns on their heads and toilet paper hidden in their cloaks. He could feel the energy of what was surely a magical night outside and knew he would have to content himself with watching it through the window. Only a few groups of kids trick-or-treated in

the complex, less rang their doorbell to get candy from his mom.

He woke early the next morning. When he came downstairs his mother was sitting at the kitchen table drinking coffee.

"Hey, hon," she said.

"Morning."

"Sleep okay?"

"Yeah, fine."

"Does it still hurt?"

"It itches more than anything."

"We have some Benadryl."

"Thanks."

He made himself a bowl of cereal and joined her at the table. She spoke in between the loud crunching.

"I'm worried about you," she said.

He looked at her and had the urge to stare back into the bowl of cereal and ignore the uncomfortable situation. He didn't though; he checked himself and instead looked her in the eye. The pointlessness of trying to hold anything back now was too apparent.

"Yeah?" he said, placing the spoon down on the table.

"What do you mean 'yeah'? Of course I am!" Her voice had risen and tears were at her eyes.

"Alright, alright. Take it easy."

"Don't tell me to take it easy! What happened to you? Where have you been?! I was going to have the police out looking for you!"

"When did you get back?"

"Last Tuesday. I've been here for almost a week and no call from you, nothing!"

"I've been gone since the beginning of the month. At least."

"*Gone?*"

"Yeah. I left. I was living on the streets."

She nodded her head slowly. He could see the tendons taught in her neck, her jaw bones flexing.

"I'm not kidding," he continued. "It's not just an expression."

She sniffed back the tears, coughing involuntarily in the process. "Go on."

"I couldn't stay here any longer. I couldn't stand my life anymore. I had to get away. From everything."

His mother looked at him blankly, like she

didn't know where to begin. He suffered from the same problem and didn't say anything, either.

"That was a really dumb thing of you to do," she said finally. "A really dumb thing to do."

"Yeah, I know."

"So why did you do it? You think it's some kind of joke? You could have been killed."

He looked down at his lap. Underneath the baggy T-shirt he wore, the wound pulsated. Heat came from under the collar.

"It's no joke."

"I don't understand this," she said. "Were you trying to hurt me? What did I do to make you run away?"

"Run away? Mom, I'm twenty years old. I can't run away."

"Well you did! You left this house to go live out on the streets. I want to know why. I want to know what was so bad about living here."

"I couldn't take it anymore, okay? The life I was living, everything was just all fucked up. I couldn't accept it anymore."

She clucked her tongue. "You'll have to be more specific."

He sighed and composed himself.

"I had nothing to hold onto anymore. School was for shit – I had no idea what I was even doing there, taking meaningless classes – I don't play competitive sports anymore, my friends are all over the place, mainly getting involved in a scene I hate with my entire soul. I wanted to throw it all away. Get rid of it all and just go off by myself."

"What about finishing your degree? You're not one to give up on something as important as that. You don't realize how lucky you are, how good you have it. Do you think everyone has the same opportunities as you? This is your life we're talking about. You don't throw that away."

"I wanted to."

"You were always under so much pressure with sports your whole childhood. I told you it would have a negative impact. And the kids you hang around, smoking dope and drinking all the time. No wonder you feel the way you do. You need to find people that make your life better, not hang around with deadbeats."

"I've had most the same friends since

elementary school, they've been there for me."

"Yeah, it really sounds like it."

"Whatever, mom. You wish I would have been some softy artist and gone to science camp. That's not me, okay? And I'm not some impressionable idiot that does things just to fit in. I do what I want, if I want to experience something I will."

"Well you have a shitty idea of what experience is. What about drawing and gardening? You used to be interested in those things. We could have done those things together. I offered to teach you how to cook Persian food so many times and you never gave it any consideration."

He had to suppress a shudder. "Look, mom, we're getting off the point. It's not as simple as just finding new things to do. At one point I believed in my life. I believed in sports and my academic ability. I believed in my friends. Then one day I woke up and realized what I believed in was gone and I had just been going through the motions. There wasn't anything to be proud of anymore."

"Then do something about it. You don't throw all your advantages away. You don't disrespect what has been given to you and just quit."

"It's more than that, though. Those things were my life. They used to make me happy. They had meaning. And they don't anymore. What do you do when nothing matters, anymore? I wasn't excelling, true, but even if I was, I didn't want that success. I didn't want that life anymore."

"So you go and live on the streets? Put your *life* in danger? I just don't get it."

He sat a moment and stirred his soggy cereal. His mother continued to wait for an answer.

"Life had given me this situation. Once I realized it, my answer was 'No.' I wanted to rebel against life itself. I wanted to punish myself for all of my regret and stand against where life was headed. Stand against the world."

She looked at him from the other end of the table.

"The world goes on without you," she said.

"I know."

She got up and rinsed out her cup in the sink. He wanted to tell her about all of the good times he had had out on the streets, the moments of bliss he'd experienced when he'd let everything go and wasn't worried anymore. He wanted to explain to her the pain-killing release of believing in nothing. But he couldn't find the words. As he sat there and thought, he realized that all the good times and moments of peace, as well as the hellish dangers of the outside world, were completely out of his control. Standing against the ultrawave of time was hopeless. The world goes on without you.

She came from behind him and put a hand lightly on his shoulder.

"By the way, hon, we're showing the house today. The realtor is going to bring some people by later this afternoon. I need you to clean your room if you're feeling up to it."

After all the theoretical talking, the sinking feeling of reality was like a punch in the gut.

"I was gunna ask you about that. So the house is for sale?"

"It's been on the market a few weeks now."

"You know the market is at a low right now. Is it the best time to sell?"

She gave him a look of such vitriol that he dropped that line of questioning.

"I need to be in Arizona full time now. John and I are getting married."

"Yeah. I got the message."

"We never got a chance to talk about it. I'm here if you have any questions."

"It's all pretty straight forward. You can do whatever you want, mom."

"But I want to talk about it. I want you to be happy for me."

"I'm happy if you're happy."

"You'll have to come visit us. It's really nice in the spring, before it gets too hot."

He shrugged.

"The wedding is going to be…"

She trailed off into a lengthy description of the wedding and the procedures for selling the house and the plans for the future but he didn't hear any of it. He wouldn't be attending the wedding. He would never visit. While she listed her plans he sighed on the inside. The reconciliation that had occurred when he first arrived began to dissipate. She had been there for him when he needed her most. Now she was leaving.

His thoughts went back to the streets. Past the huge park outside their complex, the one that had been gutted of its green fields and now stood like a gravel plant or bulldozed mountain, past Verdant Hills and

Southern Highlands, he drifted over the folds of alien mountains, across the endless terrain of blank desert and the fields of sagebrush kissed by summer storms. He floated further and further until he was gone.

She left for Arizona a few days later. He promised to stay in touch with the real estate agent so she could show the house. When his mother pulled out of the driveway and turned the corner, he went upstairs and got ready. He took a long, hot shower, with less pain this time, then changed into his best clothes: A crisp new pair of boxer briefs and sturdy jeans, a T-shirt, a hoody, and a windbreaker to put over it. Most importantly he got his best tennis shoes and the most padded socks he could find. When he was dressed he came back out the front door.

The comfortable home life flashed before him one last time but the sign in the lawn and the empty garage was more than enough to vanquish any last desire he had for the old house.

THIRTY-FOUR

On the forgotten street of Patrick the path was only a dusty two-lane road. He walked along the gravel shoulder amongst the barren fields of front yards. Del La Sol High School loomed above the rooftops, the same architectural design as all the other schools of its era, of which there were many. When the new school was built it took the last of the upper-middle class kids from where Cameron had gone, Charnell High. His alma mater was only a few miles away, but now had the dubious distinction of being an "inner-city" school. When he'd attended classes there it was a modest, good school. Now there were rumors of race riots. He'd heard that Principal Morgan had been thrown down the stairs, but he didn't know if it was true.

The small strip of road used to be a short-cut linking László's house to the parties in Verdant Hills.

He wasn't thinking about those days now, though. It was only when he stopped at the light that the memories started flooding back. No cars were on the road but he waited for the walk sign, anyway. From where he stood he could see the nursing home.

"Chillpointe 1" was what they used to call it, the nursing home parking lot with the gazebo in the corner. They used to sit under the gazebo's metal roof and smoke pot after school. It was also where Cameron had found his best friend, Nick Niño, brutally murdered. The night he'd done so much to forget, leaving the party at Rik's house after Antonio and Justin had cut him out of their circle, after Kate had completely ignored him, when he had experienced humanity at its most horrendous. A high school party with disastrous consequences.

The gazebo was gone now. He wondered if it was because of the murder or because of budget cuts. After Nick's death, a vigil had been placed on the picnic table, a giant yearbook photo of Nick surrounded by flowers and candles. He'd gone to the gazebo the whole summer after junior year to sit in front of the picture and tell Nick he was sorry. To come across such a venerable site now, and find the whole tributary apparatus missing, made him feel disheartened.

He crossed the street and walked to the corner where the gazebo used to be. He closed his eyes and

began to pray silently for Nick's soul, hoping it was in peace and at rest.

Then he heard a sound. A distant calling blew into his ears.

"Hoody Hooooooo….."

He looked all around to see where the sound was coming from. He got on his tip-toes and tried to look into the backyards behind the parking lot. Maybe it was a kid messing with him, or one of the angry neighbors that used to threaten to call the cops.

Again he heard the sound.

"Hoo-dee-HoooOooOoo…."

It sounded as if it was coming from right behind him no matter what direction he turned. He spun frantically until, right in front of him, sitting atop the wall that many a blunt roach had been tossed over, was Nick, sitting nonchalantly, like he'd been there the whole time.

A pounding in Cameron's heart made every one

of his veins sizzle.

"Are you a ghost," he whispered, blinking slowly many times to make sure he wasn't hallucinating.

Nick didn't say anything, only motioned him closer. He waved a mirage of a hand, ushering Cameron forward.

Cameron stepped to the wall slowly. Nick gave him a wry smirk, the same half smile he gave all of Cameron's sarcastic comments back in high school.

"Come here, man. Come closer," Nick said.

Cameron walked right up to the wall. Nick's transparent legs swung by his face. When Nick looked down at him his face was silhouetted in pure sunlight.

"You hear that?" Nick asked.

"What? Hear what?" Tears fell from Cameron's eyes beside themselves. He pinched his eyes closed and strained his ears to hear. He strained so hard he thought the buzzing of the ohm would make his head explode.

"Listen now," Nick said. "Listen close."

Cameron strained even harder.

Pppppfffffbblllllbbpppffffffffff.

The fart lasted as long as air could travel

through Nick's mile-long ghost guts.

"Oh you gotta be kidding me!" Cameron yelled in a high-pitched squeal. The last tears rolled down his face pinched off at the ducts. Nick was laughing so hard it was impossible that he managed to stay perched on the wall.

"It stinks!" Nick cheered. His voice cracked with excitement. "I can't believe it! It still stinks! It smells like shit!"

Cameron shook his head and covered his nose and mouth with his shirt.

"Oh, man… I can't believe you fell for that one," Nick said, doubled up in laughter.

"You sonofabitch," Cameron replied. His head felt dizzy with adrenaline. He swatted at Nick's legs but in death Nick was an expert dodger.

"I tell ya, man. It never gets old," Nick said with a sigh.

Cameron wagged a finger at him. "You… why you old…"

They laughed at this for a moment longer.

"What gives, man, seriously," Cameron said next. "Where have you been?"

Nick raised his eyebrows and smiled his

trademark laidback smile. "Dog, you don't even know." He shaded his eyes with his hand. "Shit is too real."

"Man, I bet," Cameron responded. "Is it sick? Is it as dope as we always talked about?"

The sun filtered the picture of Nick in beautifully soft sky blue tones. His striped shirt and bluejeans fit perfectly against the stone wall and the shiny leather of his PS Flyers. He nodded at Cameron and blinked.

"I've missed you, man," Cameron said. "I mean, I've been walking all over this place, you wouldn't believe the changes."

"Yeah, I guess I never would have expected things to turn out like this," Nick replied. "But then again I can't say I'm surprised, either. To me, man, everything is that junior year of high school. No matter what changes, the feelings are the same. And the memories that inspire those feelings..." He looked off into the sunny horizon where everything was blotted out in egg-yolk resplendence. "I see those memories so vividly that it's like I'm always living them."

When he finished he looked at Cameron with a smile that was pure light.

Cameron was filled with the climactic ecstasy of an epiphany. He smiled too and felt perfectly calm. All the memories of times he'd shared with Nick went off in his mind like fireworks. He remembered how in fifth grade they were obsessed with Star Wars and video games, and used to draw their own comics at lunchtime. Nick had created a character called Ghostfriend, a spirit of smoke that brought good luck to worthy friends. As they got older and became more concerned with girls and parties, they still talked about Ghostfriend and joked about what would happen if they summoned him. The joke usually involved Ghostfriend smoking them out with endless amounts of futuristic weed. He thought he'd test Nick one last time to see if he still remembered.

"So, man, I don't suppose you'd like to blaze one real quick…"

"Oh come now, playboy, you know I'm always down."

"What was that weed the homie Ghostfriend used to slang back in the dizzy?   Aexon-119 or something…"

"Aexon-190."

"Yeah!   Aexon-190. You wouldn't happen to

have some of that turbo, would you?"

Nick gave him a cheeky sidelong glance. "A'ight, dawgy, I gotchoo."

Nick reached into his pocket and pulled out a giant joint, already lit. The cherried tip blew in Cameron's face an abundant cloud that smelled like Texas mountain laurel.

"Whoo, playboy! It smells so sweet!"

"Just like the purple drank, whoadey. Rip this one time." He held the other end of the joint out for Cameron to inhale. As Cameron took a long toke, the smoke pooled from about the joint, but also the hand, and Nick's entity himself.

"This is that fire for sure for sure, my damie," Cameron said choking and laughing and choking some more. The headchange was instantaneous.

Nick bobbed his head, smiling. "Por supuesto, mija."

Cameron was high, high like the very first time. "This is amazing," he said. The greens of every leaf shined like there was silver in the trees. All around him the flora bobbed and weaved and waved their leaves at him ghostly high fives. A feeling of peace washed over him, submerging him completely. He felt free of every need.

"Too-da-LoOoOOoo…."

The goodbye sounded at first just as close as the greeting but dipped and disappeared into the sky before Cameron could even turn his head to watch it go. The only semblance left of Nick was the voice echoing behind the clouds.

He watched Nick's spirit gleam off every rolling pillar of cumulous, the clouds all blending into one another like colliding mountains until the sky was a solid greyish sheet all comingled and indistinguishable. He stood in the center of the parking lot looking up at the sky, surrounded by the blissful pain of nostalgia, the true knowledge of what once was never again to be. And in his heart he knew that Nick would always be with him. The feeling he felt now, of true happiness, of utter acceptance, of bliss, of loneliness and loss, would never be gone completely. It was the same feeling that made him go on this journey and it was the same feeling that ultimately confirmed all of his blessings and all that was cursed.

THIRTY-FIVE

Down the hill on Flamingo with the stormclouds chasing him, Cameron slowed his steps under a freeway overpass. Someone was laying in the crux where the concrete slope met the underside of the bridge. He'd thought he saw the figure from a block or so away. Now that he was close he could see it was a young boy, lying with arms folded over his chest pretending to be asleep.

"Oi," he called out to the boy.

The boy peeled open an eyelid and looked at Cameron with caution. "What is it?" he asked. The voice tried to sound stern but it was too high-pitched to intimidate.

"I'm just passin' through," Cameron called back. "I saw you layin' there from back that-aways. Just checkin' to see you're okay."

"I'm alright," the boy answered curtly. "I'm

fine." He forced his eyes shut and went back to pretending he was asleep.

"Glad to hear it. I'm heading east for the moment. Probably gunna stay on Flamingo until it ends. So if you need company, I'll be on the road."

The boy nodded, forgetting he was supposed to be asleep, and hugged himself tighter.

The storm was still hundreds of miles to the west but coming fast. Under the bridge a warm breeze swooshed now and again as if a fan in the sky was rotating past them in a semi-circle. The air smelt like rain. Outside the shadow of the bridge the grey sky gave everything a dull shine. Cameron smiled out of the corner of his mouth and kept walking.

He passed streets with familiar names. Seville and Grace. Down the street he could see where the roads used to lead to friends' houses. There was a dilapidation to the houses that wasn't there back when he was a kid, when this was a fancy neighborhood. The faded paint and chipped siding didn't look out of place in the dirty midday overcast.

A couple of blocks later and he was next to his old elementary school. He stood looking through the fence at where his fifth grade class had been. Through the black tinted windows he could see his friends and himself goofing off and stealing candy when the teacher wasn't looking. Outside the outfield and blacktop were empty. A tetherball lolled in the wind, circling the pole. A phantom hay wagon plowed the grass field, the same one that took kids on rides for five cents during the annual carnival. Across the street, where parents used to wait for their kids, only empty-looking houses sat with their screen doors hissing open and shut again.

Further east he came upon an old Mexican leaning against the brick wall on the corner of the road. Boxes of oranges were at his feet. His face was shaded by a frayed baseball cap.

"Chau, compa," Cameron said as he walked by.

"Tardes," replied the man. "Com' esta?"

"Bien, gracias." He reached into his pocket for a crumpled one dollar bill. "Tengo solamente un dollar, par las naranjas." He pointed at the box by the man's feet.

"Si, si," said the man, pushing himself off the wall. He leaned over and grabbed a bag of oranges by the orange netting. "Tome estós." He held the bag out to Cameron.

"No, no, no necesito—" Cameron said, trying to defer but not able to translate his thoughts quick enough.

"Take it. Es for you," said the man. He nodded and smiled.

Cameron took the bag of oranges from the man. He held out the dollar in return but the man refused. He gave Cameron a paternal look and patted him on the shoulder. "Es okay," he said.

"Muchas gracias," Cameron said. "Muchisimas gracias." He nodded vigorously, almost reaching out to shake the man's hand.

The man ushered him onward with a smile. "De nada."

A block away he stopped outside an abandoned Pizza Hut and began to peel an orange. He could see the man from where he sat. A Suburban had stopped and looked to be buying the whole supply of oranges.

"He's on the karma payment plan."

Sitting in front of the decrepit pizza parlor, in a mostly vacant shopping center that had become a naked canvass for ceaseless tagging, he sat and watched the cars and people that passed by. Windows were rolled down and he caught the frayed radio signals from inside. He bit into the flesh of the orange and chewed slowly, savoring the moment.

The boy's voice sounded at first like just another rogue transmission.

"Hey."

Cameron turned to see the kid from the underpass standing in front of him.

"Well, hey. You made it."

The kid scuffed his feet on the pavement.

Cameron extended the bag of oranges toward him. "Want an orange?"

The kid was bashful but eventually took a seat next to Cameron and fished an orange out of the bag. He had curly ginger hair and pale skin. A brown spotting of freckles shone through the light down on his forearms. He looked at Cameron with reptilian eyes that never seemed to fully open, giving his face an incredulous disposition. The baggy T-shirt and cargo pants he wore made him seem smaller than he really was. He was silent as he peeled the orange.

"Eat up, brother. I got plenty."

The kid looked at Cameron, smiling behind his ears. "Thanks."

"I got 'em from the Mexican on the corner over

there. He gave them to me for free. Nice dude."

"Yeah, he's cool," said the kid. "He gives me oranges too sometimes."

"You stay around here?"

"Yeah, mostly."

"Is it safe? I used to go to school around here when I was a kid. Even then it wasn't the best of neighborhoods."

The boy shrugged, somnambulant. "I guess so."

They sat awhile enjoying their oranges and the calm afternoon.

"Well, amigo," Cameron said finally. "Like I said, I'm just passin' through. Just passing through this city in general I suppose…"

The boy cut him off before his address turned into a soliloquy.

"Wanna go for a walk?"

Cameron looked at him and smiled. "Yeah. Let's do it."

"I just need to make a quick stop up the road if that's cool, then we can head out."

"Okay."

"It will only be a second."

"No problem, mate."

They went south on Boulder Highway, a street that demarcated its own distinct sub-city between regular Las Vegas and the mountains of Valhalla. The buildings for glass repair shops, RV parks and boat wholesalers were mostly run down. They serviced a demographic that was autonomous from the average Las Vegan: people who'd moved to Nevada to escape the federal government, second-rate poker scammers with criminal records, and pensioners with penchants for cheap booze and ninety-nine cent breakfasts.

When they came to a barracks of projects the kid asked Cameron to wait by the road. He disappeared inside the concrete puebla and came back a few minutes later. He didn't explain and they kept walking. Past mobile home complexes and dive bars, a place that was actually called The Roadhouse where motorcycles were lined up in front of the entrance menacingly, the old skating rink that used to host parties for the nearby schools.

Cameron kept to the sidewalk while the kid bounced from the parking lots of the vendors to the oversized median out in the street. He asked fellow pedestrians for money or sprinted toward a gleaming object on the ground that could be a coin. Cameron kept pace, watching the clouds as they came in, "I Came as a Rat" and "Dramamine" playing inside his head.

When they'd got as far as the eastern fringe of Verdant Hills they came upon a man sitting outside a gated condo community in a motorized wheelchair. He looked like he was waiting for someone to pick him up. The kid was off investigating something in the bushes and while Cameron waited for him to catch up it was only he and the man. Sitting all by himself outside of the gated community, the gate itself twisted and gnarled from someone trying to break in, one door hanging loosely ajar, the man waited for someone who was not coming. He wore a T-shirt that was too tight for his pudgy body and similarly fitting khaki shorts; he had bloated calves and his arms and face were covered almost completely with a mismatching shade of pink skin from what looked like chemical burns. His nose had been burnt into a stub and looked like a snout, his eyelids were mostly gone too; his eyes shifted uncomfortably from within the melted mask of his face.

Cameron didn't want to appear like he was staring, but while he waited for the kid it was uncomfortable to stand there without saying anything.

"Howdy," he said, lifting his hand in a hesitant wave.

The blue eyes began to move quicker and the man squirmed in his seat.

"Beautiful day, huh? I love it just before the rain comes."

The man's breath, which had risen to a pant, slowed down and he nodded his head, just barely.

Cameron lifted the bag of oranges. "Want one? They're pretty good. Nice and ripe."

The worried aura took the man again. He was unsure, afraid of a trap. People driving down Boulder Highway had thrown oranges and apples at him from their speeding cars; they'd screamed "Pig Face!" at him and pelted him with Big Gulps.

The boy returned and stood by Cameron's side. He saw the man and hesitated, not knowing what to do.

Cameron took an orange and handed the bag to the boy. He walked calmly over the man and began to dig into the peel with the long nail of his thumb.

"Really, these are good. They come from a reputable source." He wiggled his thumbnail around until the peel came off in a single husk. "All in one peel. I still got it." He then split the orange in half and handed one side toward the man.

They looked at each other. In the eyes, not the face. Cameron smiled. The man held out his hand and took the orange halve, then nodded slightly in a gesture of thanks.

"Well, amigo," Cameron said. "We gotta get going. Take it easy!"

The man watched as the duo walked down the road. His blue eyes which reflected the stormclouds and the icy blue sky, smiled too.

*   *   *

At a gas station just outside the soccer complex they sat on the curb and took a break. The kid ran in and out, handing Cameron a tallboy before sitting back down.

"How in the hell did you get this?" Cameron asked.

The boy looked at him with his alligator eyes and said nothing.

"Ah hell," Cameron said. They cracked open the

tallboy and sat drinking. "I figure we'll head over to the gypsum plant and check that out, then head over to a golf course I know of and hide out if it rains. Hopefully there's lightning, it's a great view from the course."

The boy didn't answer but Cameron could sense something was up.

"What is it?" he asked.

"I'm already too far away," he said. "I need to be getting back."

Cameron drooped a little. He had forgotten the boy was just a kid; he might have parents that were worried about him.

"Alright then," Cameron said.

"It was a good afternoon," the boy said.

"Yeah, it was, wasn't it."

The kid took a chug from his beer and stood up. "Well, take it easy."

"You too," Cameron replied. Then, when the boy had turned to go he called after him. "Hey, wait."

"Huh?"

"What's your name?"

"Tamás." He pronounced it Ta-Mash.

Cameron frowned. "What is that, Hungarian?"

"Yeah, it is. How did you know?"

Cameron shook his head. "Lucky guess."

The boy smiled his first full smile of the day. Then he turned and walked off and Cameron never saw him again.

By the time he reached the gypsum plant the sky was a glowing blue. Thunder boomed under a sheet of cloud in the distance, the breeze whirled debris in a mini-cyclone in the desert. Tall hills of black and white rock sat piled next to minarets of stained metal while arcane silos churned steam into the evening. Between the bars of the plant the casinos of the strip looked like miniature toys. Cameron tossed the empty beercan into the anonymous gravel. The boy had gone and he was left alone to keep company with the people of the world who shared it with him and all of the memories held in his heart that still existed.

THIRTY-SIX

It was early November and he was back at Sunset Park, sitting at the same bench by the lake where weeks prior he'd questioned his Shadow Self. He was now one of those bums he'd seen since childhood lounging in the grass or sleeping in the shade. The park had become a special place for him, a place where he could sit under a tree and relax, where he needn't worry about walking or finding a destination. The people he saw were just characters in the movie of his mind. If they intrigued him in any way he would ascribe them names and histories. Then they would disappear before he could ever be proven false.

He poured out some stolen sunflower kernels into his hand, the skin of which was now almost black from a lack of washing. His nails still hadn't grown into claws like the Black Lion's, but he'd grown accustomed to the squalor. Shitting in the wild and sleeping in the desert when he couldn't find a decent place to squat had become part of his life that he

accepted to the detriment of personal hygiene. Mostly though, he spent his time dreaming.

While he sat chewing the kernels, he watched disdainfully as from out of the blinding sunlight someone was approaching through the fields of grass. It was a boy about his age. He was definitely no fellow bum and he wasn't a Frisbee golfer or tennis player, either. He walked with the obvious gait of a salesman, clipboard tucked safely underneath an arm. From a hundred yards away Cameron knew the solicitor had him in his sights.

The boy raised a hand in salutation when he was ten feet away. He walked up to Cameron and greeted him with a smile. "Excuse me, sir, can I have a moment of your time?"

Cameron looked behind him, then side to side. "Oh, are you talking to me?" It was only the two of them within eye sight.

The boy chuckled a little unsurely and continued his script. "Sorry to bother you. My name's Dave. I'm with the Presidential Campaign." He held out his hand but truncated the shake when he felt the grime on Cameron's palm.

Cameron smiled a big, plastic smile. "Are you now? Are you really sorry? Cuz to me, if you were really sorry, you probably would have realized it somewhere in that field a couple of hundred yards away and you would have gone and pissed off somewhere else." He ended by chuckling himself and Dave responded with chuckling and they sat there nervously chuckling for a few more seconds.

"I don't mean to impose, mister," Dave continued, in a tone that made light of what Cameron had said and continued on. "I just wanna chat with you about the important presidential election coming up. I'm getting out the vote. Are you registered?"

Cameron sat a moment eyeing Dave. The kernels were gone and he was just grinding his teeth. "Well, since you ask, no, in fact I'm not registered to vote."

Dave's face exploded into a smile as Cameron's answer induced a Pavlovian response.

"Okay! Well I have plenty of forms here, if you can just fill one out we'll be on our way!" He fumbled in his pocket for a pen while juggling the clipboard.

"You know we don't have much time but I'll enter your info into the computer back at HQ. Mind holdin' onto this for a sec?" He held out the stack of forms. Cameron said he did mind so Dave set the forms on the picnic table. He finally wrested the pen from his shorts and held it out to Cameron.

"Okay, do you have any questions? Do you have an idea of who you're lookin' to vote for?"

Cameron didn't take the pen. "Yeah, I know exactly who I am voting for."

"Wonderful. Do you mind telling me?"

"No, I don't mind."

"Okay, then. Who?"

"Nobody."

Dave chuckled again. Cameron sat looking at him.

"Huh?" Dave said.

"I said nobody."

"Nobody?"

"I am voting for: No. Body."

Dave sighed in ebullient frustration. "You aren't voting for… *anyone*?"

"Bingo!"

"Well, why the heck not?" His demeanor changed from cheerful to slightly indignant.

"I'm exercising my rights as a citizen of this great country," Cameron said.

Dave blinked and regained his composure. He'd dealt with this type before. The ol' Wild West state's rights and no government honkeys. They were all over Nevada. Dave was from Minnesota, he had come to Vegas during the presidential primaries and stayed on for the general election. He was currently the number two ranked Field Organizer in Southern Nevada, averaging thirty-six new registered voters and twelve-hundred calls (three-hundred and ten contacts) each day. His canvassing had produced eighteen new volunteer shifts recruited daily for the past month. He looked at Cameron, studying him: he didn't fit the normal template of right-wing independent, but one never knew, there was a whole new generation of wonky libertarians and anti-government conspiracy theorists around these days.

"You know," Dave said, getting into his groove. "You aren't utilizing your rights to the full extent if you don't vote. If you don't vote you're letting others decide for you."

"That is one-hundred percent wrong," Cameron replied.

"How so?" The indignation was a bit stronger now.

"I just told you my opinion, which frankly is none of your business to begin with, and you're already trying to change it. If I gave in, and did what you want, I'd be letting *you* decide for me, wouldn't I?"

"What I'm saying is, if you don't vote you're not making a choice."

"No, you're wrong again. Not voting *is* my choice."

"That doesn't address my point, though. The democratic process isn't going to stop just because you don't vote. There will still be an election and whoever becomes President is going to have control over a lot of things that affect your life."

Cameron smirked. "Like what?"

"Well, you're in a park right now, aren't you? This is a public park. That means it is run by the government. And what about your job, are you employed?"

"Does it look like I'm employed?"

"Okay, well even better. Benefits for the unemployed. Social Services for the poor. You probably rely on those. Those issues are *majorly* affected by who is elected!"

"I don't rely on any programs," Cameron sneered. "I don't take welfare."

"How do you eat?"

"I steal."

Dave gulped. "You steal?"

"That's right. Mainly almonds or sunflower seeds from the grocery store, water, the like. Whatever I need to stay alive. It's better than panhandling, let me tell ya. That shit can be dangerous."

Dave chuckled his nervous chuckle. He thought Cameron was joking again.

"Well, if not you, what about everyone else?"

"What about them? That is their business. Unlike you, I believe people should decide for *themselves.*"

"Hey, now. My job is to educate people. There is nothing more important than an educated electorate."

"As long as it is you that decides what is correct and what will help them, right? Or not you, rather, but the Campaign. Unless, it's you that makes policy for the Campaign?"

"It's not me personally, but I believe in what the Campaign stands for. I'm fighting for the right side. I know that."

"And thus you know what is right for the people of the country. People like me."

Dave huffed in exasperation. "I don't think you understand me. We're trying to do what is right for the American People. Do you want things to continue going the way they have been? Can we afford another four years of a harmful administration?"

"No, I understand you completely. You want me to follow you because you stand for truth, justice and liberty. Therefore, if I follow you, I am following those ideals. Right?"

"Essentially, yes."

"You wouldn't be lying to me, would you?"

"Of course not," Dave moaned.

"Well in that case, where do I sign?"

"Really?!"

"Fuck no."

Dave dropped his shoulders and all the wind went out of him. "You're just trying to negate everything I say. You're not arguing the issues, you're just being sour."

"The issues have been prescribed to me, by you and your competitors. But you can't tell me what the issues are in my life. Only I can. I'm not going to choose something I don't believe in, I'm not going to take the lesser of two evils and I am not giving up the only freedom I have, which is the freedom to think the way I want."

"You think having no government would bring about a utopia? You wanna see what happens when order breaks down?"

"Down to the state of nature?"

"Exactly."

"You think your team can change the state of nature? It's your team and their team that holds that over our heads and forces us to choose. I won't sign any illegitimate social contract."

Dave stood shaking his head. "I guess that works for someone who steals for a living. No offence."

"I know the risk involved."

"Well I know what my gut tells me, and it tells me not to sit on the sidelines."

"I'm right in the thick of it, buddy. At least in my opinion. But what good is an opinion?"

"An opinion is a vote. An action."

"Opinions are meaningless."

"Our opinions are going to change the world."

"We'll see. They'll change the state of nature? That would be something, wouldn't it?"

Dave continued to shake his head. He felt sorry for Cameron, who was surely a lost cause, probably mentally ill like most homeless people. He thanked him for his time, even shook his hand again, and scurried off through the green and yellow grass that waved in the wind, over to another bum who sat with his chin on his chest and a trucker hat pulled over his face sleeping against a tree. Cameron watched as Dave shook the man awake with a nudge of the clipboard. Then he laughed, got up, and left himself.

THIRTY-SEVEN

On his way to his father's house he went through neighborhoods he'd never seen before. On bridges that arced over glistening water he stopped and looked around; if he had a camera to take a snapshot of the surroundings, he doubted anyone would ever guess it was Las Vegas. Europe, maybe. Greece. He walked down wide streets canopied by terebinths, spotted secret tennis courts that seemed to have been added to community masterplans at random. Their nets hung forlorn and limp in the middle, the frayed green tarmac flapped in the wind. Tall fences that stayed locked kept no one out but no one tried to break in.

Around a stretch of street that sent him walking a direction he didn't know any longer, another elementary school appeared amongst the houses. Just like his old one, or the one on Silver Springs. The playground and parking lot were empty, so was the enormous grass field, and for some reason that surprised him. It was getting on in the day and it could have been a weekend, but ever since he turned the corner he figured something was going on there. A festival or play like the one held by the Altar. When he reached the front office no one was there. The sound he'd heard that sounded like children laughing was only the wind wisping dead leaves across the pavement.

For a moment he stood still on the sidewalk, baffled. Something had to be going on, he was sure of it. It could be anything, the possibilities were endless. For all the expectation he'd felt, to ultimately find nothing made him feel sad. Like he had missed out on something.

He went through the gate and strolled through the grass field, then the playground and blacktop. The wake of something meaningful still hung in the air invisible but potent. Weaving between the pine trees that lined the fence he noticed thin black cables were tangled in the branches. It was bistro lighting. Where they dangled from tree to tree they looked like black spider webs, the empty bulbs poking out like transparent synthetic pine needles.

So something must have just happened, or be about to start.

He went over to a portable and sat on the metal stairs, facing the fence and the street. Paper dolls of shining green and reflective fuchsia were hung up on the portable doors. Similar non-specific decorations were draped outside of the classrooms of the main building. A party or something. Some kind of special day. He looked all around to make sure he was alone. Indeed it was just he and the breeze.

As he sat with his chin in his hands he caught something out of the corner of his eye. A tiny speck had turned the corner at the end of the street and was moving toward him. He walked to the fence and peered through the links. The car was large and boxy and it moved slowly, down the middle of the street, uncaring of streetsigns or lainpaint. As the big bodied sedan drew closer Cameron began to feel nervous.

"Who's rolling up on me like that?" he whispered to himself.

Moments later the giant boat of a Cadillac slid directly into his field of vision, still straddling the center of the two lane street. Cameron turned and began to walk back toward the portable when he heard the thunk and buzz of the passenger window roll down, letting lush tones of synthesizer flutter out into the air.

Cameron turned back around, slowly.

The driver had his head turned toward him, chin angled down. He wore a 4X sized hoodie backwards so that the hood was covering his face like a ski mask. The material of the hoodie was black, shimmered with a subtle all-over print that reflected stray bits of light in the folds. Over the face of the ghetto cloak, oversized square-rimmed black sunglasses. Cameron's appalled figure stood doubled in their lenses. He watched stunned as the driver calmly removed the sunglasses and pulled the hood down from his face. A digital gleam bounced from the gold Rolex he was wearing off the woodgrain steering wheel. The stereo system bumped the smooth beats of "Pissed Up in SE1."

Who else could it be but Rik Pollen.

The corners of his mouth turned into sharp angles. The pale bronze face smiled at Cameron, eyes covered by an identical pair of sunglasses, only these with rose-hued lenses. His hair was slicked back, immaculate, unruffled by the hood which folded neatly onto his breastbone. Rik Pollen. The high school demon lord. Unhuman twice-blessed Abraxas shadow god. He never looked out of place.

Cameron balked.

"Naahhhhhhh…."

"Čau, tyvole."

Cameron again went to the fence, put his fingers through the hexagonal wiring.

"Rik? Eres tu? En serrrrrio, güey?"

"Oui. C'est moi."   Rik replied with a slight shrug, dainty and sarcastic.

Cameron looked down the street both ways; he thought he was being pranked. No one else was around. The streets were as quiet as they were before.

"Well," he said. "What the hell?"

"You're a tough person to track down," Rik said.

"You've been looking for me?"

Rik adjusted himself in the supple oatmeal interior to face Cameron better.

"Well I heard about you. The people are going wild with rumors about you."   Rik's eyes sparkled from under the crimson mirror of the lenses.

Rumors. What rumors.

"All good things I hope," Cameron said. His nervousness was intensifying.

"Depends," Rik responded.

"Undergarments?"

Rik's smile lowered a millimeter. Cameron wriggled at the allusion. He thought he'd pulled a fast-one on the great Rik Pollen. His insides twittered with nervous glee. Rik turned his head again, like a robot moving into the pose of contemplation and said, "Oh, I get it."

"I thought you moved away," Cameron said, changing the subject. "I thought you lived in France or something."

"Hah, France. Yes. Metz, in fact. Then Lisboa, Praha." He left the sentence hanging in the air. "Here."

"Yeah, here. Here of all places. How did you find me, anyway? *I* don't even know where I am." The question bothered him. In their brief socializing during high school Cameron felt sometimes that Rik was god-gaming him, that he was somehow able to follow his every move, privy to everything he did.

"I could feel you," Rik answered. "I heard you calling."

Cameron thought back to the Altar. The

swarming clouds, the sky raging like the gods themselves were at war, and the beam of energy that shot through his body like a secret spine, sending him into blissful oblivion. Had Rik sensed that?

"We're connected you know," Rik continued.

Cameron frowned, uncomfortable. "In what way?"

"We are bound by this city."

That was Rik, always speaking in riddles. Cameron felt like he was listening to a secret and wanted to understand completely.

"But you don't live here. You're off in Prague or wherever."

"Prague, Kingston, Marseilles… just another city."

"What's that got to do with you and me?"

"We know that this city, with the mountains that bind us in, the abyss beyond, the long expanses of nothingness that pock-mark the streets, we know this city is really a macrocosm for ourselves."

Cameron stood looking at the character in the Cadillac, his forehead pressed to the fence. Rik went on:

"You ever feel like the whole city has been

emptied, that you're all alone and it is only with ghosts that you're left to interact with?"

Cameron's eyes went wide, his face a mask of horror drawn on by the dusk's shadows.

"I feel like that all the time."

"We've taken the inward path," Rik said. "How could it be that we are not alone?"

Cameron dug the toe of his shoe into the blacktop, looked down the road at nothing. What Rik was saying, the extraordinariness of their meeting, it felt supernatural and yet he believed him. Although there was blissfulness in accepting some larger force at work, the revelation left him feeling a sadness that seemed neverending.

"Cheer up, kamo," Rik answered instead. "The world is a reflection of our selves but there is an outside world. There are others like you out there, stumbling alone in the dark."

Cameron looked down at his shoe, then back at Rik. "I have been very lonesome."

Rik smiled. The evening was the purple melancholy of his smile.

"Our experiences are significant. They're like hieroglyphics on our soul that read the feelings felt since the dawn of time. They are eternal. Once you realize eternity, you'll never be lonely."

Silence took over a while. Bats were spinning overhead and bouncing off the portables. Streetlights came on, dotting the neighborhood trees with balloons of light.

"I'll leave you to it for now," Rik said. "But I do have a proposition for you."

Cameron thought about the last proposition he'd received from Rik. The one from junior year of high school; the one that had inaugurated him, however briefly, into drug-dealing; the one that he still connected to Nick's death and the one which had caused so much summer discontent.

"What is it?"

"Come to the cemetery, the one by the Discovery Museum, three nights from now. I'll tell you then." His face had turned to stone, without a hint of sarcasm or irony. "And bring a bottle of rum."

Cameron took a step back from the fence. "Okay," he said hesitantly. "I should be able to manage that."

"Good. I look forward to seeing you."

Rik slid the hood back over his face and

replaced the auxiliary pair of sunglasses over the mask. The music disappeared; the passenger window buzzed up until Cameron could see himself in its reflection.

"Yeah, you too."

The Cadillac jerked into gear and once more began rolling up the middle of the street, turning the corner as if pulled by a string or pushed by the breeze, and disappeared.

*   *   *

The Jimmy was parked out front so Cameron knew he was home. At the door he looked through the stain glass windows and saw the afternoon light refracted onto the granite fireplace in the living room. Atop the mantle a mighty bear stood on its hind legs, frozen in the act of roaring. Cameron's heart galloped as he rang the doorbell and waited.

His dad appeared from the hallway soon after. When he saw Cameron the look of surprise was unmistakable, even through the wobbly glass. He waved like he always did before unlocking both sets of locks and opening the door.

"Ehhhh, Kamran Mirzah, what are you doing

here?"

"Hey, pops. I was in the neighborhood. Thought I'd come by and check on ya."

"Come in, come in."

"Thank ya."

Cameron stepped into the house and exchanged the ritual trois-bises that was used in the region of Iran where his dad was from. They walked into the modest living room and sat in the mismatched chairs opposite a glass coffee table, his dad in the lazyboy while Cameron took the red wingback. Asian Champions League played on the TV via satellite.

"So, Mirzah. How are you?"

Cameron slunk into the thin padding and answered without taking his gaze from the TV.

"Can't complain."

His dad didn't say anything.

"Who's playing?" Cameron asked.

"Taj and Pakhtakur. Taj is playing pretty well but can't score. As usual."

"Chshhh.. same old fuckin' story."

"You want some tea? Are you hungry? I can have polo ready in an hour or so."

"I'll have some tea if you're making it."

His dad popped off the seat and went into the kitchen to prepare the samovar. When he returned again they sat in silence.

"How is school?" his father asked finally, lifting his feet to rest on the office chair in front of him.

"I don't know."

"What?"

"I don't know. I haven't been going."

His father's tension was almost audible. His face immediately turned grave. "Why not?"

"I had been going all the time, I barely missed a single day since starting. Then one day I asked myself why. Couldn't think of a reason."

"Why what? What about your degree? What about law school?"

"I don't know about that anymore," Cameron mumbled to the red padding next to his face.

His dad exhaled through his nostrils stiffly. "What don't you know anymore?"

"I don't know if I want to go to law school in the first place."

"What are you going to do then?"

There was that question again. *What are you doing? What are you going to do with your life?* This time, however, it wasn't some cop-out small talk, it was coming from a place of genuine concern. It was a valid question.

"I don't know right now," Cameron said. The words came out in a strained whisper.

His father shifted in his seat and said, "Mm." The game was in first half stoppage time so he flipped channels. The middle-east satellite offered an array of low-fi channels, mostly Arab news outlets and soap operas from central Asia's more obscure nationalities. He stopped on a Sudanese station and they sat chuckling at the black man in a white turban and robes that was gesticulating into the camera very enthusiastically.

"Man, look at those funny-looking Janjaweed," Cameron said.

"This isn't a Janjaweed. He's a northern Sudanese. They think they're Arab."

"To think someone would *want* to be Arab…"

They laughed and his father continued to flip channels.

"What about the Lebanese news?" Cameron asked.

"It's gone. State Department blocked it."

Neither of them spoke Arabic but they used to watch the news stations from all over the world just to see what was shown. It wasn't necessary to know the language to understand pictures of US armored vehicles firing indiscriminately into apartment buildings. They liked watching different country's footage; his father said it gave them a more complete picture of one-sided bullshit.

The tea was ready and his father poured two mugs full, doctoring them with lemon juice and sugar. He set Cameron's mug down on the coffee table next to him and sat back down.

"You know, I am pretty hungry actually," Cameron said.

"Okay, I'll get started."

"Nah, I'll just make a sandwich." He went to the fridge and made himself a sandwich of hotdog slices, onions and tomato on lavash bread. He had taken only a single bite when his dad resumed the questioning.

"So. You don't think you'll finish school," he said.

"I probably will, sometime. I just don't know when. I mean it's not a matter of being able to. When spring semester starts, maybe I'll go back, then."

"I don't understand, Mirzah. What are you doing in the meantime?"

"I've been walking around the city mostly."

"Mm."

His father sat waiting for him to elaborate.

"It's amazing how this city has been decimated. There are so many vacant homes, so many businesses and shopping centers that sit empty. This town's really gone to shit."

"It really has," his father said, nodding. "When I came here in '89 the I-15 was a pissy two-lane road next to the Strip. The Strip itself was only a couple of small casinos. Way out here was just desert. Remember how long it used to take just to get to Red Rock?"

"I do. And then it blew up like some tumor on steroids. The shit hit the fan and now it's all fucked. How did it ever happen?"

"A lot of people got rich, then the bubble burst," his father said in an even, unemotional way. He said it like someone who had seen the cycle repeat itself since he was his son's age.

"But who is held accountable?"

"Oh, no one is ever held accountable. They catch

a few people and put them against the wall. Make them examples. But the real people involved are never held accountable. They're off onto their next venture, making more money."

"It's such bullshit."

"The only one you can ever demand accountability from is yourself."

Their eyes met for a second.

"You have to take care of yourself," his father continued. "That's all you can do. You let yourself go the way of cities, of countries, and you'll wind up with nothing."

Cameron didn't say anything. He sat there soaking it in.

"So, back to my original question. What are you going to do?"

Cameron sighed, but it was more like a gasp.

"I believe you. I believe what you say, that we can't put responsibility in other peoples' hands. The middlemen just get fucked between every bust and boom."

"Barikala," his father said, goading him further.

"I still don't know what to do, though. I feel like one of those middlemen when I'm at school. I feel like

I'm just following the system and I'm getting fucked. There's nothing there for me that I can believe in."

His dad was looking out the window at the rolling mountains that were now so close to the city. A few cars flickered between the trees lining the highway. Above the backyard a falcon sat perched on the telephone wire, staring toward the center of town with magnified eyes, breathing in the subtle currents of a nascent winter that had begun to circulate.

"That's what you told me before, Mirzah, when you said you wanted to quit soccer."

Cameron was doubly halted by his father's words. The active daydreaming came to his mind, all the things he imagined he would have done if he never quit, all the glory. He had turned his back on those dreams back then and now according to his father he was doing it again. The same past he regretted so much, the one he'd sought refuge from by changing key facts and disappearing into the city, the whole dark history was repeating itself.

"You get your degree. You go to law school and you pass the bar. You become a lawyer and get a good job with the State Department. You live a good life, with a jacuzzi and a Mercedes."

"Bullshit my way to the top," Cameron muttered.

"Barikala! You tell people what they want to hear and you'll go right up the ranks. For someone like you who is smart it is easy."

"As long as I don't believe in anything that I say."

"Remember what my sixth grade Geometry teacher used to say? He used to complain that he had to walk to work when there were so many donkeys around. Most people are donkeys, Mirzah. You gotta ride 'em. Ride 'em all the way to the top."

Cameron laughed. "I do remember that."

"If you don't, someone else will."

"There's got to be another way, though. What about believing in what you do? What if you didn't have to bullshit people all the time just to have a comfortable living? I want something real. It may sound naïve but all I want is some truth."

His father looked at him with eyes that had seen comfortable livings wiped out in an instant, seen hard times scraping by just to pay the bills, seen history unfold for himself and the world heralding all its lessons on what to value and the fleeting impermanence of anything beautiful.

He sat in his chair and looked again out the window toward the mountains of the west.

"Of all things in this crazy world, Mirzah, the truth is most elusive."

*   *   *

When he had finished his tea Cameron took a shower. He went into the bedroom, which was his when he stayed with his dad, and found some old clothes to replace the dirty ones from before. He took a black Adidas fleece jacket and a Bayern Munich presentation kit from his dad's closet which was full with an incomparable collection of warm-up suits.

While toweling off his hair, he saw the picture of his grandfather's face. The face in the black and white photo, framed in a square of gold, embossed with blue and red flowers arranged into tiny geometrical patterns. His grandfather with perfect posture, clad in his meticulously pressed military uniform. The grey eyes stared at him, their expression shifting subtly from lighthearted salutation to disappointed frown. Cameron bowed slightly to his grandpa, the one he had only spoken to a few times when he was too young to know anything. He wondered what his grandfather was like and if he would be proud or disgusted with the way he was living his life. The photo didn't answer. The tiniest curve accented the lower lip. A Mona Lisa smile.

When he had changed into the new kit he rummaged the closet for a pair of shoes. He took a pair of leather boots that had athletic soles which were very comfortable. Then he went into his dad's study and turned on the computer. A few clicks later he had accessed his online stock portfolio.

Growing up he had always paid attention to the market, mainly watching the Nightly Business Report with his dad, so when he graduated high school his dad gave him start-up money for a small account of his own. Not an ungodly sum but enough to learn on. As soon as the computer loaded he checked his account.

His last transaction had been the purchase of 3,000 shares of Bank of America (BAC) when it was at an all-time low after the banking collapse. BofA had bought Countrywide, a major purveyor of toxic assets – many of which were in Las Vegas – and suffered for it. Since then however, it had almost tripled. Reasons varied from TARP to change of management to return of consumer confidence. Cameron didn't care because his account had benefited greatly. It now sat at a total of $34,376. He was rich.

He went back into the living room grinning from ear to ear. His father had switched the TV to local news. The faces of Dex and Julio, faces he prayed he would never have to see again, were staring at him from squares on the screen. The caption below read:

TWO OF THE MYSTERIOUS FORECLOSURE FOUR

"Can we change it, dad?" he asked, forcibly having to keep himself from trembling. His father changed it to German Bundesliga. Werder Bremen had new away kits. Cameron sat down in a complete daze.

"Sure, go ahead and take my best things," his dad joked, looking at the new outfit.

"Oh, hah, I thought I'd borrow a few things."

"I'm kidding. Take 'em."

"Thanks, pops." He waited for his heart rate to slow down. After some more tea he said he had to get going. His dad didn't press him for details. He asked for some money until he could get to the bank the next day and his dad gave him a couple of twenties. They hugged and Cameron said he would come by soon.

Leaving the neighborhood he fingered the bills in his fleece pocket. It could last him weeks if need be. With the money in his trading account he could get an apartment like he'd been thinking of, a modern flat with sleek wooden bookcases and stainless steel appliances. An awesome electronics system could play all his favorite music and movies. Maybe he'd find the porcelain bust of some character from antiquity and display it next to an art deco lamp and his reading chair. A closet full of tweed laundry and a fridge full of gin and tonic while Kings of Convenience played on the gramophone. Where would he go for these items? What did he need to do first, where did he start? All the thinking made his head hurt. Now that the dreams were possible they disgusted him.

In a patch of desert beside the HSBC compound, campaign posters littered the gravel, many of them defaced. Foremost amongst the garbage a giant sandwich board portrayed the smiling effeminate face of incumbent Dick Zermin. Re-Elect Dicky Z for State Senator District 11!

Sermen gunna laaahk you.

Cameron's flesh crawled.

He spent the night in a model home on the edge of town. He sat at the fully-furnished dinner table eating a large philly cheesesteak from Capriotti's. Plates were set at the other seats, filled with rubber chickens and plastic peas. He finished a bite and toasted his phantom family with a raised energy drink. The house was all lit up. Cozy, warm and empty. Outside, unfinished houses and newly rented units winked in the blackness. He finished his meal then went upstairs to bed.

THIRTY-EIGHT

The sun rose and fell and rose again. A heatwave straight out of the oblivion summer fell upon the city like a fever, burning up the days until finally yielding to night's shivers. In the dark he no longer looked with curiosity at the other pedestrians he encountered on the streets. Instead only cunning; sizing each one up he deduced what would be needed to escape mortal harm. On the inside pocket of his warm-up jacket he carried a nail found in the ruins of the last neighborhood he took as abode and he was confident in his willingness to use it. By day he wandered in the semi-dream state of those who sleep with both eyes open.

The abandoned RV park was littered for miles with rubble. A brick restroom stood in a pile of boulders with only the door still erect. Broken pillars dotting the pale asphalt looked like they'd been hit by a bomb, their signs painted with single letters, former designations that now signified nowhere making lean-tos stuck in the ground. Overlooking this forgotten graveyard the casinos of the Strip arose like monuments. Towers built at the height of the boom, empty pylons against the yellow desert sky next to casinos that never weren't busy. The angle of town is a crossroads between the rural wastelands of Boulder Highway and the glitz and glamor of downtown and the neon opulence of the Strip. Nearby in the grass which grew in tall yellow shoots through the asphalt an adder hissed, or a cicada, he couldn't tell which. Something slithered unseen over the vacant expanse. In the distance dope boys circled on their bikes, their baggy shirts hanging off their skeletal frames as they stood on the pedals.

He walked through the car park with the feeling he was under surveillance. Any security camera not ripped from its perch out of use although long since defunct did nothing to help this preoccupation. In the gravel near a brick wall that outlined the encampment there were the makings of a camp. Gypsy detritus, trash and soiled plastic bags, some filled with contents, a single well-used boot, a ring of barbwire that looked to be forced into a lethal ouroboros. In a patch of wild rosemary and sagebrush is where he came upon the fetus. Its naked red skin gave it the appearance of a doll. The tiny hands opened and closed slowly, its clear eyes staring at a sky so whited out by the sun, in utter confusion like a being ripped unwillingly from an other realm.

When it was in his shadow he reached down and took hold of it, doing his best to cradle it with proper support. The head hung loosely over his arm until he lifted his bicep, arms acutely akimbo in an expression of cartoon unknowing. Its tongue was shriveled to non-existence, its throat too dry to make a sound. He was surprised by how tiny it was, lighter than a cat. He tucked it under the flap of his jacket to give it some relief from the sun.

The feeling of being watched was upon him with fervor. Surrounding the park were only hostel apartment complexes, flea-ridden motels and obscure vendors for services like boat cleaning and window replacement. The hyena laughs coming from the boys on the bikes crossed the asphalt from the distance in the blow-dryer breeze. The odd walker on the sidewalk no more able to help the baby than he was.

"I don't have time."

The baby closed its walled eyes and turned into the darkness of his armpit. Soon whoever had made camp here was going to come back. He couldn't imagine what use they had for the baby, what twisted concoction of circumstances had led them to bring it here.

In the alleyway between the RV park and another unused parking lot he made his way through a series of jagged brick walls to the sidewalk. He kept the jacket flap concealing the baby facing the street. In front of him for miles no walkers were visible. If he saw one he'd have ample time to divert his path before one drew too close.

For blocks he walked with calculated calmness. Past the sprawling box store for home improvement, through scraps of a neighborhood whose houses were foreboding relics from the nuclear testing age, anachronisms with twisted wire hanging in the backyards but no laundry, only rusted hubcaps and scrap metal in the sand of the dead yards. He tried rocking the baby slowly as he walked, a technique he must have picked up from television, and with each sway the baby moved as if to evade.

Eventually they came to an enclave of english country townhomes configured into a type of barracks. Trimmed hedges lined the cheap stucco, brown lawns mowed down to the quarter of an inch. The windows all shuttered with the same color blinds. A community for the elderly. No one of any age in the parking lot or on the concrete pathways.

Between two units he scurried between the bushes and found a bifurcated spigot where landscapers connected their hoses. Holding the baby with one arm and leaning awkwardly he turned the knob, sending water out in a Y-stream. When it had turned from hot to cool he cupped tiny handfuls and tried to pour them into the baby's mouth. It choked and gagged as it struggled to rid its mouth of the phlegm the water created. It wriggled from under his arm like a worm as he pinned it to his chest and when it had finally swallowed it began to wail.

It screamed ceaselessly and tried to wriggle out of his arms, its whole being a backlash against being placed in this world. While he fought to hold onto it, trying to get a few last drops in its mouth so sunburnt and dried out it was he didn't see that from the walking path he was being observed. An old woman and her boston terrier stood in frozen indignation, the woman's curdled lips slightly parted in an expression of disbelief. She hadn't seen the baby, only Cameron's back, but she heard the screaming and anyway, the vision of a weatherbeaten vagabond crouching in the bushes was enough to set off her internal alarms. When he faced her and she saw what he carried her already pale face turned white.

Realizing his absurdity but helpless to soothe her impatient inquisitions all he could do was regard her with a crazed look in his eye. What was meant to be urgency came off as psychopathic to the fearful old woman. With the adrenaline produced for survival wracking his body he made a few cautious steps toward her, causing her to jolt back in two successive fencer's retreats. Only an ingrained sense of duty to uphold community rules kept her from fleeing the scene completely.

"Can you help it?" he said. "Can you call an ambulance?"

"What is that you got there?"

Her dog sensed the tension and had begun yapping wildly, creating along with the baby's moans a polyrhythmic cacophony of screams. She stuck her chin out and looked at him as if from over an invisible wall while the dog tried with all its might to yank the leash from her hand. As she took her time determining the moral turpitude of the figure before her Cameron shouted at her with impatience.

"Lady! This is serious. This baby needs help. Do you have a phone?!"

"Don't you yell at me."

"I'm sorry, I didn't mean to yell. As you can see this baby needs urgent medical attention."

The woman raised a crooked hand to her mouth, aghast and growingly fearful of the situation.

"Get your phone. Please," he said with stern effort to sound composed.

"Ju-just a minute, there. Don't move." And with an attitude more concerned with holding up the appearance of authority she reached into her fanny pack and began to dig around for a cell phone.

"We really don't have much time," Cameron said, trying to sound reassuring, like a guilty child explaining to his teacher. "I don't know how long it has been out like this."

"One minute," she snapped. He watched as she unflipped her phone and pressed three digits. "Yes," she said after a painfully long intermission. "I need the police."

"You cunt," he hissed. Immediately he began to walk with pace from where he stood. The woman shouted into the phone, "He has a baby with him! He's broken into our neighborhood and he has a baby! Send someone quick!"

He didn't wait to hear her explain the rest of the strange case to the police. This avenue of help had been compromised.

"Get back here this instant!" she screamed, but her petulant voice and spastic figure receded further and further into the distance until he was out of the neighborhood and back on the streets. The nearest hospital he knew of was on Maryland Parkway, five miles away at least. He made his way in that direction, trying not to slap his feet against the pavement too hard and disturb any further the pouch of guts and soft bones he held in his arms. Its moans turned to quiet whimpers and he could feel time running out. At this rate they would never make it. Every establishment he passed he looked for a place to leave it, somewhere where someone would rush it right away to the hospital or know how to console it and keep it safe.

Door after door he passed and they all looked like coffins for such a new soul so alone.

At a crowded stoplight he stood amongst a couple of pre-teens headed to or from school and a girl that looked his age covered in tattoos and torn clothing. They looked at the queer father figure holding his naked baby but made no claims of wrongdoing and avoided his eyes. Walking across the street he felt the astonished gaze of every passenger stopped at the light boring into him. Two blocks away a McDonalds. That was it, he told himself. He would find someone there to take it and whatever happened to him be damned. But as he neared the restaurant he saw a crowd of hoodlums blocking the entrance. They stood around the doors joshing each other and playing grab-ass, littering the atmosphere with shoves and loud obscenities. Inside, crowded lines and preoccupied workers stressed under the heat of rush hour, none able to concentrate on anything but that which was directly in front of them. He could feel in his bones that no help would be found there and could not justify it as a suitable place to entrust so young a life.

As he scuttled past the McDonalds one of the hoodlums caught sight of his tortured expression and returned it with a dirty look. He nudged a buddy with the back of his hand and called out a taunt that Cameron pretended to ignore. He dare not look back to see what they were planning.

"Christ," he whispered. He couldn't tell if the shaking was from his own nerves or if the baby had begun to convulse. The sound of a police siren coming from an unknown direction almost paralyzed him. His face contorted into an agony of tearless weeping.

Up Sahara the child and he walked covered in dust, burnt refugees against the wind. In the open gravel lot on the side of the road the only structure standing was a stucco masjid whose outer façade and minarets were so worn out by the sun they blended into the desert like camouflage. Cars were parked in the lot but everyone was inside for Friday prayer. As he moved closer he could hear the call of the imam, see inside the people sitting on the floors.

"Fuck it," he said and made his way toward the entrance resolutely. He was almost at the door when from another room inside the church came a woman wearing a black hijab pushing a giant stroller.

She was frozen in abject fear as the two of them almost came face to face. Inside the carriage below her, another baby dozed in ignorant bliss and watched the zoo animals spin above on the mobile.

He stood there shaking, his face pleading, and lifted the baby toward her. A beggar beseeching, appealing to her faith for the life of a child. She looked at his ridiculous outfit so covered in dust he looked like an ancient daguerreotype come to life. She saw his sunken cheeks caked over with such a confluence of dirt and patchy stubble his age was indeterminate. But his eyes were severe. They were bloodshot and watered around the lids but they stared at her with an intentness that gave his presence a distinction of its own.

"Please lady," he whispered. "You have to take it. You can save it."

His chest heaved with deep breaths as he awaited her answer. She muttered something in Urdu he couldn't understand.

"Please."

He moved to her slowly, still holding the baby out in front of him in supplication. The horrified look remained on her face until the naked thing was in her arms. She held it like it was her own; feral kin to the youngling sleeping in the carriage. He looked at her again as if by meeting her gaze would be to impart an urgent message. In the interminable seconds he prayed for understanding.

She hitched the baby up, cradling it with the naturalness of a mother. Only then did he turn slowly, composedly, and walk back to the street. He waited for the police siren to sound again or to hear the cries from the mosque demanding his head but none ever came.

As dusk fell over the streets of Northtown he was standing in the shadow of the Angel Inn. The spinning angel mascot with the big tits in the blue dress spun from her pole atop the front office, her halo missing. He leaned against a string of broken vending machines for USA Today. The windows had all been broken and the copies stolen, the outsides plastered with stickers advertising pornography. In the murk of twilight subtly accented with brakelights he wondered if the baby's luck had been pre-ordained and if it were luck at all. It had made its way to this earth and survived the first test. Now its predicament was life.

THIRTY-NINE

Three days from the meeting with Rik at the school, Cameron sat at the gas station across the street from the graveyard, munching from a bag of dill pickle chips. He was eavesdropping on the conversation held by a few young men who stood by the ice chest. Their conversation was all in Spanish; it was full of laughing and exclamations.

He tried to translate the conversation as best as possible, but their slang and fast speaking were foreign to him. He couldn't even get the gist. At that point, sitting in the run down part of town where the Strip becomes Northtown, he felt that all of his attempts to incorporate other cultures had been a waste. His first instinct, when he heard people speaking Spanish, was to look at the people and wonder from what hell they or their family had to come from in order to get to this country. The absurd bloodlust carried out by the cartels in Mexico, the horrors of civil wars in Central America during the 80's, the dirty wars in South America in the 70s, La Violencia. But what did he know of those tribulations? At best his empathy was only ethnocentric condescension.

If he were somehow able to know what the young men at the ice chest were saying however, he would have realized that two of them, Juan Carlos and Diego Fernando, were brothers; their family came from Colombia. They joked around, using their own brand of made up cuss words, with Oscar Abrego, who was Salvadoran. All three were born in the United States.

Juan Carlos and Diego's family had come from Colombia when the brothers' grandfather, a prominent jockey in Bogota in the 80s was thrown from his horse and severely paralyzed. Dealing with the repercussions, the loss of employment and medical bills, caused the family estate to evaporate quickly and before long they had moved out to Connecticut. First to arrive was Mariana, Juan Carlos and Diego's mother, then her mother Manuela along with her husband, the paralyzed Estefan. The family received citizenship after the Reagan amnesty, but by then Juan Carlos was already born an American citizen and two years later

Diego Fernando was as well. The kids grew up speaking Spanish in their house but at school they had American friends and spoke English with no accent. The whole family moved to Las Vegas in the mid-90's when Mariana remarried an insurance claims adjustor, himself born in the US but of Austrian and Italian origin.

Oscar Abrego was born in Las Vegas. His parents Adelmo and Dominga were undocumented but both had jobs, the former in construction while the latter was a maid in one of the big casinos on the Strip. They made decent money, enough to pay Oscar's team fees for the nationally-ranked soccer team he played for as well as new cleats and other living expenses associated with a teenager. Their migration from San Salvador through Guatemala and Mexico to Texas and eventually Las Vegas had been arduous; a misadventure of their former lives they never spoke about with Oscar or his brothers Eric and Patrick. Oscar's friends at school were black, white, Latino and one of them was from Slovenia. The three friends at the ice chest knew each other from soccer; they were actually getting Gatorades after having played a Sunday league match. They shot the shit and teased each other about football: Oscar was a Raiders fan while the brothers liked the Patriots.

Cameron of course didn't know any of this. He was busy thinking of the tribulations for which he would never fully understand. He didn't speak the language fluently and could never know the people. What would happen if he did? What difference would it make? And what about him? He didn't even know his own ancestral tongue nor did he have any idea about the lineage he came from. He was often mistaken for being Mexican by white people while amongst Latinos they all called him "pinchi wedo" and "cabronsito." He didn't know anything about the great Houshang or Zoroaster.

The thoughts flowed shamefully down the muddy river of his mind. He was a citizen of no race. He used to admire that quality about himself, musing that if he ever went to Brazil or Spain, people could take him for a local. Instead, everywhere he went it was obvious he was an outsider. No one could figure out what he was and it bothered them, he had the face of a party foul. The cultures of the world passed over him like clouds over the endless desert of skin, over strange lacerations that made ravines of flesh and forests of singed hair burnt into steel wool that wouldn't grow anymore, familiar landscapes rendered to look like the harsh terrain of distant planets. A horrifying body image.

It was a goddess' hand that traced over him then, personified as the afternoon breeze. Her face appeared silhouetted against the dusty sky, half skin, half bone; she lowered her embrace upon her devoted mongrel. He couldn't see her with his eyes but he felt her all the time because he was no one.

FORTY

When darkness had fallen Cameron was waiting at the cemetery gates. He held the bottle of rum in its paper bag and looked both ways down Las Vegas Boulevard, expecting Rik's Cadillac. Across the street at the bus stop outside Catholic Charities, a black man with a beard of white lambswool swatted psychotically at the invisible spirits before him, decrying the falsehoods that filled his ears and swearing to god. The two of them stood on opposite sides of the street in the hyper-vividness of the evening. Before long, the amber shine of the streetlight next to Cameron was reflected off the polished black wax of the limousine.

Window after window slid by him, his reflection bouncing from one to the next, until the limousine ceased to move and he was staring into the triple-limo tint of the ultimate window.

There was a suction cup sound followed by a

buzz as the window slid down. Rik's statuesque presence appeared from the blackness inside, jaw churning a tuft of betel. He leaned out the window slightly and shot a jet of green saliva at Cameron's feet.

"Did you bring the pleasantries?"

Cameron pulled the bottle of rum from its paper sleeve and showed Rik. He could see the pointed iron bars of the gates doubled in the reflection of Rik's dark glasses.

"Get in," said Rik.

Cameron went around the back of the Lincoln Towncar limousine and got in. Inside, the upholstery gleamed like it had just been spitshined with windex.

"So, I'm here. What's the grand bargain this time?"

Rik faced him and continued to chew the betel leaves slowly, every now and then spitting into a crystal rocks glass. He wore a Burberry Prorsum tuxedo that horned upward at the shoulders almost into conspicuous points. What little light there was inside the limousine shined off the thin lapels which rested over the black ruffled shirt he wore underneath. Black trousers, patent leather shoes.

"First we must meet the Barôn," he said.

"Without his blessing, I would not have the requisite confidence."

"Confidence in what?"

"In you."

Until then Cameron hadn't realized they were moving. The heavy gates of the cemetery had been unlocked and parted into the grass on either side of the path. The limousine had passed through and was already deep into the compound. Cameron looked outside and through the black shields saw towering eucalyptus trees overhead. The other end of the limousine was completely dark: no sign of the driver or any other living person; trying to ascertain who drove the vehicle was as pointless as staring at the night sky to see the face of god.

When they stopped it was noticeable only by a slight jerk.

"We're here," Rik said.

They got out and walked to the front of the limousine. In front of them was a giant stone crypt; the pillars of its portico rose among the looping trunks of eucalyptus. Xanthus and Balius guarded the entrance on either side, clad in stone tuxedos. Rik gazed at the mausoleum through his black glasses, the lenses now looking like evil 3-D goggles. Cameron waited by his side.

Rik called out toward the gate in a foreign language Cameron didn't understand but sounded like French. Something moved in the forest of bone-colored trees behind the crypt. Then a man stumbled forth out of the thicket like some villain in a vaudeville horrorshow. He looked like the bum Cameron had seen across the street, he stumbled drunkenly until he reached the steps of the crypt, where he then leaped up by twos and threes, nimbly as a parkour champion. He sat upon the top step with an elegant composure. A tie made of golden kaftan was tied neatly in a four-in-hand on a plaid button-down shirt. He wore a tweed blazer over it with leather pads at the elbows. Cotton trousers hung down to his worn leather sandals. Atop his head was a straw hat which he wore like a crown on his cropped cookies-n-crème afro. He looked at the boys as he twirled a big green cigar. The expression on his face warned them not to disappoint.

Rik turned to Cameron.

"Give me the rum."

"Who is that?" Cameron asked.

"Shut up. Just give me the bottle." Cameron handed it over.

Rik took the bottle and approached the man. He went up the steps, carrying himself in a formal manner, and showed the man the bottle label first. The man took it from him, sniffed the contents, making a face as if repulsed. He tried to hand back the bottle but Rik refused. The man then took a swill and spit the contents into the air in a blast of mist. He tucked the cigar behind an ear and took another long chug. This time when he spit a fireball came out of his mouth, burning up in the night air. He looked at Rik, then down the steps at Cameron, the fire still reflecting in his eyes.

"Qui," he boomed. His voice was that of a vocoder devil. A terrestrial Darth Vader. "Qui arriver à chez mois?"

Rik explained in French, very diplomatically, as he gestured toward Cameron. The whites of the Barôn's eyes looked watery; his gaze saw right through them. What they were made of. His lips curled into a predatory grin. Rik motioned for Cameron to join them.

When he got up the steps Rik pulled him close. "Couldn't you have gotten a better bottle?" he hissed.

The man grumbled another sentence of distorted bass.

"Who is this?" Cameron whispered back. Goosebumps riddled his body.

"Puis-je le presenter à vous, Barôn Le Cimetière."

Cameron got the gist this time.

"Barôn Le Cimetière," he repeated. The moon shined down on the Barôn like a giant spotlight from the sky.

"He wants to know why you have come here," Rik said.

"That's funny. I was wondering that myself."

"Don't joke. Answer him."

Cameron turned toward the Barôn and did his best at an introduction. "My name is Cameron, sir, and, uh, I came here at the behest of an old friend." He motioned toward Rik. "I know my rum is a paltry gift, I could have found something better I'm sure, but the selection in Vegas isn't really that great—"

Rik elbowed him hard in the side.

"Anyway, I mean it in good faith. I'm a simple man now. I find value everywhere. I believe there is a luxury in everything."

The Barôn stared hard at Cameron, boring into his soul for hints of chicanery. A breeze blew through the thicket, making the grass moan as it swayed from side to side. He reached out a thick-skinned finger and touched Cameron's forehead, from the plexus of his brow to the bridge of his nose, leaving behind a cross of black charcoal.

"Cámu," he said

The Barôn took another deep swill from the bottle and spat another pillar of fire into the air. He clapped his hands together, causing clouds of smoke to billow around them, sparkling and popping coming from within as each clap tripped the fuse of a firecracker.

Amidst the tumult Rik pulled Cameron back down the steps toward the limousine.

"What have you got me into?" Cameron yelled at him.

"Relax, just get in. We gotta go."

They jumped back into the limousine while the fireshow at the crypt raged on. Cameron thought for sure the whole thicket would go up in flames. As he shifted in his seat the limousine began to pull back out toward Las Vegas Boulevard.

"Who the fuck was that? What is going to happen now?!" Cameron fumed.

"I said take it easy," Rik shot back. "That man was filled with the spirit of Barôn Le Cimetière, the

Lord of the Cemetery."

"Oh, okay. That's just fucking great."

Rik seemed calm and offhanded in a way Cameron thought was inappropriate. "He is one shrewd business partner, that's for sure. He is also a great judge of character. I consult him before engaging anyone in collaboration."

"Collaboration?"

"Yes. À propos my proposition."

Rik made a pyramid with his fingers and looked down at Cameron.

"In one week I will depart for New York. I will begin filming a documentary of sorts on the renegade street artist TALK. You may remember him from the colorful murals he put up at our old school. Fascinating character. The film will also be a skate video along the lines of *Last Year at Marienbad*."

Cameron blinked. "Huh?"

"I want you to come with me. Shadow TALK, give me your perspective on him. You'll be a… creative consultant to the film. Meanwhile I will set you up in a condo on Central Park and pay you a stipend of three thousand dollars a week. You'll have access to the editors' room as well as the set, and you're welcome to engage as much as you want to learn the technical side of things."

"You want to give me three grand a week plus housing just to hang out around a movie set and tell you what I think?"

"I've already secured financing. If you need more we can negotiate."

"It's not that. Why do you care what I have to think?"

"I can see your worldview pouring from your eyes. Your blend of hopelessness and detachment from the world is of great value to me."

Cameron wiggled uncomfortably in his seat. "I'll have to think it over."

"Of course. I just thought that this would be right up your alley. Unless, that is, you have a schedule already in place to adhere to. Perhaps you have daily tasks to carry out, in that case I wouldn't want to disrupt your routine." Rik's glare penetrated the dark glasses.

Cameron stared back at him. Something about it didn't sit right with him. It was like something plucked straight from an active daydream and placed before him on a silver platter. There must be some cost that

Rik wasn't mentioning.

"Like I said, I have to think about it."

"Very well. If you wish to join me, meet me here again in one week. From there we will board a plane for New York and begin immediately. If night comes and you are not here, I will assume you have left fate to bring us together at some future juncture. I can be optimistic like that, can't I?"

There was a jerk as the limousine came to a halt. They were back outside the gate.

"You flatter me," Cameron said. "I'll think about it. See ya, amigo." He clicked open the door and got out. When he slammed the door shut again he didn't see Rik's contemplative glare watching him as he turned and walked away.

He walked away from the cemetery in no particular direction. Soon he had ventured into the naked city of ancient brick shacks and dilapidated projects, on into the dark blue morning with its black clouds filling the air like smoke, the breaklights from the odd passing car red slashes on the asphalt.

He sidestepped down the streets, sometimes in the middle of the lanes dodging cars coming from both sides, sometimes with his back against the brick walls like a shadow. He felt giddy, his heart racing on empty.

He came to a neighborhood of concrete homes demarcated by singular letters. The screen door of one of them was open, blue-white cathode rays beaming out onto the freezing villagers assembled on the front porch.

On the road a midnight blue Mercedes of outdated model appears at his side, moving with enough speed to track his movements and let him know it is watching him. The windows solid black. Ton Ton Macoutes. Rik's agents sent to track his movements. When he notices it he stops, the car stops too, and he blows the driverside window a fuck you kiss. The Mercedes maneuvers right, like a bird dropping its wing, across four lanes of traffic and disappears down an alleyway.

The sutured scar on his chest itches. He wonders where his mother is.

At the tracks a train cuts through the heart of the city pouring black clouds into the atmosphere, its horn baying incessantly like a baby in pain. Past the FBI building, vacant except for its continuous eyes that are always scanning the premises. Past churches of unknown denomination with their untrustworthy logos perched on their facades, preaching to no one.

In a park he's been to before but can only recall as a distant figment of hallucination, he lies in a pile of leaves and sleeps a few dreamfilled hours about running through foreign cities, places in Europe with the topography of Paris and New York, flying along the current of their underground sewers on wooden canoes with his friends while aboveground the neon hologram of a ferriswheel turns against the sky where other planets are held in silhouette.

"Hey, you don't live here," he says to the person next to him.

"Yeah, I do. We all do," answers Tabor, a friend of his he hasn't seen in years.

When he awakens the day is cold, the chill sunk deep into the concrete all around him. Figures flow out of the mist obscured by their morning cigarettes and winter jackets. Through parts of town he has never seen before he sees entire societies of people he never considered. Schoolbells ring like the alarm of incoming aerial attacks, a laser blast from all directions is just an ambulance on its way to the next job. Nothing makes an impression anymore. All of the neighborhoods and buildings and parks and city stretch on mindlessly and he never gets to the end of it all. He recognizes nothing. No more energy for imagining.

At a detention basin that is carved out of the civilization like an immense concrete gridiron he looks over the fence at the miles and miles of empty space. On the other side of the street it's undeveloped desert. The dull black sheath of dust covers the immediate surroundings in a palpable stripe, if you crouch you are below it in the fields of dust and gravel with the dead flowers and dusty pollen. From far enough away you'd see where the dark line ceases and clear air can be found again, but from the vantage point of anyone standing head-height in the smoke, they can't tell what they are breathing from anything else and you can't see past the tall buildings high enough to know if it gets any better or worse. The sun shines through the layered ether as a glowless ball radiating heat only known to exist by the light shining off your sweaty forearms which are now coated in an unseen layer of mud. In this transparent atmosphere through the cracks of skyscrapers and office buildings are expanses of open fields and blasted earth undeveloped and primitive with big chunks of boulders strewn about as if they've been mortared and gravel that stretches on as far as the eye can see disappearing into the dust of the sky. Walking through this alien terrain is like sauntering through a tombstoneless graveyard punctuated with dried and crackling flowers, the figures emerging from the dust could be ghosts or a mirage, the wavering horizon an optical illusion or the result of watering eyes. Out there in the middle of that desert anyone would be just a speck of wildlife with any sign of civilization merely ruins made of broken elements waiting to crumble back to the earth. The skeletons of foliage point their stick fingers in every direction and it is impossible to know if you are travelling in circles but to stare at the sun and follow its trajectory as it makes circles around you. You're hiking and travelling by foot for hours, the earth never runs out, cars whizz by in the distance but look like flying insects and the sky purples as lights come on in the city sparkling in a wonderful homage to life. The gravel now a soft nude skin color and the stripe of smog blended into the darkening clouds that invertedly overflow into space and the lights of stars and planes. A mattress, ripped open on one side lies naked amongst the rubble as does a destroyed television so you watch it using the light from the burning husk of a vehicle to warm yourself as the climate flattens and freezes and you doze off into the sleep of a tired nomad in a busy world.